D0778457

Her lips were incredibly soft and oh, so arousing. Shann felt weak, as though only Angie's touch was holding her together as she drowned in the velvety softness of her mouth. Angie drew back a little, and Shann swayed toward her. She nuzzled Angie's bottom lip, teased it delicately between her teeth, and sucked it gently. Then she drew back again and Angie took Shann's guitar and leant it against the wall before kissing Shann again. She ran her tongue tip over Shann's lips, paused at the corner of her mouth, then sought the sweetness within. Shann moaned softly, at least Shann thought it was her. But it might have been Angie. Then they were straining together, their kiss deepening, breast to breast, stomach to stomach, thighs to thighs. Shann slid her hands inside Angie's denim jacket, her fingers luxuriating in the smooth warmth of Angie's skin. Eventually they drew slightly apart again, both breathing raggedly.

"I don't think I could have gone another night without doing that," Angie said thickly.

"I thought it was only me," Shann managed to get out.

Angie gave a soft, throaty laugh. "Oh, no. Believe me. It wasn't just you." She slid her fingers into Shann's hair, cradling her face, and kissed her slowly, deeply, again.

Visit

Bella Books

at

BellaBooks.com

or call our toll-free number

1-800-729-4992

Always *and* Forever

LYN DENISON

Bella
BOOKS

2006

Copyright© 2006 by Lyn Denison

Bella Books, Inc.
P.O. Box 10543
Tallahassee, FL 32302

All rights reserved. No part of this book may be reproduced or transmitted in any form or by any means, electronic or mechanical, including photocopying, without permission in writing from the publisher.

Printed in the United States of America on acid-free paper
First Edition

Editor: Anna Chinappi
Cover designer: Sandy Knowles

ISBN 1-59493-049-X

For Glenda, my LT

And
For Lorelle F
cousin and friend
and the very best supporter
of women's literature and music
You are greatly missed by us all

About the Author

Lyn Denison lives in a renovated old "Queenslander" house in Brisbane, the capital of Queensland, Australia's Sunshine State. Before becoming a writer Lyn was a librarian. Lyn and Glenda, her partner of eighteen years, enjoy reading, modern country music and traveling. Lyn is also obsessive about scrap-booking, but she can't convince Glenda to get involved in that.

CHAPTER ONE

"What if they don't like me?"

Shann drew her not so comfortable thoughts back to the present. She turned sideways in the stationary car and looked at the young boy in the passenger seat beside her.

"What's not to like?" She touched his upturned nose with its sprinkling of light freckles. "Cute nose. Big blue eyes. Trendy hairdo. Definitely Mel Gibson material. They'll love you."

Corey grinned. "I think you're a bit prejudiced, Mum."

"You think so?" Shann took a bite of her sandwich.

"I reckon." He sobered. "I hope they do like me, though."

"They will." Shann forced her own disquiet aside. She desperately hoped they would accept her son. For Corey's sake. He was the innocent party in the total mess she'd made of her life back then. He was only nine, or almost ten, as Corey would remind her, and there was no need to burden him with the intricacies of the dysfunctional Delaney clan. Well, they weren't all dysfunctional, but those who were did a pretty good job of it.

"Tell me about them again." Corey munched on his apple.

"Oh, love, I've often talked about them," she began, and Corey gave a disbelieving laugh.

"Yeah, right, Mum. I didn't even know I had a grandfather until Aunty Liz came down that first time."

"Your aunt first saw you the day after you were born."

"Well, when I first *remembered*," he emphasized, "her visiting us."

Shann sighed. "Corey, there's a lot of stuff that goes on in families, most of it good, but sometimes, some's not so good. Before you were born, well, there was some bad feeling between your grandfather and me."

"Like you were pregnant with me and not married to my dad?"

Shann hesitated, not wanting to think about that time, about the pain of it all. "Your grandfather was," she paused again, "disappointed I wasn't married."

"Didn't he know you were a lesbian?"

"Not exactly. And I'd rather we just kept that for discussion between ourselves while we're visiting. Okay?"

"You mean you haven't told them?"

"Not in so many words," Shann said.

Corey regarded her levelly. "Why not?"

"Things were, well," she made a helpless gesture with her hand, "they were different then."

Corey shrugged. "But it's who you are. Can't they see that?"

"Not everyone's as open-minded as my wonderful son," she said and gave him a hug. "And you know I told you some people don't understand about all that."

"Yeah." Corey nodded. "But I still don't see what all the fuss is about. You're pretty neat no matter what, and even if I could I wouldn't swap you for a different mother. Honest. Not even a really, really rich one," he added with a cheeky grin.

"I'm glad you wouldn't, you old smoothie." Shann ran her hand over his spiky dark hair. "Besides, you lucky guy, you're stuck with me."

"I know." Corey gave a theatrical sigh. "I'm just making the most of it."

Shann chuckled.

"So, Mum. Maybe they, the family, I mean, were confused because you were with my dad. Do you think?"

Shann almost choked on her mouthful of sandwich. "Maybe they were," she finally agreed feebly. What could she say in the face of that sort of logic?

"So tell me about them again," Corey persisted. "Who'll be there, besides Aunty Liz and Amy?"

"Well, Aunt Liz will be in the hospital for a while, so we'll be looking after the house for her and Uncle Rhys and your cousins, Gerard and Amy."

"And Grandpa with his hip replacement?"

Shann nodded. "And your grandfather. Ruth, my stepmother, is away in England visiting her mother."

"Will Aunty Liz be okay?" Corey frowned. "I mean, it must be pretty serious this operation she's having."

"It is a fairly big operation so she'll need some time to recuperate. That's where we come in. We'll be chief cooks and bottle washers."

"There aren't any kids my age, are there?"

"No. Amy's fifteen, but you got on pretty well with her when she came down with your aunt last year. Gerard's seventeen, and he'll be tied up with his schoolwork I'd imagine so we probably won't see much of him."

"And Uncle Pat's not coming home?"

Shann's brother Pat and his wife and daughter had called in to see them on their last visit home. Pat had worked overseas for the Australian Embassy since he finished university. He'd met and married his wife in London and their only daughter had been born in Canada.

"I like Uncle Pat. He's funny." Corey laughed. "He told some great jokes."

Shann smiled. "He was always like that. The family jester." Pat had never come to terms with his father's remarriage after their mother died, and he just couldn't get on with their stepmother, Ruth. Joking about it had seemed to be his defense mechanism.

Their mother had died from cancer when Shann was only nine. Ruth had been a widow with a son of her own when their father had married her barely a year later. At thirteen, Pat had been resentful and difficult while Shannon, just nine years old, had been confused and unhappy.

Not that Ruth had been unkind to them. She had simply moved in and expected them to go on as though their mother had never existed. Shann remembered once asking Ruth why her mother had to leave them to go to heaven. Ruth had said she was their mother now and that Shann just had to accept it.

The same way she'd had to accept Ruth's son, Billy, as a new brother. Shann had never liked him and neither had Pat. She swallowed and pushed thoughts of Billy back into the dark recesses of her mind.

Only Liz, older than Shann by twelve years, had seemed to sail through unscathed. Of course, with hindsight, Shann knew that she hadn't. Liz had been in the middle of her nursing training and was already living away from home. The only time Shann had seen her break down had been when Shann had repeated her question about her mother going to heaven. Their mother had been really sick, Liz had said, and then she'd hugged Shann, and they'd cried together.

Looking back, Shann realized it had been an incredibly sad time for them all. But life had gone on the way it always seemed to do and in their own way they had all done what they had to do to get through it. Liz became the nurturer, Pat the joker and Shann, well, she wasn't sure what she'd done. Perhaps she'd simply held the hurt of her mother's loss inside her. Until Leigh Callahan had—no, she told herself forcefully, don't go there. Not now when they were so close to home.

"Why didn't you just stay at home and have me?" Corey broke into Shann's reminiscences.

She glanced at her son and away again, uncertain how much she should tell him, wondering if perhaps she should have prepared him a little better for this acquaintance with her family. But how much should she tell him? Although she knew he was mature for his age, he was, after all, still a child. It was something that never failed to amaze her, that she could raise such a well-adjusted child. But he was still a child.

She took his hand in hers. "I didn't think that was an option, love. I thought I'd upset my parents and my family enough, and, well, I just felt I needed to get away."

"Did you tell them about me?"

Shann shook her head. "Not in the beginning. No. But I did later. I didn't want them to pressure me into doing anything I didn't want to do."

"Like marrying my father?"

"Partly that," Shann said carefully. She knew that hadn't been an option either, but she couldn't tell Corey that. And she'd been terrified they'd want her to have an abortion. Not that she hadn't considered an abortion herself. At first. But she hadn't been able to do it.

So she'd run away. Or tried to. But Pat had found her walking aimlessly around the shopping center, and he'd brought her home. That's when she'd told them she was pregnant, and her father had been even angrier.

He'd demanded to know who the father of her child was and she'd angrily told him she didn't know, that it could be anyone. That statement hadn't gone down especially well, even if it had been the truth. She hadn't known who Corey's father was back then. She'd blanked the whole sordid incident out of her mind. With hindsight she knew she should have told her father what had happened ten years ago, but she'd been too scared, too ashamed. She'd only discovered the awful truth two years later when it all came back to her in harrowing detail.

However, if they'd known the true circumstances, who knew what Ruth and her father would have done. And Shann herself had been too fragile to fight them. Flight had been the only solution she could see. So she'd run away again, this time successfully.

She found out later from Liz that her parents had been frantic until her mother's only sister, to whom she'd run, had let them know Shann was safe with her.

After much discussion, argument and recrimination, they'd decided it was for the best that Shann stay with her Aunt Millie until they'd all had a cooling off time. Especially her father, who had been devastated over Shann's pregnancy and even angrier that his daughter had run to his sister-in-law, Millie. Jim Delaney and Millie, Shann's mother's only sister, had disliked each other on sight, and when he moved his family interstate before Pat was born, Millie had never forgiven him for what she saw as his theft of her only sister.

Shann sighed and turned to her son again. He was gazing at her with his big eyes, mirrors of her own. "We've had this discussion about your father, Corey. You know I couldn't marry him, even if I'd wanted to."

Corey nodded. "Because he was already married."

"Yes." She couldn't tell him any more. How did you tell a child, a child you loved more than life itself, that he should never have been born, that his father was nothing but a rapist. She'd wanted to end her life, and had planned to as soon as he was born, but when she'd held his tiny body in her arms, felt his warmth, the sweet baby smell of him, she'd been filled with wonder. And a burning need to protect him. Her son had virtually saved her life.

Corey gave a heartfelt sigh. "And then he died."

"Yes, he died," Shann said gently.

"As I see it," Corey continued, "it would have been so much easier for you if you could have married my father. Then you wouldn't have had to leave your family."

"Perhaps. But we've managed okay, haven't we?"

"Course we have." He was silent for a moment. "Does Grandpa know you're famous?"

Shann laughed. "Famous? To quote you, yeah, right."

Corey chuckled, too. "Well, you are. You'll just have to live with it, Mum. And besides, all the kids at school think you're famous. Everyone knows the theme from *The Kelly Boys*."

"Oh, sure. Now, enough of that. Let's head off so we can get there before dark. So buckle up." Shann switched on the engine and drove out of the rest area where they'd stopped for lunch. She turned left, heading north on Highway 1.

They made good time up the Pacific Highway. Reluctantly bypassing most of the Gold Coast to save traveling time, Shann promised herself she'd spend some time down at the beach with Corey. She had fond memories of family holidays there before her mother died.

Now they were almost on the outskirts of Brisbane, and Shann was grateful they were heading into the city, rather than joining the stream of traffic outbound. At least she thought they were on the outskirts of the city. It all seemed so different, especially the freeway. She couldn't seem to find a familiar landmark. Buildings must have been torn down and others erected and, of course, the trees would have grown in the intervening ten years.

Her hands tightened on the steering wheel of her new four-wheel drive. Liz had said she shouldn't have any trouble getting through the city, but it was nothing like she remembered it to be. Still, if she just followed the signs she should be all right.

"Do you know where we're going, Mum?" Corey asked as the other three lanes of traffic surged past them.

"Do I know where I'm going? How can you ask that? I was born here." Shann grimaced. "Yes. And no. So you'd better help me look out for signs."

"Well, first up I'd suggest the left lane," Corey said matter-of-factly. "The speed limit in this one seems to be for racing cars."

Shann laughed and eased the car over. And then the road swept around a gentle curve and the high-rise buildings of the city center appeared before them. "There's my old hometown."

Corey snickered. "Some hometown. It's a lot bigger than I thought it would be."

"And probably bigger than when I left ten years ago. For some reason the buildings look taller."

The traffic bunched up, and Shann fell silent as she concentrated on her driving. The freeway skirted the Brisbane River and she pointed out Southbank on the other side of the river, with its walkways, tropical palms, and colorful bougainvillea. Corey craned his neck to see over the guardrails.

"There's even a man-made swimming pool with its own sandy beach," she told Corey. "It's built on the site of Expo 88."

The traffic had backed up and they crawled along. "Not far now," Shann said, more for her own benefit than her son's, and she tried to relax her tightening stomach muscles.

She veered off Coronation Drive and joined the traffic on Milton Road. Then she was turning onto the street of her childhood. She'd come back after ten long years, after vowing never to return.

The street was wide compared to most of the surrounding ones in the inner city suburb, and huge jacaranda and poinsiana trees grew in the center nature strip and on the footpaths, providing a leafy canopy. The old homes, referred to as Queenslanders, snuggled among the greenery of trees and shrubs and picket fences.

A few of the houses dated back to the late 1800s but most were the smaller workers cottages, early 1900s vintage. All had been renovated over the years, verandas closed in, outsides encased in faux brick cladding. By the time Shannon had left home the new renovators were moving in. The cladding was being removed and the verandas replaced, as people restored the houses to their former glory.

Shann's own family home had been built in 1935 by her grandparents. They'd married quite late in life and Shann's father had been their only child. When her grandparents died within months of each other, not long after Shann's sister Liz was born, her father had inherited the house. He'd moved his family back to Queensland and into his childhood home.

When Shann was born her father had built two extra bedrooms onto the back of the house, and later he'd added a covered back deck. But the front of the house was still in original condition, with its gabled roof and leadlight glass in the windows.

Shann slowed the car, pulling to the side of the road, letting the engine idle as she gazed at the rambling old house.

"Which one is it?" Corey asked, and Shann heard the thread of apprehension in his young voice.

She reached over and gave his hand a sympathetic squeeze before she pointed to the house two doors down, on the opposite side of the road. "The cream one there, with the pale green roof."

A riot of red, white and yellow flowers grew on the footpath along the low fence, and Shann knew Liz would be responsible for them. It didn't matter what the season Liz would have a garden blooming. Just like their mother had. The shrubs Shann could see in the front yard were tidily trimmed.

The house itself had been painted rich cream for as long as Shann could remember, with the typical heritage green and red trim. Her father had refused to consider an alternative color scheme.

Two years ago Liz and her husband and family had moved in with their father and stepmother, after her father had had his first knee replacement. Liz's doctor husband had finally taken a job in the city after years of working in rural hospitals, joining the cancer research team at the Wesley Hospital only a suburb away. Liz was a relief nursing sister, and it had fitted in so well.

The street, the houses were achingly familiar to Shann, and she'd grown up knowing every family living here. Although the houses were built relatively close to each other, the blocks themselves were deceptively large, the long narrow lots giving the houses large back yards, ideal for young families.

Shann dragged her eyes from her house and made herself focus on the house next door. It was older than theirs, with wide verandas on the front and down one side. She knew there was a huge covered deck on the back, and there used to be a large hammock, big enough for two. She hastily pushed those memories back into the darkest corner of her mind. It wouldn't do to think about that when she had her meeting with her father to face.

The trees in the backyards of both houses had grown, too, and she could see the backdrop of the old mango trees, huge now, and the tall silky oak that grew on the fence line.

She couldn't help wondering if the Callahans still lived there. Surely Liz would have told her if they'd moved. Then again, maybe not.

Suddenly the door to the Callahan's house swung open, and Shann tensed, her knuckles white where she clutched the steering wheel. A tall slim figure jogged across the veranda and down the wide front steps—fairish hair, short and thick, shone to a burnished gold in the late afternoon sunlight.

For one heart-stopping moment Shann thought it was Leigh and something inside her twisted, the sharp pain spreading with such easy familiarity. The rational part of her mind told her that the figure was taller, thinner, the jean-clad legs longer. But a little voice inside her told her all that could have changed in ten years. Yet, there *was* something almost familiar.

A hazy picture began to form in Shann's mind, but it retreated just as quickly, and she half believed she'd imagined it.

The woman crossed the footpath, stepped over the closed door of the old MG and slid into the driver's seat. The engine purred to life and the antique sports car drove off down the street, its British racing green paintwork gleaming like new.

"Neat car," Corey commented beside her, and Shann nodded.

She put the four-wheel drive into gear, checked to make sure the road was clear and continued on, turning into the driveway so she could reverse and park at the curb in front of the house. "Well," she turned to her son, "guess this is it." She attempted a cheery grin. "Chin up. Level gaze. Deep breath."

Corey drew in an exaggeratedly noisy breath and Shann chuckled, smoothing the tuft of dark hair that persisted in standing on end above his forehead. "If you dare to spit on that, Mum, I swear I'm going to run away to a new family."

"Gee! How many new families do you want, Corey Delaney?" she laughed.

He frowned. "You have a point. One's more than enough."

"Exactly. And that cowlick is rather cute anyway."

"Mum!" Corey gave a long-suffering sigh. And then he looked past her, and a smile lit his face. He slid out of his seatbelt, opened the door and jumped out of the car. "Aunty Liz. Hi!" Then he was around the car and throwing himself into the welcoming arms of Shann's older sister.

"Corey, love." Liz held him away from her and studied him with exaggerated care. "I don't believe it. I think you've grown a foot since I last saw you."

"And now I have two foots," Corey said, bouncing from one sneaker-clad foot to the other, and then Corey and his aunt dissolved into gales of laughter.

Shann groaned.

"Do you get it, Mum?" Corey smirked. "One foot. Two foot?"

"I swear that so-called comic routine is no better today than it was the last time you two dredged it up."

This comment only brought more laughter, and Shann waited patiently until her son and her sister had pulled themselves together.

Liz turned and hugged Shann. "Now, now, you old sourpuss. You know you think we're funny."

"Oh. Funny. All right. But," Shann held up her hand, "funny ha ha or funny peculiar? That's the big question."

"Ha! Ha!" said Corey with mock seriousness. He looked at his aunt, and they both lost it again.

"Talk about Abbot and Costello," Shann muttered, trying to keep a straight face.

"Ah, Mum, if you joined us we could be the Three Stooges." Corey mimed a few moves from the old television shows.

Shann groaned again, and Liz laughed. "You're the one who introduced him to those old slapstick shows so don't blame me." She sobered. "It's so good to see you both," she said sincerely, one arm around her sister's waist, the other holding her nephew against her.

"And it's good to see you too, Liz. How are you feeling?" Shann asked. Her sister was due to go into hospital next week. Five years ago she'd had benign fibroids removed from her uterus and now the fibrous tumors had grown back, and it was decided they needed to be removed again. This time she was to have a hysterectomy.

"I'm fine. All prepared?" Liz glanced toward the house. "Dad's waiting to see you."

Shann raised her dark eyebrow, wanting to question her sister, but not in front of Corey.

At that moment a large black and brown dog came bounding around the corner of the house, pink tongue lolling. He slid to a halt and gave a deep woof.

"It's a dog!" Corey said excitedly. "Is he yours, Aunty Liz? Can I pat him?"

Shann put her hand on her son's shoulder when he would have approached the large animal.

"Tiger, you've snuck through the fence again, haven't you?" Liz reprimanded and the dog hung his head. "He belongs next door," Liz told Corey. "The Callahans are dog sitting him, and he's a big softy, so it's quite safe to pat him," she added for Shann's benefit.

Corey stepped over and tentatively ran a hand over the dog's gleaming body and was rewarded with a lick of the pink tongue. "Hi, Tiger. I'm Corey. Look, Mum, I think he likes me."

"Is Dad, well, is he okay?" Shann asked her sister quietly as they watched Corey and the dog get acquainted.

"Of course. He hates being incapacitated, of course, but apart from that, he's really well."

"I mean, with us, Corey and me, turning up?"

"He's been looking forward to you coming."

"I'm sure," Shann said dryly, trying not to be skeptical.

"He has. Really." Liz touched her arm. "Shann, give him a chance. He wants to mend fences with you. He's wanted that for a long time."

"Are you sure that's not just the wishful thinking of your soft heart?"

"No. Truly." Liz hurried to reassure her. "Dad just—well, you know he finds it difficult to express his feelings."

"He did a pretty good job of expressing them ten years ago," Shann remarked, and Liz shook her head.

"As he saw it, you'd given him just cause to be upset. The trouble with you and Dad is that you're too much alike."

"Me? And Dad? No way," Shann said emphatically.

"In lots of ways you are."

Shann went to comment and Liz squeezed her arm. "Let's not get into that, Shann. Just promise you'll give him the opportunity to make amends. Okay? He wants to. I know he does," Liz finished earnestly.

Shann frowned.

"If not for yourself, then for Corey."

Shann expelled a breath. "Low blow, Liz."

"I use what I have to." Liz smiled crookedly. "But Corey can only benefit from having his family around him. He should get to know his grandfather. And he's such a wonderful child, Shann, Dad should get to know him."

"He is a great kid," Shann agreed and sighed. "I can't disagree with you there. Don't know how I managed it, do you? Do you suppose he was mixed up in the hospital, that some other poor woman has got my tearaway?"

Liz smiled and shook her head. "Oh, no. He's your son all right. He looks just like you. And I do know how you brought him up to be the person he is."

"Oh, yeah?"

"Yeah. And don't you go saying anything negative about my baby sister either or you'll have me to contend with." She gave Shann a playful shove.

"Mum, isn't he the greatest dog?" Corey ran up, the dog beside him.

The large dog flopped on the grass and gazed up adoringly at Corey.

"I've always wanted a dog," Corey said and rubbed the dog's

ears. "Do you think the people who own him will mind if he's friends with me?"

"I shouldn't think so." Liz ruffled Corey's hair. "And it looks like Tiger has chosen a new friend already. But your grandfather's waiting so now it's time for him to go home." Liz took the dog by the collar and led him over to the gate in the fence between the two houses. "Home, Tiger," she said firmly and closed the gate after him. The dog gave a mournful whine, and Liz shook her head. "He gets like this when there's no one home."

"Will he be okay?" Corey asked, loathe to leave his new friend.

"He'll be fine," his aunt assured him. "If we look out in five minutes he'll be asleep. Now, come on, let's go inside."

They climbed the steps, and Shann paused, gazing at the familiar veranda, the leadlight windows of the main bedroom, her step-mother's clay wind chimes. Shann reached up, gently moved them, and they tinkled softly.

"Liz?" A deep voice called from inside the house.

"Yes, Dad. It's me." She glanced encouragingly at her sister. "Shann and Corey have arrived."

Taking Corey's hand Shann followed her sister into the foyer, down the hallway and into the living room.

The man in the room had obviously struggled out of his chair and was leaning on crutches.

Shann gazed at her father. This couldn't be him. Her father was taller surely, and thickset, with thick dark hair. The man who faced her was much thinner and his hair was completely gray. Then her blue eyes met his, and she knew it *was* him. Steady, clear blue eyes, eyes just like her own, held her gaze.

She became aware of Corey's hand in hers, and she drew herself together. She gave her son's hand an encouraging squeeze. "Well, Dad. You look pretty good. Nice to see you."

For long moments no one spoke, and only the sound of the ticking of the grandfather clock in the corner echoed around the room.

"It's good to see you, too, Shannon," Jim Delaney said at last, and Shann expelled the breath she hadn't been aware she'd been holding. "Thanks for coming to help out," he added softly.

"That's okay. I—you seem to be doing pretty well." Shann indicated his hip, and he nodded.

"Can't complain. At least I knew what to expect this time after having my knee done a couple of years ago."

"I suppose so."

"It takes time. To heal and so forth." His eyes flicked to Corey and back to Shann.

She drew Corey forward, resting her hands lightly on his shoulders. "Dad, this is my son, Corey," she said, her stomach clenching as she waited for her father's reaction to the grandchild he hadn't wanted ten years ago.

Jim Delaney turned his attention to Corey, and Shann felt a small tremor pass through Corey's body.

Then her son was bravely stepping forward. He held out his hand to his grandfather. "Nice to meet you, sir. Um, I mean, Grandfather. I'm Corey. Corey James Delaney. The 'James' is after you and the 'Corey', well, that's just mine."

Shann's heart swelled with pride as Jim Delaney continued to look at his grandson. And then he slowly reached out and shook Corey's outstretched hand.

"It's nice to meet you, too, Corey," he said, and Shann heard the roughness of emotion in his voice.

"I'm nearly ten," Corey told him and his grandfather nodded.

"I know. You'll be ten in a couple of weeks. On the eighteenth, isn't it?"

Corey smiled. "That's right, Grandfather. My birthday's on the day after yours."

Jim Delaney nodded. "Grandfather's quite a mouthful. Gerard and Amy, they call me Pop. I think you might as well call me Pop, too."

Corey's grin broadened. "That would be excellent." He turned to his mother. "Wouldn't it, Mum?"

15

Shann swallowed a lump in her throat. "Sounds like a great idea."

"Well." Liz rubbed her hands together. "I think this calls for a cuppa. Dad? Shann? Tea?"

"Yes. Thanks. Can I help?" Shann asked.

"No. I have it all ready. But maybe Corey could help me carry in the biscuits."

"Okay. Did you make them Aunty Liz?" Corey asked as he followed her. "Are they chocolate chip cookies like you brought us last time you visited us?"

Shann stood in the living room, part of her registering that the lounge suite was new, but the carpet square on the polished wooden floor was the same. She'd sat on the rug and played games on rainy days and on cold winter nights with the warmth from the blazing fire in the old brick fireplace. Snap. Monopoly. Paper dolls. They'd set up Patrick's electric train set. Her mother had read her stories in this room. And in this room she'd had that final devastating argument with her father. So many memories.

And now she was alone with him, ten years on, with all those memories swirling around inside her head.

She ran her damp palms down the sides of her jeans and nervously brushed back a strand of her long dark hair. Swallowing, she faced him. "Thanks, Dad," she said softly.

"For what?"

Her whole sensory system was alert to his tone, but she could find nothing confrontational in his voice. Old habits died hard, she reflected wryly. It seemed she was looking for criticisms that weren't there. "Thanks for being, well, nice to Corey."

She watched as her father slowly and painfully sat himself back in his chair. Stepping forward, she moved his crutches to the side of his chair, within reach if he needed them. Yes, her father was definitely thinner. And older.

"You thought I wouldn't be nice to the boy?" he asked thickly.

She shrugged her shoulders realizing she'd upset him by suggesting it. "Yes. No. I didn't know how you'd feel. Seeing us . . .

16

seeing me again. I thought you might be, well . . . you were angry with me."

He remained silent for long moments, and Shann saw his Adam's apple move as he swallowed. "Yes, I was angry with you. We all seemed to be angry back then. But I wouldn't take that out on the boy. I'm sorry you thought I would."

Their eyes locked again, and Shann nodded slightly and sat on the lounge chair opposite her father. "I hoped you wouldn't because Corey's the innocent party in all this. And because he's, well, I'm very proud of Corey."

"I can see that. And I can see why." He paused. "He looks just like you did at that age."

Shann gave her father a crooked smile. "But he's heaps smarter than I was."

A faint grin moved over her father's face. "You were pretty smart yourself, make no mistake about that."

"I guess I just made some not-so-smart choices."

Jim Delaney nodded. "You weren't alone there. We're all guilty of making those sorts of choices in our lives. But it's how you handle yourself afterward, what you make of your life in the face of adversity, that's what counts. I haven't always handled myself well," he added, and Shann could see it was difficult for him to admit it. She could see her father was flipping through his own memories just as she was.

"I still don't think I fully understand what went on with you ten years ago, Shann," he continued. "But I . . . since then, well, I'm proud of you."

Shann stood up, crossed to her father, leaned down to hug him, and he held her tightly for a long moment. When she returned to her seat they regarded each other a little self-consciously. "I'm sorry I upset you, Dad," she said carefully.

"And I'm sorry I wasn't more—" He gave a negating shake of his head. "I know we both said things we shouldn't have, but I'd like us to try to put it all behind us." He looked across at his daughter.

Shann nodded. "There is one thing though, Dad. I want you to know I could never be sorry I had Corey."

What her father would have said she would never know because Liz returned at that moment, Corey following behind her, frowning as he concentrated on carrying a plate of Liz's homemade cookies.

By dinnertime they'd settled in. Shann was in her old room at the back of the house, and they'd put a single bed in her father's small study so Corey could have his own space.

Liz had collected Amy from school and as their father liked an early dinner, they all sat down around the dining room table just after five o'clock. Liz's son Gerard was away on a school orienteering trip until the weekend, and her husband Rhys was still on duty at the hospital.

Memories flooded back as Shann sat eating the meal Liz had prepared. Her father always sat at the head of the table, her stepmother Ruth at the other end, with Liz and Shann on one side and her brother Pat and Billy, Ruth's son, on the other. Just one big happy family, Shann thought wryly.

As they ate it was left to Liz and Corey, and occasionally Amy to carry the conversation. Not that her father had ever been much for chatting over a meal. And yet, in the dim recesses of her mind Shann had a feeling her father used to laugh as they all sat in here. When their mother was alive. She couldn't swear that that was an actual memory or simply something she wished had happened. She'd have to ask Liz. Maybe she would remember.

"We probably won't see much of Rhys for the rest of the week," Liz was saying. "He's busy organizing things so he can have some time off next week."

Shann began to feel some guilt for her silence. "This stir-fry is really delicious." She complimented her sister. "I think I should warn you all in advance that I'm not the world's best chef."

"You're not that bad, Mum," Corey said loyally before he gave Shann a teasing grin. "Except we won't ask Mum to cook rice pudding, though. That would be a bad move." He screwed up his nose, and Shann laughed.

"Not fair, Corey. That was the one and only time I let anything burn."

Liz related a few of her culinary disasters, and by the time they were eating dessert, they were all far more relaxed.

"Guess what, Pop?" Corey turned to his grandfather. "I got to meet Tiger before."

"Tiger?" Jim Delaney looked perplexed.

"The big dog next door," Corey explained.

Jim looked at Liz. "The Callahans have a dog?"

"Not exactly. They're dog sitting. I thought I told you."

"So that's where the barking's coming from. I heard it on and off all day yesterday." He frowned.

"Uh! Oh!" Amy said in mock fear. "Old Mrs. Jones will be making complaints about the noise."

"She still lives across the street?" Shann was amazed. "She must be over a hundred."

"Ninety-seven," said Liz. "Her daughter lives with her now but she still gets about. Catches the bus down to the shops and the Senior Citizens Club."

"But she hates noise," Amy persisted. "So they'll have to keep Tiger quiet."

"Is it Robbie's dog?" asked their father.

"Ah. No." Liz began moving her cutlery around, not meeting Shann's eyes. "It's the Radfords. They've gone to New Zealand. I think that's where Ann said they were going."

"The Radfords?" Jim frowned.

Shann felt the tension in the dining room reverberate, bouncing from wall to wall as the name hung in the air. Yet her father didn't seem to notice. But Shann knew Liz did.

"Oh. Leigh and her husband." Jim seemed to realize what he'd said and looked across at Shann and just as quickly away.

Leigh Callahan. The name echoed inside Shann. No, not Callahan. Not anymore. Leigh Radford.

Shann's heartbeats flipped over themselves, and she replaced her spoon on her plate, knowing she would be unable to swallow anything at that moment. Not if her life depended on it.

19

"Yes. They've gone to New Zealand." Liz said quickly. "Touring in a motor home. The South Island I believe."

"They've left their car next door with Aunt Ann and Uncle Mike, too," added Amy. "It's a Jag."

"Wow! What model?" asked Corey, and Amy pulled a face at him.

"No idea. I just know it's sort of metallic red if that helps."

"They're pretty expensive cars," Corey told his cousin seriously. "It'd cost the earth in running expenses."

"And what do you know about running expenses, young man?" his grandfather asked him lightly enough.

"Well, you know, insurance, rego, petrol, and stuff. Mum and I researched all that before we bought our four-wheel drive."

"I'm pleased to hear that," Jim said with a genuine smile.

"Oh, yes." Corey nodded. "And a Jag would cost heaps."

"I don't think that would worry Leigh and Evan," remarked Amy. "They're really rich."

"Amy!" Liz admonished. "It's hardly nice to gossip about people in that way."

"Oh, Mum." Amy gave her mother an exasperated look. "Everyone knows how rich they are. Evan developed some machinery or other to do with cutting sugar cane, and he sold it for heaps of money. It was in the local paper."

That was one paper Liz hadn't sent on, Shann reflected. Liz, always the protector.

"I think I'll have my coffee in the living room." Jim Delaney moved slowly to his feet. Corey ran around and passed him his crutches. His grandfather ruffled his hair. "Thanks, Corey. I don't want to miss the news." He shuffled out of the room.

"Can I go and watch the news with Pop?" Corey asked, and Shann nodded.

"But don't talk while the reports are on," she warned him, and he gave her an old-fashioned look.

"Oh, Mum! Like I would."

"And Amy, you can take Pop's coffee in to him before you start your homework." Liz passed her daughter a cup of coffee.

Amy rolled her eyes and, taking the cup, she headed out of the room.

"Well," exclaimed Liz brightly. "That wasn't too bad, was it? Better than I'd hoped. Sure you don't want some coffee yourself, Shann?"

Shann shook her head. "No, thanks. I'll be awake all night if I drink coffee after lunch."

"How about some tea then?"

"No. Don't worry, Liz. You don't have to wait on me. You've done enough. Just relax and finish your coffee."

Liz patted Shann's hand. "I'm just pleased to have you here. I know Amy's fifteen and probably old enough to stand in for me, but I didn't want her schooling interrupted and, well, as I said, I'm just pleased to have you here. I really am."

Shann laughed. "Okay. I'm beginning to believe you."

Liz sipped her coffee, then absently rubbed at the lipstick smudge left on the rim. "Shann? About Leigh?"

Shann stiffened.

"They'll be away for the next month or so, and there's no reason why you need to see them when they return."

"No. I know."

"And I had no idea they were going to be anywhere near here. They live up north and hardly ever visit Ann and Mike."

"It's a free country, Liz," Shann shrugged. "I can't dictate where they go or don't go."

"I know. But—"

"It's in the past, Liz."

"Is it? Are you sure?"

Shann nodded. "Ten years is a long time," she said flatly.

"I suppose so." Liz sighed. "They got married about a year after you left. Everyone was surprised she chose Evan Radford."

Shann had been, too. And devastated. Anyone but Evan Radford.

"But the marriage has lasted," Liz continued. "Evan's done very well for himself. And I think he has improved with age."

"I find that a bit of a stretch," Shann put in dryly and Liz gave a laugh.

"No. He really has. Who knows? Maybe Leigh's been good for him?"

A knife sliced somewhere in the region of Shann's heart. Shann had been so sure Leigh had been good for her, too.

"They have two kids," added Liz. "A boy and a girl."

She tried to analyze her feelings about that, about Leigh having children. Evan's children. But all she felt was a heavy numbness.

"They seem nice little kids. Blond and blue eyed. Look like Leigh."

Shann's gaze met her sister's, and Liz grinned. "Lucky about that, hey? Because Evan Radford was never an oil painting in the looks department."

A reluctant smile tugged at the corners of Shann's mouth. "No, he wasn't," she acknowledged. They'd all gone to school together, and Evan had never been liked. He was a total nonentity. Tall. Thin. Awkward. But smart in a sneaky, underhand way. Evan had the knack of using any situation to his own advantage. And if he was slighted he waited and sought his revenge. Shann knew this better than anyone.

That familiar feeling of panic rose inside her, and she wiped a hand over her face, feeling the sudden chill that always passed over her when she thought about—

"And who would have laid bets that Evan Radford would have made anything of himself?" Liz broke into Shann's tortured thoughts. "I mean, snaky little Evan Radford! But do you know what? He was at last year's school reunion and surprised everyone by being quite nice, according to Mary Lenton. Remember her? From your year? She married an Italian and lives up in Mareeba now." Liz talked on about people they both knew.

Shann made herself concentrate. At least then she wouldn't have to think about Evan Radford. Or about Leigh.

"I have to cut back on this," Liz said ruefully as she poured herself another cup of coffee. She looked across at Shann, her gaze levelly holding her sister's. "You know, when I asked you to come up here I never considered that you might have someone special you'd be leaving behind. Is there? Someone special?"

"No." Shann shook her head. "No one special."

Actually, if she had simply said, no, no one, it would have been a more accurate reply.

A couple of times in the past ten years she'd met someone and thought it might work out. But it never had. At one stage she'd even thought perhaps she needed to come back and face Leigh, lay her ghost. But, of course, she couldn't. Among other things, Leigh had accused Shann of breaking her heart. It was a moot point, Shann reflected wryly, about who had broken whose heart.

"Has there ever been?"

Shann drew her thoughts back to the present and raised an inquiring dark eyebrow.

"Anyone special? Since you left?" Liz expanded, and Shann shook her head again. "I never have asked you." Liz gave a self-deprecating laugh. "If I were honest I'd have to admit that part of it was that I wasn't sure I could, well, cope with what you'd say." She looked at Shann and Shann sighed.

"When Corey was three I met Toni," she began.

"Tony?" Liz repeated hopefully.

"Toni. With an i. She couldn't come to terms with an instant family. So—"

"Oh. She?"

"Yes. I'm a lesbian, Liz. It will always be *she* with me."

"I guess I've never brought the subject up with you because I wasn't sure. I mean, you and Leigh were little more than kids. And later I didn't know if you wanted to talk about it."

Shann picked up a teaspoon and turned it over and over in her fingers. "I'm far more comfortable with myself these days, Liz," she said, knowing that at least was true.

Liz nodded slowly. "I can't really say I understand why you feel that way, Shann. I mean, men can be trying, I'll give you that, but, well, I can't get past the sex thing."

Shann laughed lightly. "It's not just about sex, although I've got no complaints about that. It's just a . . . I don't quite know how to explain it. An affinity, I guess. I define myself with women the way I never can with men."

Liz nodded again. "I accept that you feel that way, love, even if I don't understand it. I suppose what's really important is not who you love, but that you love someone and you're happy. You're my sister, and I love you. Even if you're something of a mystery to me."

"I love you, too, Liz, and I appreciate your support. And for the record, I can't explain why I feel that way either. I just do."

"But what about Corey?" Liz asked gently. "How do you think he'll react when you tell him?"

"He already knows. And he's fine with it."

"He is?"

"Yes. He knows it's part of who I am. Besides," Shann smiled, "there were three other kids in his class who had two mothers. And one who had two dads."

"There were?" Liz grinned. "Well, that puts me in my place and reminds me I'm twelve years older than you are. I'm almost from another generation."

"Hardly." Shann laughed. Her sister could pass for thirty, certainly didn't look like a woman who had already turned forty.

"Kids certainly get a more eclectic education than I did. Sometimes some of the things Amy tells me totally flummox me." She laughed. "I've developed quite an acceptable acting technique over the years just so she doesn't think I'm a crusty old fuddy duddy. It's not easy."

"I suppose it isn't. I do admit to being slightly apprehensive about facing Corey's teenage years when I think about my own."

"Oh, Corey will be okay. I can tell."

"I hope you're right. For my own selfish reasons." Shann laughed and then sobered. "Do Amy and Gerard know I'm a lesbian?"

"I have no idea." Liz frowned. "I haven't told them. The opportunity never came up."

"What about Dad?"

"Well, I don't know. He knew about, well, you and Leigh. But when he found out you were pregnant—"

"It sort of confused the issue?"

"Sort of." Liz set her coffee cup down. "Shann. About Corey's father. You never said . . . what happened?"

A million answers churned inside Shann. She'd never talked about it. Not even to Aunt Millie. And never to Corey.

She remembered her father shouting, demanding the name of the man involved. But Shann had never told him, had never told anyone. Her stepmother Ruth had tried a quieter, woman-to-woman approach. Her brother Pat, at home on holiday from his job in London, had offered to drag this excuse for a guy to the altar if that had been what Shann wanted. But she hadn't, and that had been the problem that had ended in that last terrible fight with her father.

"It's not important who Corey's father is," she said flatly and Liz reached across and clasped Shann's hand.

"It might be to Corey," she said softly.

Shann stood up and paced the length of the dining room. "I can't . . . I don't want to talk about it, Liz."

"Oh, Shann." Liz stood up, concerned. "I didn't mean to upset you, love."

"It's all right. Don't worry, Liz. Look, let me clear the table for you." Shann picked up a plate just as the doorbell rang. She replaced the plate and waved Liz back into her chair. "Stay there and finish your coffee. I'll go."

Her long strides took her down the hallway into the foyer, and she reached out and swung open the door. Before her stood a tall slim woman with short fair hair and incredible green eyes. She wore faded blue jeans and a soft gray windcheater with a small black logo over one breast. Then the woman's wide mouth lifted in a delighted smile.

"Shannon Delaney. It's been a long time."

Shann's eyes moved over the woman again. She was incredibly attractive. How could Shann have forgotten her?

And then firm arms wrapped around Shann and she felt the thrust of breasts, of hips and thighs, as she was drawn into a close embrace.

CHAPTER TWO

Long forgotten responses woke inside Shann as the warm body held her close. And those responses frightened. and yet excited her at the same time.

She wanted to step quickly away, break this confusing contact, put protective space between herself and this stranger. Stranger? It was obvious this woman was not unknown to her, and part of Shann recognized that she should know who she was. It only served to unsettle her even more.

The woman's arms slowly released their hold, and she stepped away from Shann. Just as suddenly Shann wanted her back, yearned for the warmth again. It had been so long since she'd held a woman close to her, and her emotions seesawed wildly.

Shann drew a quick breath, tried to calm her erratic heartbeats. She had to say something. What would the other woman be thinking of her? She met the level green gaze again and she felt a warm flush wash her cheeks.

"You don't remember me, do you?" asked a pure, liquid voice, and the green eyes crinkled at the corners, bright with amusement.

Those eyes. They were so familiar. Shann knew those eyes. A small frown gathered on her brow and then her mouth opened slightly in total dismay. "Angelina?" she said incredulously. "Angelina Callahan? My God! Angelina."

"One and the same," laughed the other woman delightedly. "All growed up."

"All growed up all right," Shann repeated, amazed. "I can't believe it's you. You must have been what, thirteen, when I saw you last?"

"Fourteen, nearly fifteen actually. But who's counting?"

Shann searched her memories. Images of the young Angelina came flooding back with such vivid clarity that it took her aback. Angelina at ten when she first came to live with her aunt and uncle next door. A gangly child, all arms and legs, pale skin, and huge green eyes. And her last memory of Angelina, still tall and pencil thin, those big green eyes filled with concern.

"She doesn't mean it, Shann," Angelina was saying earnestly. "You'll see. She'll get over it." While Shann stood desperately looking after Leigh as she'd flounced away leaving Shann standing there with "You've broken my heart, Shann Delaney," ringing so unfairly in her ears.

Shann blinked the memory away, and she was back in the present, ten years later. She became aware of Leigh's young cousin watching her. "Wow!" she said, her eyes moving unconsciously over the other woman. Black boots, jean-clad legs, long long legs, the figure-molding gray sweatshirt that did little to hide the curve of her hips, the swell of her breasts. And that face. Could this beautiful woman be the shy, quiet, almost sorrowful young girl who was part of and yet not quite part of Shann's youth? "You look," she paused, "sensational."

Their eyes met again, and Shann was conscious of a flicker of awareness. She felt the air between them shift just slightly, and her pulse rate picked up again.

"Thanks," said Angelina softly. "You look pretty sensational yourself."

Shann's mouth went dry, and she swallowed convulsively, not knowing quite what to say now. Had she imagined that frisson of cognizance? Did the other woman feel it too? Was Angelina Callahan—?

Shann had a totally irrational urge to pull this beautiful woman back into her arms, move against her, cover her lips with her own. She almost recoiled in horror at her wayward thoughts. They were so uncharacteristic, so foreign to the cautious, steady person she'd become. It was too fast, too frightening.

"Who is it, Shann?" Liz walked into the foyer behind Shann.

Shann was never more relieved to see her sister. She stepped awkwardly aside.

Liz smiled a welcome. "Angie! How are you? Come on in out of the cold. I see you've met Shann." She hit her forehead lightly with the palm of her hand. "What am I saying? You two have known each other for years."

Angelina laughed, and the sound played over Shann, warming her, reaching inside her. "I don't think Shann recognized me at first, but in her defense it has been at least ten years since we've seen each other." She looked across at Shann. "I knew you straight away though. You've scarcely changed. Although your hair wasn't as long then, and I somehow thought you were shorter. Were you always as tall as I was?"

"From memory you were both always taller than average, taller than the rest of our families." Liz waved a hand. "But come on in, Angie. Dad always likes to see you. Would you like some coffee?"

"No. But thanks anyway, Liz," Angie picked up the paper bag she'd set down beside her and stepped into the foyer. "If I drink coffee after lunch it keeps me awake all night."

Liz grinned. "It does the same to Shann, doesn't it, Shann?"

"Mmm. Hypes me up. Not a pretty sight." Shann's voice sounded thin in her ears.

Those green eyes moved over Shann again, this time taking in

29

Shann's own jean-clad legs, the long-sleeved red T-shirt she wore. As Angie's eyes moved over Shann's breasts she felt her nipples begin to harden, and she could feel herself flushing again. In confusion she turned quickly to lead them down the hallway.

When they walked into the living room Jim Delaney and Corey looked up, and Shann saw the first really genuine smile light her father's face.

"Angie. How you doing?" He muted the television with the remote control. "I thought you were away on business."

"Got back this morning."

"How about some tea, Liz?" their father suggested, but Angie held up her hand.

"Not for me, thanks, Uncle Jim. I just bought these books over for Amy. For her assignment." She set the paper bag on the coffee table. "I didn't realize Shann was already home."

"They only arrived this afternoon," Liz said and turned to Corey who stood regarding the stranger with interest. "And this is Shann's son, Corey. Corey, meet Angie Callahan from next door."

Corey grinned at her as they shook hands. "You're the lady with the neat MG, aren't you? We saw you this afternoon as we were arriving. Are you Tiger's dog sitter, too?"

Angie laughed. "Yes, to the MG and no, to the dog sitter. My aunt has that dubious honor."

"He's a great dog," Corey said enthusiastically.

"You think so?" Angie pulled a face. "So long as you don't want a veggie garden, shoes or clean washing on the line."

"Oh no," said Liz. "I knew he'd dug up Mike's garden and chewed a few shoes. What happened with the washing?"

"Apparently yesterday Ann had just hung out the sheets, and Tiger decided it would be fun to pull them off the line and drag them through the ruined garden."

"Oh, dear." Liz commiserated. "He's such a cute pup, too."

"Cute or not Ann's going to try to get him into puppy school, and if he doesn't knuckle down I think he'll be off to a kennel somewhere. If he lasts that long," Angie added ominously.

"I could play with him," Corey offered, "and try to keep him out of mischief."

"Now don't encourage that dog over here, Corey," put in his grandfather. "I don't want him getting up to any shenanigans in our yard."

"Maybe I could go to the library and get a book on how to train dogs." Corey turned to Jim Delaney. "Is there a library round here, Pop?"

"Just up the road." He looked thoughtfully at Corey. "So you like to read?"

"I love it. And guess what?" Corey looked at them all. "I'm getting the next Harry Potter book for my birthday. Aren't I, Mum?"

"That's supposed to be a secret." Shann smiled at him.

"I love the Harry Potter books," said Angie and proceeded to discuss the various characters and plots with Corey.

"Mum and I read them together. At night." Corey's eyes widened. "Wow! The bit in the bathroom with the troll. Yuck! And the snake. Now that snake was mega scary, wasn't it, Mum?" Corey appealed. "And the movie, phew! We could hardly watch it."

"It was mega scary all right," agreed Angie. "I have to admit I covered my eyes with my hands and sort of snuck a peek through my fingers."

She put her hands to her face, and Shann wondered if she was the only one who noticed how the soft gray sweatshirt moved across the other woman's full breasts. An ache started in the pit of Shann's stomach and spiraled teasingly downward. She shifted from one foot to the other, totally disconcerted when Angie peered at her through her fingers. Then Angie dropped her hands, her eyes still holding Shann's gaze. And Shann couldn't seem to look away. She desperately hoped none of her traitorous feelings were visible, although she suspected this gorgeous woman knew just how unsettled she was making Shann feel. How could she not know?

"Mum and I hid behind our hands, too," said Corey in amazement.

"We'd better change the subject," said Angie to Corey. "I think we're scaring your mother."

Corey turned to his mother and took her hand. "No," he said loyally. "Mum's really brave."

"Why don't you all sit down," Jim Delaney suggested. "I'm getting a crick in my neck looking up at you all."

They all moved to sit down.

"Sorry, Uncle Jim." Angie sat opposite Shann. "That must drive you nuts."

"Oh, it gives me a chance to boss everyone round," he said with a smile.

"As if you ever need an excuse, Dad," Liz teased him good-naturedly.

"So what are you doing these days, Angelina?" Shann asked the other woman. She did a mental tally. Angelina Callahan must be about twenty-five so she'd possibly finished studying.

"Please call me Angie, Shann. I never could stand Angelina." She wrinkled her nose. "It's such a mouthful. And I run a hardware store. The one here on James Street."

Shann frowned. "You mean Grossman's?"

"Yes. And I love it. Of course, it's a little more up market than it used to be. We've had a name change, and we've expanded. All in all we're doing quite well."

"Have you still got some of those tomato stakes?" Jim Delaney asked. "Liz was saying she could use some more of them."

"Sure," Angie said easily. "Want me to bring a bundle home tomorrow, Liz?"

"That would be great. If it's not too much trouble, Angie. Just put it on my account."

"You should come down again, Liz. We've got these new secateurs in stock that are to die for. Mrs. Jorgens told her garden club about them, and I've had to reorder them. We sell them as soon as we get them in store."

The conversation went on in a similar vein for a few moments, and then Angie turned back to Shann.

"What about you, Shann?"

"Oh, I've done a bit of everything I guess. Packed shelves in supermarkets. Done some landscaping. Waited tables."

"So a bit of a Jill of all trades, so to speak," said Angie. Shann felt Corey's eyes on her, and she gave him what she hoped he'd read as a warning look.

"And are you still songwriting?" Angie continued.

"Oh, I do a little here and there," she replied vaguely.

Corey chuckled. "Mum's famous."

"Famous?" Liz looked from her nephew to her sister.

"Corey's teasing," Shann said quickly, willing her son to take the hint.

"No, I'm not, Mum. You are famous."

"What's the lad talking about, Shann?" put in her father.

"Nothing much, Dad. I've had a bit of success with a few of my songs, that's all."

"I always knew you would," said Angie. "I used to think you were great. Would we have heard any of them?"

"Well, that depends. Probably not though."

"Do you watch *The Kelly Boys* on TV," Corey warmed to the subject.

"Amy and I watch it every week," said Liz. "You've been watching it, too, Dad."

"Mum wrote the theme song." Corey told them.

"You wrote that?" asked Liz. "It's a great song."

"And that's not all," continued Corey. "Mum's going to be singing herself at the Gympie Country Music Muster this year. And," he paused for emphasis, "Adam Harvey and Beccy Cole have both recorded Mum's songs."

"Corey. Enough." Shann said. "Anyone would think you were my manager. Besides, not everyone likes country music."

"What's wrong with country music?" Angie grinned at Corey. "And I love Beccy Cole and Adam Harvey. Which of their songs did you write, Shann?"

"They haven't been released yet. They're on the albums they're both bringing out for the Muster."

"And they pay you for these songs?" her father asked.

"Of course," Shann told him.

"Enough to live on?"

"Well, things are improving. Having them use my song for *The Kelly Boys* was a big break for me."

"We could get a new car just before we came up here," Corey told his grandfather. "And I got a new bike. We left it with Aunt Millie."

"Good for you, Corey." Angie leaned back in her chair, and she smiled across at Shann. "And do you know, I think I used to be your mother's biggest fan."

That night, stretched out on her old single bed, Shann could almost imagine she had slipped back in time, that the ensuing ten years had never been. She watched the familiar light patterns dance across the ceiling as the breeze gently rustled the silky oak branches in the moonlight outside her window.

On her left was a wall of bookcases containing her books, swimming trophies, and various other paraphernalia from her childhood. It had taken her aback to realize her father and Ruth hadn't packed her things away. Her desk was still between the door and her closet with its mirrored doors. And she'd set her guitar case back on the carved trunk at the foot of her bed where she'd always kept it. Except that Corey now had her old guitar, and she had a new one.

Shann slipped out of bed and shrugged on her cord jacket over the old T-shirt she slept in. She tiptoed into the study next door to check on her son. He was curled up in his striped pajamas, hugging an extra pillow the way he always did. She gently pulled the blankets back over him before returning to her room.

The curtains billowed slightly as the breeze gusted, and she crossed the room to gaze out into the night. The moon was nearly full and so bright she could almost discern colors. Shann leaned on the windowsill and took in the scents of her childhood.

Of course her eyes were drawn to the house next door. The

large covered deck on the back matched their own. Shann's father was a builder by trade, and he'd done the renovations for the Callahans. She knew the neighbors had a gas barbecue, and wooden table and chairs just like they did. In summer, all families on the street lived out on their back decks.

The light caught the faint movement of the hammock that swung from the rafters next door. Shann had spent hours swinging in that hammock, nestled beside Leigh as they talked, made plans for the future.

Shann shifted her gaze. The room opposite her own used to be Leigh's bedroom. Sometimes they'd shout across the fence at each other, but neither set of parents had cared for that. After the 'telephone' they'd made using string and tin cans had broken, they'd developed an intricate system of hand signals. Shann smiled at that memory. Their communication system would have done international spies proud. Eat your heart out, *Charlie's Angels*.

With a sigh Shann pulled her jacket around her as the cold breeze shifted. She'd known the Callahans all her life. Well, almost all her life. Mike and Ann Callahan had bought the house when Shann and Leigh were two years old. The girls had gone to kindergarten, preschool, started first grade together and their mothers were friends. Their fathers went fishing together, and Shann couldn't remember a time when she didn't love Leigh Callahan. They were best friends.

When they were fifteen Leigh had started to notice boys. Not that boys hadn't already been noticing them. They had. It had been a source of great amusement to Shann and Leigh. Then suddenly, Leigh's attitude changed, and she seemed to find them fascinating.

"Oh, come on, Shann," she'd said with a giggle. "Don't you often wonder what it would be like to go out on a date?"

"No." Shann was sure. And she was suffering the first pangs of a new emotion. Jealousy.

"Don't you think about getting married? Having kids?"

"Married? I guess," Shann admitted reluctantly. How could she say it all seemed just a little surreal to her? That it happened to other people. She just couldn't see herself in a frilly white dress and a veil.

"I'm going to have two children," Leigh was continuing. "A boy and then a girl. What about you?"

"I haven't really thought about it," Shann said honestly.

"You are so out of it, Shann. I sometimes wonder what you *do* think about," Leigh said exasperatedly.

Shann shifted uncomfortably. You, she wanted to say. "My music, I guess."

"What about boys?" Leigh asked.

"What about them?"

Leigh rolled her eyes. "Don't you think about them?"

"Not really. Just that most of them are pains in the neck. Why?"

"Don't you think Lex is cute?" Leigh asked, and Shann frowned in disbelief.

"Lex Ellis? You have to be kidding, Leigh. He's an absolute thug and a bully."

"Well, what about Evan Radford? I think he's cute."

Shann grimaced. "He's a sneak. He weasels his way out of everything."

"But he's got nice blond hair, and he's smart," Leigh said with a small smile on her face.

"You have to be kidding!"

"Who do you think is cute then?"

"You, I guess," Shann said without giving herself time to think about how the other girl would take this revelation.

"Me?" Leigh laughed. "Shann! I mean guys."

"I don't think I find any guys cute."

Leigh sobered and looked across at Shann. "Not at all?"

Shann shook her head. "I think I must be a lesbian."

"Of course you're not a lesbian," Leigh admonished her. "That would be awful."

"Why would it? There are lots of great lesbians."

"Oh, yes?" Leigh grimaced. "Like who?"

"Well." Shann gave it some thought. "Lots of old women writers are lesbians. Then there's Martina Navratilova. And what about Ellen DeGeneres who came out on that TV show. That was hilarious."

"It was funny." Leigh frowned again. "But in real life people make jokes about lesbians."

"Which people?"

"Guys do."

"Which is why I'm not too fussed on guys," Shann put in. "But apart from that, people don't just make jokes about lesbians, they make jokes about anyone who's different. Remember yesterday those kids teasing Angelina because she's taller than the boys in her class?"

"Not after you'd had a go at them for doing it," Leigh said. "Angelina's quite capable of fighting her own battles, you know, Shann."

"But it does prove my point about anyone who's different. It doesn't matter what it is. Green hair. Preferring girls. Whatever."

"People can also be cruel, Shann. I mean physically cruel. I've heard of lesbians getting bashed up."

"Don't forget my brown belt in judo," Shann struck a kung fu pose.

"Shann, be serious."

"I am."

"You're not a lesbian," Leigh repeated firmly, and Shann expelled a breath exasperatedly. "Have you ever even kissed a girl?" Leigh asked.

"No. Of course not."

"Ha! Then how do you know?"

"Well, I'd sure rather kiss you than any guy I know," Shann stated.

"All right. Let's prove it. Kiss me now."

Shann stared at Leigh as she stood there in her denim shorts and crop top, her tanned midriff bare. "But—" She looked around.

They were in Leigh's room, and they were alone in the house. Robbie was across the road playing computer games with a friend, and Leigh's parents had taken Angelina late night shopping for new netball shoes. "What if someone sees us?"

"Who's going to see us? We're alone." Leigh gave Shann a smug look. "You're chicken. And it proves you're not a lesbian!"

"I am not chicken." Shann stepped across the floor before she had a chance to lose her nerve. She rested her hands on Leigh's bare shoulders, reached forward and put her lips to Leigh's.

For one startled moment they both stood there stiffly, almost frozen. Then the softness of Leigh's lips registered, and Shann gave a low moan, leaned into her, her tongue-tip seeking, deepening the kiss. And Leigh didn't push her away. Her hands slid around Shann's waist and when they finally drew apart they were breathless.

"Where did you learn to kiss like that?" Leigh asked softly and then she leaned forward, kissed Shann again.

Shann was having trouble believing it was really happening. She was holding Leigh in her arms, and it was so much more than she ever imagined it would be. Her body was on fire and the way Leigh was moving in her arms must mean that, incredibly, she felt the same way. Shann slid her hands from Leigh's back to the indentation of her waist, over the smooth bare skin of her midriff, upward, cupping her small breasts covered by the thin material of her short crop top.

Just as suddenly there was space between them, and Leigh had moved away, had wrapped her arms around her body. "Shann, we have to stop this."

"Why?" Shann's voice was thick. "It was wonderful. Really wonderful." When Leigh made no reply Shann gave a crooked smile. "Do you suppose I really am a lesbian?"

Leigh brushed her shoulder length fair hair back from her flushed face, but there was no answering smile there. "The trouble is, I'm not," she said softly.

"You were enjoying kissing me," Shann said, her heart sinking.

"You're very good at it but—" She shrugged.

"Better than Evan Radford?" Shann said in a half-hearted attempt at a joke, but she felt far from amused.

"I haven't kissed him yet."

"Yet? Do you intend to?"

Leigh shrugged again.

"What about us?"

"We're friends."

Shann gave a derisive laugh. "Friends don't kiss like that."

"We won't be doing it again."

"You don't mean that." Shann said flatly. "Do you?"

"Shann, I can't . . . I don't want to be, well, that different. I need to . . ." She stopped and looked helplessly at Shann.

"Conform?" Shann finished bitterly.

"Call it what you like. I just think we should forget this ever happened."

"Can you?" Shann asked her, the ache of tears in her throat. She knew it was impossible on her part, and she suspected Leigh wouldn't find it as easy as she thought it would.

"We have to forget it if we still want to be friends."

And it was a whole year before Shann kissed Leigh again.

Shann sighed. For a long time she'd regretted that she'd allowed Leigh to dictate the terms of their relationship. Or non-relationship. But what could she have done? She hadn't wanted to lose Leigh altogether.

She'd had to stand by and watch as Leigh went out first with Lex Ellis and then, after she broke up with him, with Evan Radford.

Yet all the while Leigh found small ways to touch Shann. An arm around her waist. Leaning against her as they watched Angie play softball. Getting Shann to teach her to slow dance. It had been exquisite torture for Shann. She'd told herself she was a fool to allow Leigh to get to her, but Shann was in love with her.

Then Leigh had had an argument with Evan, and she'd cried on Shann's shoulder. Shann had hugged her comfortingly and after a while, Leigh's tears had stopped. She'd looked at Shann for long moments before leaning forward and kissing her. After that when they managed some time alone they'd kiss and cuddle. Sometimes Leigh would let Shann caress her breasts, but anything below the waist was taboo. After all, Leigh explained, she wasn't a lesbian.

The breeze gusted again, and Shann shivered. She should get to bed. She was weary from driving and emotionally exhausted from her meeting with her father. It had gone so much better than she'd anticipated, and she was so grateful for that. Still it had worn her out.

She straightened from the window, but as she did she caught a movement out of the corner of her eye. Someone was moving on the Callahans' back deck. The figure crossed to the railings, and Shann drew instinctively back into the shadows. She recognized the tall figure immediately. She still wore the dark jeans and the light gray sweatshirt. Her short fair hair gleamed in the moonlight.

Angie Callahan had her hands in her pockets, and there was an air of defeat in her stance as she leaned against the veranda post. As Shann watched she turned and walked slowly back toward the door. Pausing for a moment, she touched the hammock, making it swing slowly back and forward before she continued on, disappearing into the house. The light in what used to be Leigh's bedroom came on and then went off.

Shann let out the breath she hadn't realized she was holding.

CHAPTER THREE

As the next few days passed Shann and Corey settled in with their family. Shann enrolled Corey in her old school, and he had already made some new friends, including a little girl who lived down the street.

Shann met the capable woman from a family assist group who came each morning to help her father with his shower and Derek, the young physiotherapist who worked with her father three times a week. She supposed she would describe her new relationship with her father as an armed truce. They both walked carefully, fearful of upsetting their newfound suspension of hostilities.

Corey was definitely their saving grace. With each passing day she could see that grandfather and grandson grew closer. Not that she was surprised. Corey was a joy to have around. He was interested in anything and everything and had a wacky sense of humor.

Liz was saying as much as they sat on the back deck sharing a pot of tea. Corey was at school, and their father was resting after his physio session.

"Corey's so special, Shann," Liz said. "And did you notice Gerard actually held a conversation with him last night? I was speechless." Liz's son had arrived home the day before.

Shann chuckled. "I think Gerard was amazed that Corey even knew what orienteering was. I couldn't believe how much like Pat Gerard looks."

Liz nodded. "But he's quiet like Rhys. Getting information out of them both is like pulling teeth. I learned more about his week away listening to his conversation with Corey than I did questioning him when I picked him up." Liz looked up and waved. "Morning, Angie."

Shann turned in her seat to see Angie Callahan on the deck next door.

"Feel like a cuppa?" Liz called, and Angie nodded.

She jogged easily down the steps, vaulted the low fence and walked up onto their deck. "This is very civilized," she said with a grin. "Taking tea in the fresh air."

Today she wore a pair of dark gray slacks and a white tailored shirt, open at the throat, the V of her neckline disappearing into the tantalizing shadow of her cleavage.

"Morning, Shann." She smiled, her eyes crinkling, and Shann felt that same disquieting spark of attraction.

As Angie sat down Liz went inside to get another teacup.

"Settled in all right?" Angie asked Shann easily, and Shann pulled herself together to reply.

"Just about. Seems a bit weird though. Sometimes I feel as though the last ten years never happened. Then I look in the mirror," Shann laughed derisively. "That brings everything into perspective."

Angie's gaze moved over Shann's face. "As I said before you haven't changed that much. Your hair's longer. That's about it."

"Don't forget the character lines."

Angie laughed softly again.

And once again that low, so enticing sound played havoc with Shann's composure. A small fire began inside her, tingling along her nerve endings, awakening feelings she thought would lay dormant forever.

"Character lines? Now what can I say to that?" Angie appealed. "Whatever I say you'd end up either wrinkled or characterless. And you're neither."

"Thank you, you charmer, you." Shann inclined her head. "But you're the one who's changed, you know."

"You mean I've grown up?"

Shann shook her head. "Not just that. You were always so, well—" She sought a description that accurately defined the young girl Angie had been ten years earlier.

"So dull and boring?" Angie suggested.

"No. Definitely not dull, or boring. I was thinking shy, quiet, and retiring."

"Well, she's not shy and retiring now," stated Liz as she rejoined them.

"Absolutely not retiring," Angie agreed. "And everyone probably wishes I was still quiet."

Liz handed Angie a cup of tea. "So how come you're not hard at work?"

Angie rolled her eyes. "Mike's playing golf, and Ann's got a dental appointment so I'm babysitting the dog from hell for a couple of hours." She motioned toward the deck, and Shann noticed Tiger sprawled out in a patch of sun, fast asleep. "I took him for a run, and now he's resting. I've showered and have to get back to work. Apparently it *is* a dog's life."

"You must have an understanding boss if you can have time off work when you want it," Shann said, and Liz and Angie burst out laughing.

"I guess I do," Angie said still grinning.

"Shann, Angie is the boss," Liz explained, and Shann stared at the other girl in surprise.

"You are? I drove by the shop. It's huge now."

"Not only is she the boss, but she's the owner of the whole kit and caboodle."

"You own it?" Shann was now totally astounded.

Angie nodded. "Lock, stock, and overdraft."

"How long . . . What made you want to own a hardware store?"

"I worked there part time when I was going to Uni. Then the owners said they were going to close the place down and retire. Well, there were a lot of jobs that would be lost, and I had the opportunity to buy it," Angie shrugged. "So I did."

"But it used to be a small corner store. When did they extend it?" Shann asked.

"I did that. I acquired a couple of properties adjacent to the shop and extended the building. It was a much-needed extension, too. It was necessary to augment the stock, diversify, if you like, for me to stay competitive." She gave Shann another of her level looks. "You'll have to call in, and I'll give you a guided tour."

"I'll hold you to that. I love hardware stores." Shann flushed a little. "Corey always ends up having to drag me out of them."

"Oh," said Angie, continuing to hold Shann's gaze as she lifted her teacup to her mouth.

And Shann couldn't seem to look away. She was almost mesmerized by the way Angie's lips pursed, sipped her tea, and then her tongue tip dampened her lips. A shaft of pure desire clutched at Shann, and she grew suddenly hot, her nerve endings clamoring. She wanted to reach out, replace that inanimate teacup with her own tingling lips. "I'll hold you to the guided tour," she said to diffuse some of the tension Angie must surely feel crackling in the air between them.

At that moment Tiger stumbled to his feet and gave a loud woof.

"Oh ho! My intrepid watchdog tells me either Ann is home or we're being robbed. I'd better get home and investigate." She glanced at her watch and stood up. "And I'd better get back to work before I'm forced to fire myself."

"Well, don't do it until I get my tour," Shann said lightly enough.

"No, I won't." Angie laughed and lightly touched Shann's arm.

Shann fancied she could feel the heat of that light touch burning through the flannelette of her shirt.

"Thanks for the tea, Liz. See you, Shann." She crossed to the steps and paused, glanced back. "Call in any time, Shann," she said, and then she was gone. She waved from the deck next door and then disappeared into the house with Tiger scrambling behind her.

"I don't hold out much hope for that dog graduating from puppy school," Shann remarked, and Liz grimaced.

"Well, we do have backup there. Corey's diligently reading his *How to Train Your Puppy* book." Liz refilled her cup from the large teapot.

"I'm amazed that Angie owns a hardware store." Shann commented as casually as she could. "When did all that happen?"

"About three years ago. She inherited money from her grandmother."

Shann raised her eyebrows. "Her grandmother? You mean, her mother's mother? I thought she had no other relatives besides her parents and Ann and Mike."

"So we all thought," Liz concurred. "Angie's mother always said her parents were dead. That's why Angie was given into Ann and Mike's custody when Angie's mother went to jail."

"Did the grandparents know about Angie?"

"Apparently not. Angie's mother had problems with drugs as a teenager. She ran away from home when she was sixteen, and I have no idea why her parents didn't try to find her. She was their only child." Liz shook her head. "After the father died the mother must have had a change of heart, willed her estate to her daughter, Angie's mother. It was a considerable estate, too."

"When did the grandmother die?"

"A few weeks before her daughter it seems. Remember I told you Angie's mother died about five years ago. That's when they discovered the letter from the grandmother's solicitors. Angie's mother hadn't even opened it. There were a couple of years of legal mumbo jumbo, and then Angie was recognized as the sole beneficiary. And it couldn't have happened to a nicer kid."

45

Shann nodded.

"She had a hell of a life before she came to live with the Callahans. She was taken out of her mother's care half a dozen times and put into foster care. Every time the mother would go into drug rehab, come out, take Angie home, and it would start again."

"What about her father? Wasn't he Mike Callahan's brother?"

"Stepbrother or half brother or something," Liz frowned. "He barely acknowledged Angie's existence from what Ann told me. He certainly didn't marry Angie's mother. They had an on-again off-again sort of relationship. Angie hasn't seen him since he left when she was six. No one knows where he is or even if he's alive."

"No wonder Angie was such a quiet little thing."

Liz nodded. "She was always such a good kid though, and really smart. Even with all the schooling she missed it didn't take her long to catch up once she got settled with the Callahans, and she hasn't looked back."

"I remember helping her with her math once." Shann remembered Leigh was supposed to do it, but she wanted to go down to the shopping center. They'd argued, and Shann had ended up staying with Angie. "Not that I could help her all that much." She laughed. "It was so embarrassing. She was better than I was. She could have tutored me."

"She has a degree in business management or something."

Casually Shann took a sip of her now lukewarm tea. "Is she—? I didn't notice a ring. Is she seeing anyone?"

"I don't think so. Not that Angie would tell us. She's always kept that side of her life fairly private."

"She's so attractive, and she has such an outgoing personality you'd expect guys would be beating down her door." Part of Shann cringed at the way she was pumping her sister for information but she couldn't seem to stop herself.

"Oh, Angie has lots of friends but no one special I don't think. I know Ann's worried about her, wants to see her settled down and happy. You know what mothers are like." Liz giggled. "I shouldn't laugh, but not long ago Ann tried to set Angie up with the son of a friend at her bridge club. Angie was dead against it, but Ann persisted until Angie gave in and went out with the guy."

"And?"

Liz smothered a laugh. "Angie went off on a week's holiday next day. She told Ann she needed a week away to get over it and to cease and desist with the matchmaking."

"So the guy didn't measure up?"

"No. Angie told me he was a nice enough guy, but she wasn't interested."

"Hmmm." Shann said noncommittally.

"You think Angie's gay, don't you?" Liz whispered.

"Why do you say that?" Shann asked in surprise.

"I don't know. She doesn't look gay. Maybe it's that you watch her." Liz shifted uncomfortably in her chair. "I don't know why I asked you that. Perhaps I shouldn't have."

"Gay people don't always look stereotypically gay, Liz. Apart from that, I don't know if Angie's a lesbian or not. I haven't seen her for ten years, and I'm just amazed at the change in her. And apart from that, how do you know anyone's sexual orientation just by looking at him or her? We don't all wave rainbow flags," Shann said, admonishing her sister.

"I suppose that's true. You'd never know with you." Liz paused. "You're sure you still are?"

Shann sighed. Her sister was certainly persistent. "It's not something you turn on and off, Liz. I can't change even if I wanted to. Which I don't."

"The rational part of me knows that, but when it equates down to my little sister I, well, I worry about you. I just want you to be happy."

"I am happy. And if someone special comes along who knows?"

"But it's so hard for you, Shann. Life's geared to being heterosexual. You're just expected to meet a guy, settle down, have kids."

"So, what's wrong with meet a woman and settle down?"

"But there are people who hate gays."

"I know. But I can't live my life being dictated to by people like that."

"I still worry."

"Try not to, Liz. Look, I'm not going to shout it from the rooftops, but I'm certainly not going to deny it. Even to Dad," she added flatly.

"He's never spoken about it. Not to me."

"It's okay, Liz. I know how he feels about it. He told me in no uncertain terms years ago."

"Shann, he was upset then, and, just for the record, he was far more upset about not knowing where you were than he was about, well, anything else."

"You know the sad part is that when we had that last argument the only thing he accused me of that was true was being a lesbian."

"You never really told me what happened."

"Just the usual screaming match that fluctuated between accusations of lesbianism and loose morals and quiet denunciations that I'd let everyone down."

"Oh Shann." Liz's expression was heavy with distress. "I'm sorry."

"It's in the past, Liz. There's no point in dredging it up again."

"Perhaps not." Liz reached out and squeezed Shann's hand. "But you know I'm here if you do need to talk."

"Thanks, Liz."

"So." She rested her chin on her hands and grinned at Shann. "Are you attracted to Angie?" she asked, her voice conspiratorially low.

Taken by surprise, Shann felt herself blush. Wasn't that the problem she kept refusing to acknowledge since she'd come face to face with Angie Callahan her first night home? She was attracted to Angie, and she had no idea what she was going to do about it. "Come on, Liz. I'm too old for her."

"Too old? That's rubbish," stated Liz. "She's only what? Three or four years younger than you? Rhys is five years older than I am. Dad was four years older than Mum, and he's eight years older than Ruth."

"Yes, well, let's just agree that anyone would find Angie attractive, female or male. And talking of Ruth, when's she actually due home?"

"Okay, we'll change the subject. About eight weeks. She did want to postpone her trip, but Dad wouldn't let her. I don't think he could have sat in the plane for the long trip to the UK anyway. And, of course, we didn't know then that I'd have to have this surgery. That's what caused the problem, threw the spanner in the works, so to speak."

"You said Ruth hadn't been home since she emigrated from the UK nearly forty years ago?"

"No. And she's been planning the trip all year. Her family was really looking forward to seeing her, especially her mother who will be turning eighty while Ruth's there."

"In retrospect I can see we, Pat and I, may have made it difficult for Ruth when she married Dad."

"You were just kids, Shann, kids who'd just lost their mother. I've always felt Ruth could have handled the situation better and, let's face it, Billy was a big part of the problem. Ruth couldn't see her son was a spoilt little troublemaker. But what mother would want to see how unappealing Billy was."

They paused for a moment, each lost in the past.

"Did I tell you I spoke to Janice, Billy's second wife, when I went up to Darwin with Ruth for Billy's funeral?" Liz asked, and Shann shook her head, not wanting to think about her stepbrother. "She said they'd actually broken up before he was killed in the accident. She seemed quite nice. Heaven only knows what she ever saw in Billy. I know I shouldn't speak ill of the dead, but I never liked him as a child and that didn't change as he grew up. And I use the term *grew up* very loosely. At least Janice and Billy didn't have any children."

"Does Ruth ever see her granddaughter?" Shann asked carefully.

"No. And Billy didn't see his daughter either. His first wife remarried and now lives in New Zealand. Billy wasn't interested enough to keep in touch with the poor kid." Liz checked the time.

49

"Oh, is it that late? I'd better get going or I'll be late for my doctor's appointment. I'll be back before you need to collect Corey from school."

Liz went into hospital the next day and came through her operation well. The next week was busy for them all as they dovetailed looking after Shann's father and visiting Liz in hospital. By the time Liz came home they were all organized. Gerard and Amy were a big help, and they settled into a routine.

On Thursday Amy had a study day so she was at home, enabling Shann to run the few errands she had to do.

"I've got my mobile phone with me so ring if you need me."

Liz was sitting on the back deck, and she assured Shann they'd be fine. "I'm going to stay out here on the deck and do some cross-stitch, and Dad can sit with me after Derek leaves. Amy will make us morning tea so take your time, Shann."

Shann drove down to the shopping center, paid bills for her father, bought a couple of school books Corey needed as well as a new school uniform. When she left the shopping complex she found herself heading toward Angie's hardware store.

It wouldn't hurt to have a look around. She could pretend she was looking to buy something. An electric drill, suggested her inner voice, and Shann bit back a laugh. That should send the conversation in the right direction.

She turned into the parking area and switching off the engine, she sat looking at the impressive building. Forklifts darted about loading and unloading, customers came and went. Tradesmen in utes, handymen in station wagons, couples in family sedans. If the fullness of the car park was any indication Angie had a successful business.

Maybe Shann shouldn't interrupt her. Angie was probably busy. And Shann should get back to Liz and her father. She checked the time. Perhaps just ten minutes wouldn't hurt. She could have a look around and then leave.

Shann climbed out of the car and bleeped the locking mechanism. She followed a couple of workmen in through the large entry doors. Inside, she was amazed at the range of merchandise. Gone was the small corner store selling bolts and nails. Signs designated areas for electrical, bathroom fittings, gardening, and, of course, power tools. The signs went on. And there seemed to be customers everywhere.

"Can I help you?" asked a pleasant young man in a blue staff shirt with the name *Joe* embroidered on the pocket.

"I'm just browsing," Shann said quickly, and he frowned.

"Aren't you Shann Delaney?"

Shann turned back to the man, really looking at him, realizing he was vaguely familiar.

"I'm Joe Radford. Evan's brother. I was a couple of years below you at school."

"Oh. Yes. Joe. I remember you." He did look a little like Evan, although his hair was much darker than his brother's. "Have you worked here long?" Shann asked politely.

"Since Angie extended the place. I was working at a hardware chain on the other side of town so I jumped at the chance of a job closer to home." He made a sweeping motion with his arm. "Bit different to what it used to be, isn't it?"

"Yes. Unrecognizable."

"How long have you been home?" Joe asked.

"Nearly two weeks."

"Oh. That's why I hadn't heard. You would have missed seeing Evan and Leigh before they left for New Zealand."

Shann stiffened. "Yes. Angie said they were on holidays."

"Combined with one of Evan's business trips. So what are you doing with yourself these days?" Joe continued as Shann tried to find an excuse to leave.

"I've had lots of different jobs," she said vaguely.

"Oh. Married?"

And they said women could gossip, Shann thought, and then felt a little ungracious. Joe was only being friendly. Shann shook her head. "No. Still single."

"Well, I can recommend married life," Joe continued pleasantly. "Remember Kylie Farmer? I think her sister Jeanette was in your year. We've been married for two years. Had our first child at Christmas. A boy. Eight pounds. Joseph Junior."

"Congratulations."

"Are you staying in town long?"

"No. I'm just here while my father recuperates from a hip replacement. Oh, Joe, could you point me in the direction of Angie's office?"

"Sure. Go down this aisle. Turn right and keep going. I can show you."

"No. That's okay." Shann held up her hand. "I'll find it. And I don't want to keep you from your customers." She indicated an elderly woman hovering near them.

"Okay. I'll see you around, Shann." He headed over to the woman.

Shann breathed a sigh of relief that Joe Radford was a conscientious worker. She turned right and saw a group of offices along the end wall. Shann took a couple of strides forward and stopped. Should she approach Angie? Now might not be convenient. Perhaps she should simply leave.

"Does madam need assistance?" asked a soft low voice off to her right.

Shann turned to see Angie leaning casually against a rack of painting paraphernalia. She was wearing dark slacks and a matching jacket over a pale blue shirt, and her smile was full of welcome. That now familiar glow of awareness warmed Shann, and she shifted from one foot to the other. "I was just trying to decide if I should or shouldn't bother you. I mean, if you're busy—"

"No. I'm not too busy to see you," Angie said quickly. "Actually I came down to rescue you from Joe." She pointed to the mezzanine level up above them. "I saw you come in and get waylaid. Joe's a pretty good talker."

Shann laughed. "That he is."

"He's a good salesman, but I sometimes think customers just buy whatever to get away from him. He's a nice guy, though."

"Yes. I only vaguely remember him from school."

"Me, too. But do you want the promised tour or would you prefer a cup of our famous coffee?"

Shann looked around. "I thought I smelled coffee."

"Come on." Angie motioned for Shann to follow her. "I'll show you our coffee shop. It's only been running for a month, but it's a big success. Especially at the weekend."

In the corner of the building near the offices there was a cordoned off area with a dozen or so small tables and chairs. Half the tables were filled, and a delicious aroma wafted on the air.

"What will you have?" Angie asked as she indicated a free table away from the other coffee shop patrons.

"Skinny cappuccino if you have them." Shann reached for her wallet.

"Put that away. My shout," Angie said lightly as she walked across to the counter. She came back with two plates holding vanilla slices. "I hope you still like these. I can recommend them."

"Vanilla slice." Shann took the plate Angie handed her. "They were my favorites."

"I know," Angie said softly as she sat down opposite Shann.

"You remember that?"

"Yes." Angie looked down as she cut her slice in two. "I remember a lot about you." Then she looked up, and her clear green eyes met and held Shann's.

That heady tension surged between them, and Shann had to fight the urge to lean across the small intimate table and put her lips to the other woman's soft, so inviting mouth.

"You do?" she asked, and her voice sounded barely recognizable as her own.

"I do."

The low resonance seemed to flow gently down the length of Shann's spine, as though Angie's soft fingers were moving physically over her.

Angie took a bite of her vanilla slice, murmured her enjoyment and then swallowed. She wiped her mouth with her napkin. "You also loved netball, swimming, violet crumble bars, playing your guitar." She chuckled. "But not mathematics."

"Definitely not math," Shann agreed. "Unlike you. Do you know you completely humiliated me that afternoon I tried to help you with your homework."

Angie wrinkled her nose. "I was a bit precocious, wasn't I?"

"You were smart, I'll give you that."

"Sorry about that not-so-attractive exhibition of my flawed character," Angie said with mock seriousness, and then she sighed. "Truthfully, Shann, I took my anger out on you when it was Leigh I was mad with that afternoon. I was angry with her for not staying to help me when she was supposed to. And it was my biology and not my math. I just said math to get to you because I knew you hated that subject. Heaven only knows why I did it because you were always the one who was there while Leigh always seemed to weasel her way out of things."

Deep down Shann knew what Angie was saying was true. Leigh was very accomplished at getting her own way. But they had all allowed her to. It was part of Leigh's charm.

"So will you accept a belated apology?" Angie was asking with a smile.

Shann smiled back. "Sure. What's an ego dent anyway? It was probably very character building. And talking about netball, you were no slouch yourself." Shann seemed to recall Angie was part of the winning team in the lower age group the year Shann left. "Did you continue playing?"

"Until I did my knee. Once I got that patched up I decided not to chance more damage, and I changed to softball."

"Oh. Probably wise."

"Then I sprained my ankle," Angie remarked derisively. "So I decided sport was far too dangerous and became a complete nerd."

Shann laughed. "But you didn't give it up completely though. Didn't you say you went running with the dog the other day?"

"Mmm. But that's only so I can guiltlessly eat the occasional vanilla slice." Angie popped another piece into her mouth.

54

"I don't think you need worry about putting on weight." Shann's eyes slid downward, touched on the rise of Angie's breasts and skated away again. When she looked up she knew Angie had seen her assessing regard, and she felt herself flush.

"Oh, I can pack it on if I'm not careful."

Shann shook her head. "That I don't believe. You're just saying that to make me feel better because you remember too many of these go straight to my hips."

Angie pulled a face. "Okay. So I just don't want to take the chance. But if you'll cast your mind back I always told you that you were imagining the thickening hips thing."

A scene flashed into Shann's mind, obviously the one Angie was referring to. Shann had just bought some new jeans. She'd saved up for a proper pair, as they called them, a name rather than a generic brand, and she'd raced over to show Leigh.

A small frown gathered on Leigh's brow and she pursed her lips. "Turn around. Did you get a smaller size?"

"No. Why?" Shann glanced at her reflection in Leigh's mirror.

"Oh. Nothing."

"No. Why? Come on Leigh," Shann persisted. "Don't they look okay?"

"Well, they make you look a little big in the hips, don't you think."

"They look fine to me," said Angie who was sitting cross-legged on Leigh's bed. "Don't listen to her, Shann. She's only jealous because Aunt Ann said she couldn't have a new pair."

"Don't you have some study to do, Angelina. Or some boring book to read." Leigh dismissed her young cousin and turned back to Shann. "I was only thinking you might have put on a bit of weight, that's all. You said as much yourself the other day."

Shann had said that. She glanced again at her reflection, trying to swivel round to get a better look at her rear view.

Angie gave an exclamation of disgust as she pushed herself to her feet. "You look absolutely fine, Shann," she said as she left the room, closing the door firmly behind her.

Leigh had then run across and flipped the lock. "I knew that would get rid of her. I thought she'd never leave us alone." And she'd walked across and pulled Shann into her arms, nibbling quick kisses along Shann's jawline.

"I think my little cousin has a big fat crush on you, Shann Delaney."

"What are you talking about, Leigh?" Shann was suddenly flustered, recalling the clear green intensity of Angelina's level looks. "She's just a kid."

"Now don't pretend you haven't noticed. She hangs on your every word."

"Leigh! You're being ridiculous."

"You wouldn't kiss anyone else the way you kiss me, would you?" Leigh asked, looking up at Shann with a half-teasing, half-serious gleam in her eyes.

"No. Never," she said, and drowned in the feel of Leigh's lips on her own.

Shann drew her mind back to the present. Angie was watching her, and Shann was relieved the other woman couldn't see into her thoughts. Or could she? Something flickered in Angie's green eyes but was gone before Shann could define it.

Just then the young waitress put frothy cappuccinos down in front of them, and Angie thanked her. "So what about you," she asked, turning back to Shann. "Are you on the exercise bandwagon?"

"I try to walk a couple of times a week. Occasionally I go for a run. And Corey and I like to play soccer in the park." Shann took a sip of her coffee and then licked the foam from her lip. "Yum. This is delicious. I'm glad I called in."

"So am I."

There was that tension again. It seemed to Shann to hover just below the surface when she was with Angie, waiting to swell between them and set Shann's nerve endings clamoring.

"All this is quite impressive," Shann motioned to encompass the store.

Angie sipped her own coffee. "I'll admit it was something of a gamble, but I thought it was worth the chance and, touch wood," she lightly rapped the tabletop, "it seems to be paying off."

"But why hardware?"

"Why not?" Angie laughed. "The Grossmans who owned this place taught me every aspect of the business when I was working for them and, besides, I loved fooling around with power tools. It always seemed so, well, butch."

CHAPTER FOUR

The word reverberated between them, and Shann's breath caught somewhere in her throat. Was Angie giving Shann the clue she was looking for? Or was it just an innocent comment? Shann had no way of knowing if Angie was aware of the huge family drama that unfolded ten years ago. Possibly she didn't know about it, but in all probability she did.

Ask her, suggested a voice inside Shann, but she somehow couldn't bring herself to do so. What would she ask anyway? By the way, Angie, did you know your cousin Leigh and I were supposed to have had a lurid sexual lesbian affair?

"You remember the stuff I made for Ann and Mike in woodwork and metalwork classes?" Angie was saying. "I don't think the house was big enough to hold it all. Your parents ended up with the second coffee table I made, and they still use it out on the deck."

Shann gathered herself together. "Yes, I do remember that. And the coffee table is beautifully made."

"I got an A for that one," Angie grimaced.

"I didn't know you did metal work, too."

"Oh, yes. Can't you see me with my face mask, my gloves, wielding my welder?"

The trouble was, Shann thought almost hysterically, she could.

"I did all that macho stuff, much to Ann's horror. I even considered teaching the subjects." Angie grinned. "But only for a minute. So, as you can see, all this," she waved her arm around, "suits me fine. If I was a cat you'd say I'd fallen on my feet."

"It's obvious how much you love it. I can hear it in your voice."

"You can?" Angie's fingers fiddled absently with her empty coffee cup. "Am I that transparent?"

"No. Definitely not generally. Only about your work. And you're lucky to be working at something you love. Most people just have to put in their eight or more hours."

"That's true. And I really do enjoy all this." She paused. "Did Liz tell you about my grandmother?"

"Yes. That must have been a surprise."

"It was. I didn't even know I had grandparents. My mother certainly didn't mention them. Apparently she ran away from home when she was sixteen, and they never saw her again. No one could tell me if my grandparents tried to find her, only that she was something of a problem child from the moment she was born. She had me when she was eighteen, and that didn't work out for her either."

"Which was hardly your fault, Angie," Shann said, trying to reassure her.

"I know that now, but it caused me a lot of heartache when I was a child. The turning point in my life was coming to live with Ann and Mike. I do wish I could have met my grandparents though. And I'm very grateful to them for providing me with the opportunity to try to make a go of this." Angie sighed. "So what about you, Shann? Do you enjoy doing what you do?"

"Well, in the past I've had a few jobs I didn't much care for, but they were a means to an end," Shann told her. "As in, Corey and I had to eat. But mostly, I found something to enjoy with my various jobs."

"No. I mean your songwriting."

"Now *that* I've always loved, and I'm so lucky it's starting to pay off."

"I knew back then it was your passion. You were always strumming your guitar."

"I guess I drove everyone nuts."

"Not me." Angie's fingers returned to twisting her empty cup. "I used to sneak over and listen to you most afternoons."

"Sneak over where?"

"Over the fence. I had a spot behind a grevillea bush underneath your bedroom window. I loved your songs. As I told you the other night, I was one of your biggest fans."

Shann didn't know what to say as a glow of pleasure grew inside her. "I . . . you sat listening?"

Angie nodded. "I told Ann and Leigh you'd be famous one day."

"I wish you'd told me." Shann laughed. "I could have used some encouragement. My parents thought it was a mammoth waste of time I could have used studying." So much so that Shann had confined her guitar practice to the hours after school and before her father and Ruth came home from work. And while Leigh was at sports practice. Leigh hadn't cared for Shann's guitar playing either and had once accused Shann of caring more about her precious guitar than she did about Leigh. "I lacked a lot of self confidence back then," she finished flatly.

"I don't know why. You were fantastic, and I'm not surprised at your success."

"There's been a certain amount of luck involved," Shann began.

"Luck? Luck doesn't come into it unless you have talent. And no matter how much you downplay it, Shann, you do have talent. You always did."

"Thanks. But if I hadn't been lucky enough to do *The Kelly Boys* theme I'd still be a struggling songwriter," Shann said honestly.

"How did that come about?"

"As I said, luck. Just being in the right place at the right time. I was taking a songwriting course. I'd felt I was a bit stale, couldn't come up with anything new or fresh, and Corey saw the ad for the course in the paper. So I applied, got a place, and was thoroughly enjoying it. The teacher was quite well known and did a lot of television work. He told us about the proposed show and gave us the project to write a theme song. He really liked mine and passed it on to a friend who was working on the show and," Shann shrugged, "the rest is history. I was lucky."

"And you wrote a fantastic song," Angie said sincerely. "I particularly watched the show the other night so I'm speaking with full knowledge, so to speak."

"Well, thanks. That's nice of you to say that."

"Sorry to interrupt, Angie." A young woman had approached them and stood apologetically beside their table. "That distributor you wanted to talk to is on the phone."

Angie looked as though she was about to refuse to take the call, and Shann stood up, glancing at her wristwatch. "I should be going anyway. Liz will be wondering where I am. Thanks for the coffee."

"My pleasure." Angie stood up too, and a rueful smiled lifted the corners of her mouth.

Her very kissable mouth. The thought hit Shann like a blow to the solar plexus. This attraction she felt for the other woman was getting way out of hand. She knew she'd have to put a stop to it before she did or said something they might both regret. Perhaps it was better if she made sure she didn't see any more of Angie than she had to. And at that particular thought something painful shifted in the region of her heart.

"Call in any time. For coffee or whatever," Angie added softly and then smiled. "I have a fairly reasonable boss. However, I should get this call. It was good to see you. Bye, Shann."

Shann hurried outside, jumped into her car and headed the short distance home. As she turned into the driveway she realized she was humming the tune of the song she was working on. And she felt more alive than she had in years. She knew she'd not been as attracted to anyone in a very long time.

But attracted to Angie Callahan? She still couldn't believe that the shy, retiring teen had blossomed into an attractive, vivacious young woman. Yet when she thought about it, Angie had always been special. She'd overcome her less-than-perfect childhood and simply got on with life. But Angie Callahan. It was too difficult. Wasn't it?

She acknowledged that small—very small—rational voice inside her that told her she should simply cool it, keep as much distance as possible between herself and the other woman. The whole thing was fraught with emotional pitfalls, not the least being that Angie was Leigh's cousin.

She switched off the engine and sat for a moment looking at the house next door. Shann had spent a lot of years totally in love with Leigh Callahan, but Leigh had been lost to her all those years ago. If she'd ever had Leigh, said that same small voice inside her. Now Leigh was married with a family. She'd rejected Shann when she was at her lowest ebb, and Shann told herself she'd put that painful part of her life behind her. She had to move on. She was single and so, it would seem, was Angie.

Was Angie a lesbian? The word *butch* echoed inside her again. Had that been a hint from Angie? Or a warning? Shann had no way of knowing and unless she asked Angie herself how would she know?

We need a mark, Shann reflected irreverently as she climbed from the car and collected her purchases from the boot. Perhaps a large *L* in the middle of the forehead that only another lesbian could see. Or a secret handshake like the Masons. Now something like that would make it easier.

Shann laughed at herself as she jogged up the steps. Maybe there was some secret symbol or sign, and she'd been away from the scene so long she didn't know about it. She'd have to call Gina and ask her.

Later after she'd settled her father in his room for a nap and she'd satisfied herself that Liz was also resting on the veranda,

Shann went into the bedroom with the handheld phone and dialed Gina's number.

Gina Carlisle was the first out lesbian Shann had met. She owned a bar in town, and it was here that Shann had made her singing debut.

It started when Shann had seen a sign for a position as a kitchen hand on the notice board in the area's first alternative café. The small coffee shop served organic food, sold crystals and played very different music. New Age hippies, her father labeled them. Shann sometimes called in there and the fact that her parents frowned on the place made it far more exciting. So when she saw the job advertised, she rang and got an interview.

"You won't be working out in the bar," said the owner, "but I want someone over eighteen."

Shann guiltily fingered the fake ID she had in her pocket. "I had my birthday last week," she said, refraining from mentioning it was her seventeenth and not her eighteenth. Because she was tall she rarely had trouble appearing older than she was. As yet she'd never been asked to show the ID that a friend of Leigh's had acquired for them. "I have ID."

She just had to be confident, she told herself as she knocked on the back entrance of The Blue Moon. The door opened and Shann smiled at the huge woman who was eyeing her suspiciously.

"I have an appointment with Gina Carlisle at four p.m.," Shann told her.

The woman, Jess, the cook, Shann later learned, looked Shann up and down again before opening the door wide and motioning her inside. "Second door on the left."

Shann swallowed and strode down the hallway. She took a deep breath. Be confident, she reminded herself as she rapped on the door.

"Come in." Gina Carlisle stood up as Shann stepped into the room. She was barely five feet tall, with dark hair and olive skin. She also did nothing to disguise her voluptuous figure. Blue jeans hugged her rounded hips and the low neckline of her sleeveless shirt barely covered the swell of her full breasts.

At the time Gina was on the right side of forty, and her dark eyes narrowed as she sized Shann up. "Wow! You're a tall one," she said.

"I'm five-ten," Shann told her.

"Well, sit down and let's get started." She reseated herself and looked levelly across the desk as she began firing questions about Shann's previous work experience. She took down phone numbers to check Shann's references and named an hourly rate that was slightly higher than the going amount.

"Well, if your references check out the job's yours," Gina said after what seemed to Shann to be fairly casual conversation rather than an interview. "As long as you're not concerned about working here."

"Concerned?" Shann frowned, perplexed. "About what?"

"You do know this is a lesbian bar?"

Shann had had no idea, wasn't aware that such places existed. Her mouth dried, and she swallowed, knowing a flush had colored her face. "Of course." She rallied. "That's no problem."

Gina gave her another piercing look. "Okay. Unless you hear from me you can start tomorrow at five p.m. Jess out in the kitchen will tell you everything you need to know."

It took a week for Shann to get up the nerve to venture out into the bar after her shift in the kitchen ended. She looked around, peering into the slightly dimmed lights. Women of all shapes, sizes, and ages danced together on the small dance floor or sat talking in groups at tables. Shann hastily looked away as two women began to kiss passionately in a darkened corner.

She walked nervously up to the bar and ordered a Coke with a slice of lemon from the attractive bartender. The woman had bare muscular arms with a tattooed pattern encircling one bicep.

"One Coke with a slice of lemon," said the woman and, embarrassed, Shann paid for the drink. She'd only just got her license and her father allowed her to use her brother's old car. She had no intention of being caught drunk driving. Apart from that Shann thought the taste of most alcohol was very overrated.

Shann took a sip and swiveled around on her stool so she could survey the room again. If she told Leigh about this place, would she come with her one night? Shann wasn't confident Leigh would but how wonderfully freeing it would be to dance close to Leigh and not have to worry about anyone knocking on the door, interrupting them.

"I haven't seen you here before," said a deep, throaty voice beside Shann, and she nearly dropped her drink.

The woman who slipped onto the stool beside her wore black leather pants and a leather vest that fit snuggly over her breasts, the open top two buttons displaying an impressive cleavage. A diamond stud sparkled beneath her full bottom lip, and a silver ring hung from one eyebrow.

"Oh. I . . . no, I haven't been here before," Shann stammered, blushing furiously.

"No. You sure haven't. I'd have remembered you," said the woman, leaning closer to Shann, running her finger down Shann's bare arm.

"Okay, Laurie. Knock it off." Gina Carlisle walked up to them, and the other woman pouted.

"Sorry. Didn't mean to tread on your turf, Gina." She turned to Shann with a rueful smirk. "Pity," she said as she moved off to join a group of women.

Gina looked at Shann and shook her head. "I hope that's not alcohol you're drinking," she said, and Shann hastily assured her it wasn't and that she was driving home.

Sitting on the stool the other woman had vacated, Gina lit up a cigarette. "You know, I suspect I'd be in big trouble if anyone saw you in here, Shann Delaney. So how old are you really? No." She held up her hand. "It's best you don't tell me."

"I have my ID," Shann began. "It's a really good one. You can't tell it's—"

Gina held up her hand again. "Don't tell me."

"I really need the job, Gina."

"What sort of trouble are you in, honey?" Gina asked.

"No trouble. Honestly. But I need the money. To make a good quality demo of some of my songs. I'm saving to do that. That's all. I write songs."

"What sort of songs?"

"All sorts but mainly modern country."

"You don't mean my baby done left me, my horse has gone lame, and mama's in jail?"

Shann laughed. "Sort of. Without the horse and the lawless mama."

Gina grinned. "Are you any good?"

"Yes," Shann said. "I think, well, I hope so."

"You have the look of that sexy Terri Clark, all dark hair and legs up to your eyes." Gina drew on her cigarette. "We have a talent search here every Friday night at nine. Fifty dollars for the performer the crowd chooses. Then once a month on a Saturday night we have a final with a hundred-dollar pot. Why don't you try it?"

"That would be great." Shann bit her lip. "But what about, well, the ID?"

"So keep that on you and no alcohol. That way I can talk myself out of it if the cops decide to do a spot check."

"Do I need to put my name down for the talent search?"

"No. I'll tell them to expect you. Just turn up on Friday before nine p.m. And Shann, be selective who you talk to in here, just for my peace of mind. Okay?"

"Okay."

"Some of these women would eat you up and spit you out. And all puns are intended."

Shann blushed again, and Gina patted her arm.

"Come on. I'll introduce you to some nice people."

Shann had played and sang at The Blue Moon talent search and impressed everyone enough to win her heat and then the final. Gina then offered her a permanent gig a couple of nights a week.

Now, ten years later Shann listened to the phone ringing.

"The Blue Moon," said a gravelly voice.

"Is your chili still so hot it makes your eyes water for days, Jess?" Shann asked lightly.

"Who is this?"

"Sheez! How quickly they forget. It's only been ten years."

"Ten years? At my age I'm lucky to remember what happened yesterday, let alone ten years ago."

"It's Shann."

"Shann Delaney?" she said incredulously. "Good God, kid. You back in town?"

"Yes. So how are you?"

"Oh, I'm fine. I lost weight then it found me again and brought along a parcel of relatives." Jess laughed. "You coming in to see us?"

"That's the general idea," Shann told her. "Is Gina there?"

"Sure. Isn't she always? You know Cassie died a couple of years ago?"

"Yes. I heard. How's Gina coping?" Gina and Cassie had been together for twenty years.

"She just puts one foot in front of the other. Wish they could find a cure for this bloody cancer."

"Amen to that," Shann said with feeling.

"I'll put you through to Gina. She'll be pleased to hear from you. And Shann, you come over to see us soon."

"I will, Jess." Shann waited, heard a moment's taped music then Gina's voice came on the line.

"Shann Delaney. Where are you?"

Shann laughed. "Stretched out on my bed wearing tight blue jeans and a big smile."

"You big teaser. When did you get back?"

"Last week. I'm helping the family out. My father and my older sister have both had surgery."

"You're playing nurse? To your family?"

"Dad and I have a sort of armed truce going. But I wanted him

67

to meet Corey, and that's working out really well. Ah, Gina, I was sorry to hear about Cassie."

Gina sighed. "Yes. Life's a bitch, isn't it? Has you wondering about the scheme of things, doesn't it? Cassie never hurt a living soul."

"No. She was one of the nicest, kindest people I've ever met." Shann paused. "So how are you holding up?"

"Okay, honey. Part of me went with Cassie, but the rest of me keeps on plodding along." She sighed. "So when are you coming in to see us? And will we get to meet Corey?"

"Sure you will. How about I bring him in one day after he finishes school? He's dying to meet you."

"He is? You've told him about, well, about us?"

"Of course. Corey's a special boy, even if I do say so myself."

"Shann, that's wonderful. And why wouldn't he be a special boy? He has a special mother, too."

"I've missed you all, Gina." Shann felt the rush of tears in her eyes.

"We've missed you, too. And are you going to do a couple of gigs for me?"

"If you like."

"Good. I'll make up some posters. Everyone will be stoked to have a real live star performer."

"Star performer? You have bigger stars than me all the time, and you know it."

"You'll have to do the theme from *The Kelly Boys*."

Shann groaned. "How did you hear about that?"

"Read it in the *TV Week*. I'm even hooked on the show now. I always tell the TV screen that I gave you your first big break."

"You gave me more than that, Gina. You gave me a sense of self and a sense of belonging. I felt like some sort of freak until I met you."

"A very cute little baby dyke freak," Gina laughed. "Seriously, Shann. We'll all be pleased to see you."

"Liz's husband has a few hours off tomorrow so I'll come over after lunch if that's all right with you. Say about two. I don't have to collect Corey from school until four because he's got soccer practice."

"Two is fine. We'll see you then, shall we?"

"Looking forward to it. Bye, Gina."

"Bye, honey."

Shann set down the receiver and smiled. It would be so good to get reacquainted with her friends.

A few days later, Shann asked Liz if she'd mind if she asked Amy to babysit Corey. "He'll be in bed before I leave," Shann told her. "I wouldn't ask, but I know you said Rhys would be home. Otherwise I'd be worried if you and Dad were on your own."

"Rhys will be home at ten so we'll be fine, Shann." Liz assured her. "Where are you going? Catching up with friends?"

"Yes." Shann paused and then decided she wanted no secrets. "And I've got a singing gig."

"That's great, Shann. Whereabouts?"

"At a club called The Blue Moon. About fifteen minutes drive from here."

"The Blue Moon?" Liz frowned. "I don't think I've heard of that."

"It's a lesbian bar."

"You're going to be singing in a lesbian bar?" Liz had dropped her voice and paused with her teacup halfway to her lips. "There's a gay bar near here?"

"Not that near," Shann said dryly. "Don't worry, only those of us in the sisterhood can pass within." Liz's eyes widened, and Shann chuckled. "I'm having a go at you, Liz."

"I knew that." Liz took a studied sip of her tea.

"Actually I used to sing there ten years ago. You could say I made my debut there."

"You did?" Liz sat her cup on its saucer. "But ten years ago? You weren't old enough to be in a bar, were you?"

"Not technically. But according to my fake ID I was."

"You had a fake ID?" Liz was incredulous. "Shann, what were you thinking, and where did you get it?"

"Most of us had them and, as to my supplier, my lips are sealed."

"Shann! Good grief! Did Dad know?"

"About the fake ID or The Blue Moon?"

Liz gave her a playful shove.

"Not about either actually. But relax, Liz. Gina, the owner of the club, watched out for me, and I never drank alcohol."

"Well, I can be grateful for small mercies," Liz said, rolling her eyes.

"Seriously, Liz. Gina gave me my first gig. She paid me, and I got lots of tips, made a lot of money for a seventeen-year-old. Where do you think I got the money to fly down to Aunt Millie's?"

"I guess I didn't think," Liz shrugged. "I just thought Millie had sent it to you."

Shann shook her head. "It was my own money."

"I can't believe Dad didn't know anything about where you were working."

"Come on, Liz. Could you see me telling him I was playing guitar at a lesbian bar? He'd have freaked. I told him I was work-ing in McDonald's."

"Didn't you worry he'd check up on you?"

Shann laughed. "Not too much. Dad hates McDonald's. He says the food gives him indigestion."

"But Shann, you were taking a heck of a chance."

"I know. But it was worth it to me. It was so wonderful to be there, Liz, with women who were just like me." Shann looked across at her sister. "I felt like I'd come home."

"Oh, Shann." Liz touched her hand. "Did we make you feel like an outsider?"

"Only—" Shann sighed. "Not really, Liz. I loved you, my family. I just wished I could be more, well, more open. Down at the club I could be myself."

"Was it that bad? Were we so bad?"

"No, of course not. It's hard to explain, Liz. I felt . . . I don't know, like a freak. Being expected to be and do what's expected is such a huge stress when you feel different. And then to have your parents so angry, well, it was pretty devastating."

"You mean, because of that thing with Leigh Callahan?" Liz asked softly.

Shann raised her eyebrows. "How much did you know about that?"

"Only what Ruth told me on the phone." Liz looked a little embarrassed. "She said you and Leigh were caught, well, experimenting."

"Experimenting?" Shann exclaimed exasperatedly. "We weren't caught having sex, Liz. We were just kissing."

"I told Ruth they were overreacting."

"Dad was furious. I wanted to tell him I was a lesbian then, but he was so angry. So were the Callahans. I felt Ann and Mike blamed me."

"Were you and Leigh having an affair?"

Shann stood up, turned away, the pain of rejection rising inside her like bile. "I was in love with her," she said softly. "It was—" She sighed. "It was pretty innocent really." She sat down again. "Look, Liz, I don't particularly want to dredge all that up again. I've put it behind me."

"Oh, Shann. I'm sorry. I had no idea. I should have talked to you about it when Ruth told me," Liz agonized.

"No, you shouldn't. You were over a thousand miles away. You had a husband and two young kids. Ruth had no right to worry you with it." She shrugged again. "Apart from that, I probably wouldn't have discussed it. I was in a pretty bad state." And Shann hadn't even been able to talk to Gina about it. Not until after Corey was born, and she'd called her to tell her.

Liz ran her fingers through her hair. "I feel I've let you down, Shann. You think you know your family as well as you know yourself. You think you'd understand, that you'd realize when someone

71

you loved was hurting. But I never knew, Shann. You were my little sister, and I didn't know."

Shann walked around the table and gave her sister a gentle hug. "This isn't something you need to beat yourself up over. The situation was way out of your control. So give it up. Look at me. Do I look like I haven't recovered? I'm at ease with who I am, Liz. It means I don't have to take out front page ads in the papers unless I feel I want to. And as for Dad, I've adopted a don't-ask-don't-tell truce with him. So quit worrying. Dad and I will make our own peace or we won't. It's up to us."

"I know. But . . . I love you both." A tear trickled down Liz's cheek.

"I love you, too. So let's find something else to talk about. If your mild-mannered husband comes home and finds you in tears he'll have my guts for garters."

Liz laughed. "What makes you think he'd blame you?"

Shann raised her hands and let them fall. "Everyone blames me," she said and then laughed. "I should write a song about that."

"So are you getting paid to sing at this place?" Liz asked and Shann nodded.

"Oh, yes. Your sister's a professional singer." She pulled a face. "Gina wouldn't let me do it for free even though I wanted to." Shann chuckled. "She says I'm a tax deduction. You'd like Gina, Liz. Maybe I could introduce you sometime."

"I'd like to meet her, Shann," Liz said sincerely. "And whenever you want to go out you know you can. I'm doing fine. Really."

"Just don't get too cocky and overdo it, that's all." Shann admonished her.

Shann parked the car behind The Blue Moon, grabbed her guitar case and knocked on the back door. Jess let her in and gave her an enveloping hug.

"Just like old times, hey, Shann? Whoa!" She looked Shann up and down. "Now that shirt is really something."

Shann put her guitar down and spun around. She wore her best boots and black dress jeans with a silver chain belt. Her white suede shirt had a fringed yoke and fringes down the long sleeves. Around her neck she wore a silver chain with a heart-shaped locket nestling in the valley between her breasts.

Jess whistled. "You make me wish I was thirty years younger and a lesbian."

Shann kissed Jess's weathered cheek. "You old flirt, you. What would George say if he heard that?"

"He'd say I told you so. And he'd say I told you you'd catch it if you started working for those gay people. He gave me dire warnings twenty years ago when I took this job working for Gina. But I decided to stay straight and keep making his life miserable."

Shann laughed delightedly. "You can't fool me, Jess. You love that old codger to bits."

"You just keep those dangerous thoughts to yourself, young lady. Now, go on out there and wow 'em."

Shann left her guitar in Gina's office and walked through to the bar. She paused and took in the ambience of the place. The women. The music. The sound of laughter. And she could almost believe the ten years between had never been. But, of course, they had.

Tonight The Blue Moon was packed. Women danced, sat around tables, stood in groups, talking or singing along to the songs coming from the old jukebox.

Shann spied Gina at the bar and moved around to join her.

"What a relief! Our star's turned up," Gina said with mock seriousness. "And she's looking sensational." She gave Shann a hug and turned to the bartender. "Charley, a coke with a slice of lemon for the famous Shann Delaney. Do you still drink that or have you progressed to the hard stuff?"

"Coke with lemon will be fine. Besides, you know that hard stuff will rot your boots."

"Too true," acknowledged Gina. "But what a way to go. I'll have my usual hard one," she added with a wink at Charley.

73

The bartender was new. Gina had told Shann that Meg had moved over to Perth last year.

Charley smiled at Shann as she handed her her drink. "One coke with lemon. Nice to meet you, famous Shann Delaney."

"Famous? Hardly. And Gina might regret asking me to sing once you've heard me. It has been ten years. Maybe I'm getting a bit past it?"

"Oh sure!" laughed Gina, taking the gin and tonic Charley passed her. "You're not even thirty. Besides, age is all relative. Koalas are old at six."

"They are?"

Gina nodded. "As for the 'past it', my bet is you're even better."

"We can but hope." She took a sip of her coke and nodded her thanks to the bartender.

"Have you had a look around, Shann? You'll see lots of old friends." Gina sipped her own drink.

Shann glanced around at the crowd. Women raised their glasses, some waved, and Shann smiled and waved back at the familiar faces. "Now I think I'm getting nervous."

"Rubbish!" stated Gina. "Now go get your guitar, and we'll get this show on the road. We're all dying with anticipation."

Shann collected her guitar, stuck a couple of extra plectrums in her pocket, and headed for the small, brightly lit stage. Gina was just starting her introduction.

"Tonight's performer really needs no introduction to a lot of you. We remember her when she was quite literally jailbait. Really cute jailbait."

Everyone laughed, and Gina gave them a concise list of Shann's accomplishments, told them Shann had debuted at the club. "Now, come on up here, Shann."

Shann stepped up beside Gina and set her drink on the floor behind her.

"Now you'll all be pleased to hear Shann's single and, happily, now of legal age."

"And then some," laughed Shann.

Gina went on to talk about Shann's involvement with the theme song for *The Kelly Boys* as Shann looked out over the room and the mass of faces.

The door at the back opened and a latecomer moved into the room. Two women waved and each hugged her as she joined them. The trio moved into a brighter patch of light and Shann's eyes narrowed, her breath catching in her chest.

The familiar short fair hair was spiked and her green eyes seemed to lock with Shann's across the sea of women.

CHAPTER FIVE

Tonight she wore faded jeans that rode low on her hips and a short red sleeveless top that displayed a flat midsection of firm tanned skin. Something bright flashed in the region of the woman's navel, but from this distance Shann couldn't see what it was.

The red top set off the lightly tanned skin, her slightly muscular arms and the rounded neckline sat just above the swell of her breasts. She carried a dark jacket over one arm.

So was this her answer, Shann reflected, the thought making her suddenly lightheaded. Or did it only pose more questions? But the key could very well be that Angie was here, in a lesbian bar. A million thoughts skittered about inside Shann. She felt like grinning broadly but a small part of her warned her to take care. She knew there could be some other reason Angie was here. Perhaps she simply had lesbian friends? And, of course, Liz might even have told Angie that Shann was singing, and she'd come down.

Pull yourself together, she admonished herself. This whole thing with Angie Callahan was reducing her to borderline blithering idiot.

And then Gina was smiling at her, turning and leaving her alone on the small stage. The lights in the room dimmed a little, cocooning Shann on the small stage. She took a deep breath and settled her guitar strap over her shoulder.

"Nice to see so many familiar faces," she said to settle her nerves. "Seems like old times. Let's start with one of my favorites, Terri Clark's 'Girls Lie Too'." She moved around the stage to the beat of the song, had the audience laughing at the song's lyrics. Shann loved performing the song, and when she'd finished the crowd clapped and whistled their appreciation.

She continued on into Mary Chapin Carpenter's "Down at the Twist and Shout" and a couple of other fast numbers. Then she sat back on the stool Gina had left for her and plucked the intro to Trisha Yearwood's "The Song Remembers When." Later she also sang a few of her own songs, including the now famous *The Kelly Boys* theme.

After three-quarters of an hour Gina stepped in to announce they'd break and that Shann would return to perform again later in the evening. Once the lights had dimmed Shann had lost sight of Angie and now that she was back on the club floor it was impossible to find anyone in the crowd of people. Shann left her guitar propped on the stage and followed Gina across to the bar. Women congratulated her on the way.

Charley set a fresh coke and lemon on the bar top for Shann. "Nice work," she said with a grin.

Shann took a much-needed gulp of her drink grimacing as the bubbles fought on the way down.

"Nice work all right," Gina squeezed her arm. "You were fantastic. How about doing a couple of extra gigs while you're home?"

"Sure. If it fits in with Liz and my father." Shann's eyes were scanning the crowd, and Gina raised one arched eyebrow questioningly.

"Don't tell me someone's caught your eye? I don't believe it."

"What—? I don't know what you mean, Gina."

Gina gave a soft laugh. "Sure you don't! You've never been much good at subterfuge, love. Not when you were a kid and definitely not now."

Shann pulled a face. "Who me? Subterfuge? Never."

"Cassie used to say your face was an open book, and she was right. Well, can't say I'm surprised someone caught your eye. There are plenty of women here and most would be more than willing."

"You're talking complications, Gina." Yet even as she said the words Shann knew she'd be hard-pressed to give a thought to the uneasiness of entanglement where the new, grown-up Angie Callahan was concerned. "And complications I don't need right now," she added, more for her own benefit.

"What you *do* need," said a husky, amused voice behind Shann, "is a relaxing bracket of dancing."

Shann spun around to see Angie leaning on the bar. She flushed with pleasure, and was just as quickly embarrassed. Had Angie heard her comment about complications? She drew herself together. "Oh. Hi. I thought I saw you out there in the sea of faces." Shann became aware of Gina's scrutiny of the other woman, and she hurriedly made the introductions. "Gina, this is Angie Callahan, our next-door neighbor. Angie, meet Gina Carlisle, the owner of The Blue Moon."

"Hello," said Angie easily. "Nice to meet you, Gina."

"Yes." Gina nodded, but before she could comment, Angie held out her hand, palm upward, to Shann. "What about it, Shann? Care to dance?"

Shann automatically put her hand in Angie's. She nodded, excusing herself to Gina without meeting the other woman's eyes, before following Angie out onto the dance floor.

The up-tempo number had the small dance floor packed with gyrating women and Shann and Angie insinuated themselves into the crush.

"Nice show," said a woman Shann knew from the past.

"Great to see you," said another.

They'd barely started to dance when the music changed to a softer, slower number. Angie moved closer, her arms sliding lightly around Shann, their bodies moving together, not quite touching. Shann's throat was dry, and she swallowed. She slid a look at Angie. A slight smile lifted the corners of her mouth and her green eyes twinkled.

"So you don't need complications, hmmm?" Angie asked lightly.

"Oh, I . . ." Shann swallowed again. "I always tell Gina that in case she tries to matchmake. She likes to do that. Matchmake," she finished, totally disconcerted.

Angie smiled and moved a little closer to Shann. "Now, this is more like it," she said softly and Shann felt the warmth of Angie's breath on her cheek.

"Yes," Shann said, her whole body responding to the other woman's delightful proximity, and they danced quietly for a few moments. "Do you come here often?" Shann cringed when she heard the words tumble from her mouth. It was bad enough to think them, let alone actually say them. She groaned. "I can't believe I actually said that."

Angie gave a bubbly laugh. "It's not so bad as an ice breaker. And it's a valid question. Yes, I come here every so often with some friends. I don't always dance, but it's a great place to unwind. Nice people, fantastic music. Especially tonight. The music tonight is beyond compare, by the way."

"Thank you. I haven't done any performing for a couple of months."

Some of the dancers had left the floor, and they moved together with the remaining couples.

"So, are you going to ask me?" Angie asked lightly, her breath tickling Shann's ear, causing Shann to shiver slightly.

She drew back a little and regarded Angie inquiringly. "Ask you what?"

"If I'm a lesbian."

"I don't know whether I would have had the nerve to ask you that."

"No?" Angie gave a soft laugh.

The throaty, enticing sound played over Shann's tingling nerve endings, multiplying her awareness of the other girl's firm body so close to her own. And the music, the other dancers, seemed to fade into the background. "I'm not sure I'd have drummed up the courage," she said honestly.

"Coward," Angie breathed lightly as they continued dancing. "Well, in case you were going to ask, then the answer's yes," she added softly after a moment.

Shann digested this information, her feelings a mass of clamoring sensation. Now she knew her attraction to Angie had some chance of being reciprocated. Surely she wasn't imagining the interest in those incredible green eyes.

"No comment?" Angie asked, her breath fluttering over Shann's sensitive earlobe.

"I . . . I'm thinking about it," Shann managed through her constricted throat muscles, and Angie laughed again.

"Are you surprised?"

"Yes and no. Well, I guess I am. But it's a pleasant surprise," she added in a rush.

"Good," Angie said so softly that Shann had to strain to hear her.

They lapsed into silence, moving slowly to the beat of the music. Then they swayed closer, and Shann couldn't have said who closed the small distance between them.

She felt the thrust of Angie's breasts brush against hers and her nipples tingled, then Angie's thighs touched, moved against hers, and a shaft of pure desire speared through Shann, searing her senses. Angie nestled into the curve of Shann's neck, her breath teasing Shann's already heightened awareness.

Shann's hand slid downward to rest on the warm bare skin of Angie's waist. How she wanted to take her away from the crowded club, make love to her. She could hear her heart beating wildly in her chest. Or was it Angie's? The burning need to pull her so much closer was almost overwhelming.

Then the beat of the music picked up, and they moved reluctantly apart.

"Want to sit this one out?" Angie asked thickly, as though she was having trouble forming her words.

Shann nodded and, taking hold of Angie's hand again, led her from the dance floor and back to the bar. They ordered drinks and sat slightly apart from the half dozen or so women who were perched on the barstools. Gina was over at another table talking to a group of women and hadn't noticed Shann and Angie at the bar.

"How long have you known you were a lesbian?" Shann asked, and Angie gave a slight shrug.

"Most of my life would be the simple answer. But I suppose it must have been since I knew what a lesbian was. Before that I just had the sensation of being different. I guess I was about thirteen. How about you?"

"The same I guess," Shann acknowledged. "I don't remember thinking you were . . . I mean, I never discussed anything like that with you when we were younger."

"Why would you have? We never really talked about anything deep and meaningful. Except your music and my math." Angie grinned. "And besides, the three years difference in our ages was more discernible when we were teenagers, don't you think?"

"I suppose they were." And Shann knew she was focused on Leigh and no one else.

"Would you believe the day I decided I was going to tell Ann I was a lesbian I arrived home to discover Leigh had apparently stolen my thunder."

Shann stiffened slightly.

"Of course, most of it was over when I walked in, and even before I got part of the story from Leigh, I'd decided Ann wouldn't be receptive to my earth-shattering revelation. Two lesbians in the family in one day would have been two too many."

Shann met her gaze, and Angie smiled ruefully.

"But I already knew how you felt about Leigh," Angie said softly, and her green eyes reflected a deep sympathy. "I knew you loved my cousin and I suspect she broke your heart."

"It was a long time ago, Angie." Shann sighed. "We were only kids."

"Which doesn't mean it hurt any less."

"No. I suppose not. Let's just say it wasn't the best time of my life."

"I never did find out exactly what happened that day," Angie said gently. "All I knew was that Leigh had been banished to her room, and Ann was absolutely livid. She was not in the mood for my questions so I was sent to my room, too. After Mike came home they both headed over to your place. I saw them go, and Ann's body language said all hell was going to break loose."

"It did. She'd sent me home, and I had to wait for my father and Ruth to come home, too. Before I could begin to explain anything, Ann and Mike were there. Things deteriorated from that moment."

"And I went in to talk to Leigh, but she was still crying her eyes out. It wasn't such a jump to figure out that Ann had walked in on the two of you."

"We forgot to lock the door, and Ann came home early. It was pretty harrowing. And humiliating." Shann said with remembered pain. "Leigh told . . . Ann caught us kissing." And Shann had had her hand under Leigh's T-shirt.

"I gathered as much. Until that day I thought my aunt and uncle were loving, tolerant people. I didn't even consider they wouldn't accept that I was a lesbian with anything other than compassion." Angie laughed. "They gave me some extremely mixed messages over that. Apparently it was okay to love whoever you liked as long as that person was a member of the opposite sex." She looked at Shann. "They way Ann was reacting I knew Leigh hadn't been truthful. Whatever she told her mother, well, I suspected it was more like the truth with a bit of a kink in it. Leigh betrayed you, too, didn't she?"

"There was a lot . . . it was something of a shock to have her mother walk in on us. We were both scared, scared about what would happen to us. Leigh told her mother what she thought her mother wanted to hear. I don't blame her. It was self preservation I guess."

"You didn't do that."

"Maybe I was more of a fighter." Shann shrugged. "I know I had a huge fight with my father and Ruth after your aunt and uncle left."

Angie was silent for a moment. "Are you still in love with her?"

Shann looked away, then shook her head. "I haven't seen her for ten years," she said, knowing she was being evasive.

Angie looked as though she was about to say something, but Gina joined them to ask Shann if she was ready to start her second bracket. As Shann went to follow Gina to the stage Angie put her hand on Shann's arm. "What about singing your song 'Rollercoaster Love?' I used to love that one."

"She's not the one who broke your heart, is she?" Gina asked as they crossed the floor.

"No." Shann hesitated before continuing. "It was her cousin, Leigh."

"Ah, yes. Leigh." Gina turned and raised her eyebrows, but she made no comment. They reached the stage and then she reintroduced Shann.

As soon as she had finished her final bracket Shann knew she should be heading for home. It wasn't late by clubbing standards, and although Corey would be fast asleep, Shann was worried that her doctor brother-in-law might have been held up at the hospital, and either Liz or her father might need her. She packed her guitar away and looked around the still-crowded room. She couldn't see Angie anywhere, but Gina waved and joined her.

"Now you're free to party," Gina said brightly.

"Wish I could, but I should head on home."

Gina pouted. "And here I was thinking lascivious thoughts about what you and the delicious Angie would be getting up to."

Shann couldn't prevent the blush coloring her cheeks. "Knock it off, Gina. I've only just caught up with her after ten years. She was just a kid when I left."

"She's not a kid now." Gina wiggled her eyebrows suggestively. "I know a stack of women here tonight who'd race her off if given half a chance."

"I take it you've seen her in here before," Shann remarked with feigned disinterest, pretending to study the women on the dance floor.

Gina's smile told Shann she wasn't fooling anyone. "She's not what I'd call a regular, but I've seen her now and then. I'd have to be blind not to remember her. She's not what I'd describe as unattractive." Gina paused. "She keeps herself to herself from what I hear."

Shann raised her eyebrows.

"She doesn't sleep around," Gina said baldly.

Shann knew it shouldn't matter but Gina's statement pleased her more than it should. She had no right to judge anyone. Her own life wouldn't stand up to much scrutiny.

"See that couple facing us over at table twenty-eight," Gina continued.

Shann knew where to look, and she recognized the two women as the couple Angie had joined when she arrived.

"I think she was an item with the brunette quite a while ago," Gina told her. "But apparently not now. But they obviously parted as friends."

Shann tried to study the couple without seeming to stare. The brunette stood up to take drinks from the tray another woman had brought to the table. She was tall, her hair shoulder length, and she was attractive.

"Notice anything?" Gina asked.

"No. What?" Shann shrugged. "She's attractive."

84

"And she looks very much like you."

Shann turned back to the other woman.

"Oh, not as in, you look like sisters, but in, she's your style, so to speak. Tall. Dark. Good looking. Must be Angie's type."

"Angie's type? Gina!" Shann exclaimed in disbelief.

"What?" she said innocently. "We all have a type, love. Look at me. Cassie was short and blond. I always go for short and blond. In fact, see that fair-haired woman at the bar now?"

Shann followed Gina's gaze and then looked inquiringly at Gina.

Gina nodded. "It's early yet. We're both taking it slowly. She lost her partner six months before I lost Cassie." Gina sighed. "You know there'll never be anyone like Cassie for me, but Kerri and I, well, we're comfortable with each other. And, of course, the sex is pretty good."

Shann blushed, and Gina laughed as she squeezed Shann's arm. "Just teasing. I love to see you blush. It's a dying art these days. As I said, Kerri and I aren't rushing into anything right now. It's enough to have someone to talk to."

"I hope it works out, Gina. She looks really nice."

"She is. Maybe too nice for me."

Shann rolled her eyes, and Gina laughed again.

"Kerri and I are having a couple of days away next week. Who knows after that? But enough of me. Have you always fancied that gorgeous Angie?"

"Gina, she was barely fifteen years old when I last saw her and—"

"And there was her cousin," Gina finished softly.

"Yes. There was Leigh."

"Have you seen Leigh yet?"

"No." Shann shook her head. "And I don't think I want to."

"Is it likely you will? I mean, don't her parents live next door to yours?"

"Yes," Shann acceded. "But she's in New Zealand at the moment. With her husband and children. And I'll be safely at the

Gympie Muster when they return, so I'm hoping we'll miss each other."

"Perhaps you should see her, Shann. Lay old ghosts."

"It's old history, and I fancy the old ghosts might still be a trifle painful," Shann said dryly.

"All the more reason to exorcise them, wouldn't you say?"

Shann looked skeptical.

"You know, Shann, about Leigh. I never—" Gina shook her head. "As you said, old history. So, to get onto more pleasant subjects, is there any chance you and Angie might get together?"

"I really don't know. That very same old history makes it a bit complicated."

"It doesn't have to be so, does it? You're either attracted to her or you're not, and I think it's pretty clear it's the former."

"Am I so obvious?" Shann asked her.

"Only to someone who's looking. She seems nice, Shann. And you deserve to be happy, love."

"Thanks, Gina." Shann kissed her on the cheek. "But I am happy. I have Corey. My music's taking off. My father and I are talking again. It's a pretty good time for me at the moment."

"No harm in making it better, and having someone like Angie in your bed is not going to be all that hard to take, don't you think?"

Shann's traitorous body reacted to the thought. Maybe Gina was right. It had been a long time since she was close to someone, physically close. She was primed for an affair.

Yet something told her to tread carefully, that what she felt for Angie was not a casual thing, that she needed to be cautious, that there were pitfalls that could pave the road with pain. Shann didn't think her bruised heart would take another beating. And Angie was beginning to—

At that moment Shann caught sight of the other woman as she detached herself from a group in the far corner of the room and began making her way toward them.

And just as suddenly Shann knew she had already set out along that road, and she might have gone too far for her to turn back.

"Hi! You were fantastic," Angie said. "Care to have another dance?"

If she got out on the dance floor, close to Angie, she knew she wouldn't want to leave. "I'd like to but," she glanced at her wristwatch, "I should be getting home."

Angie reached out and picked up Shann's hand so she could check the time for herself.

Shann's skin burned where the other woman touched her.

"Darn! Is it that late? You're right. And I have to work tomorrow," she said ruefully.

"You do?" Shann was surprised.

"We're open seven days a week, and I do my turn at the weekend shifts. Only fair." Angie seemed to realize she was still holding Shann's hand and reluctantly released it. "How did you get here tonight? I mean, do you need a lift home?" She smiled. "It wouldn't be out of my way."

Shann shook her head, disappointment and a hint of relief mingling inside her. "No. I came in my own car."

"Me, too. Oh well, guess I'll just have to follow you home." She grinned. "We live next door to each other," she added for Gina's benefit.

"Pity," Gina said, slanting a meaningful look at Shann.

Shann gave a nervous cough, sure that Angie couldn't have missed Gina's obviousness.

"You should have carpooled," Gina finished innocently.

"We should have," Angie agreed lightly enough. "Maybe next time. Well, it was a great night. Nice to officially meet you, Gina. I'll see you again." She gave Shann a slow smile. " 'Night, Shann."

Shann nodded, not sure she could trust her voice after that smile. She watched Angie as she walked away, the artificial lights picking up the highlights in her fair hair, the curve of her neck, that strip of tanned, bare skin at her waist, the swell of her buttocks encased in her jeans, the long, nicely shaped legs. Shann's eyes returned to that expanse of smooth skin. Was that the faint hint of dimples above the top of her jeans? As she watched, Angie collected her jacket from the back of a chair, waved good-bye to her friends and headed out the door. Only then did Shann let out the breath she hadn't known she was holding.

"At the risk of repeating myself," Gina said beside her. "Pity."

Shann met her dark eyes and looked away.

"Shann, love. Don't throw something special away because of an old memory. Old memories often have a habit of taking on a rosy hue they might never have had."

Shann grimaced and gave Gina a warm hug. "If you keep this up I'll think you're nothing but an old romantic."

"Heaven forbid." Gina hugged her back. "I'll see you again, soon I hope. I meant it when I said I wanted you to play for us again."

Shann nodded. "I'll let you know how things go at home. Just let me know when you work out a schedule. And thanks, Gina."

After collecting her guitar Shann let herself out the back door. Jess had long since finished her shift. Shann turned out onto the main road and headed for home. The traffic seemed light for a Saturday night, and she was soon pulling to the curb in front of her house.

Rhys's car was in the driveway so at least he was home. She decided not to park behind him in case he had to leave early. She lifted her guitar case out of the boot and gently closed the lid. As she beeped the central locking system she heard the electronic garage door sliding closed next door.

In the glow from the street light she saw Angie walking across the front lawn. Angie paused as Shann crossed the footpath and walked through the open front gates.

"Are you sneaking in the back way like I am?" Angie whispered.

Shann laughed softly, suspecting her voice was a little high. "Yes. I don't want to wake everyone up."

"Me neither. Although Ann and Mike are pretty heavy sleepers. None of us had trouble sneaking in and out when we were younger."

Shann wasn't sure she wanted to think about that. She'd known Leigh often slipped out to meet friends. That was her explanation. To meet friends. But Shann knew it was to meet Evan Radford.

They walked quietly down beside their respective houses, their way lit by the moon.

"I only hope Ann's locked that wretched dog in the house or he's likely to slobber me to death." Angie stopped. "This is where I used to jump the fence to listen to you playing the guitar."

Shann looked up to see her open bedroom window above them.

Angie sprang lightly over the fence and landed beside Shann. "And that's my grevillea bush."

"I never knew you were there."

There was a moment's silence.

"Leigh caught me once," Angie said. "She called me a little pervert. I wasn't sure how a girl could be a pervert, but it made me stop hopping the fence for a while."

"I wouldn't have minded if you'd come inside," Shann told her.

"I wouldn't have wanted to stop you working on your music. I loved it."

Shann put her guitar case down, held it by the top. "They were all full of teenage angst and forlorn lost love."

Angie laughed softly. "And your point is?"

Shann chuckled. "I suppose the teen years are a pretty intense time in our lives." More intense for some than others, Shann thought.

"'Rollercoaster Love' was one of my favorites," Angie was saying, "and I enjoyed hearing you sing it again tonight. I also liked one called 'Till She Touched Me.' I thought it was so romantic."

Shann shifted embarrassedly. If she'd known back then that anyone was listening to that song with its impassioned lyrics she suspected she'd have been mortified. She hadn't even played it for Leigh. "I've brushed that one up quite a bit, and I've had some interest in it."

"Do you ever perform it yourself?"

"I think I might. At the Muster. Maybe at my night show. The lyrics are a bit, well, physical."

"Mmm." Angie paused. "Well, I guess I should go in."

Neither of them made a move, and Shann swallowed nervously. She could see the sparkle of Angie's eyes in the moonlight and her fingers tightened on her guitar case as though she needed its solidness to support her.

"I used to imagine you'd see me out here," Angie's voice was impossibly lower, "and that you'd come out and we'd talk. Funny how things change. Talking's the furthest thing from my mind tonight," she said thickly. She leaned slowly forward and put her lips to Shann's.

CHAPTER SIX

Her lips were incredibly soft and oh, so arousing. Shann felt weak, as though only Angie's touch was holding her together as she drowned in the velvety softness of her mouth.

Angie drew back a little, and Shann swayed toward her. She nuzzled Angie's bottom lip, teased it delicately between her teeth, and sucked it gently. Then she drew back again and Angie took Shann's guitar and leant it against the wall before kissing Shann again. She ran her tongue tip over Shann's lips, paused at the corner of her mouth, then sought the sweetness within.

Shann moaned softly, at least Shann thought it was her. But it might have been Angie. Then they were straining together, their kiss deepening, breast to breast, stomach to stomach, thighs to thighs. Shann slid her hands inside Angie's denim jacket, her fingers luxuriating in the smooth warmth of Angie's skin.

Eventually they drew slightly apart again, both breathing raggedly.

"I don't think I could have gone another night without doing that," Angie said thickly.

"I thought it was only me," Shann managed to get out.

Angie gave a soft, throaty laugh. "Oh, no. Believe me. It wasn't just you." She slid her fingers into Shann's hair, cradling her face, and kissed her slowly, deeply, again.

Shann ran her lips along the line of Angie's jaw, tasting her skin. She nibbled her sensitive earlobe, and when Angie made a low sound deep in her throat, Shann found her lips again.

"You are really something, do you know that?" Angie whispered, and Shann slid her mouth down over Angie's chin, settling her lips to the erratic beat of the pulse at the base of her throat. "God, Shann! I can hardly stand up."

Shann's hands moved from the curve of Angie's waist and up to cup her full breasts. She could feel the hardness of Angie's nipples against her hands, and she teased them with the pad of her thumbs. She let her mouth slide down from the base of Angie's throat to cover her breast, suckling the hard peak through the thin material of her shirt.

Angie clutched at Shann's head, holding her to her, then she drew Shann up again so they could kiss again. She fumbled with the buttons on Shann's shirt, pushed it aside to mold Shann's lace-covered breasts. And it was Shann's turn to moan brokenly.

Sliding one leg between Angie's, Shann moved against her. Her hands molded Angie's jean-clad buttocks, drew her impossibly closer. She heard Angie catch a ragged breath, and Shann knew Angie was as aroused as she was.

Shann's fingers fumbled for the top stud on Angie's jeans but Angie's hand shakily covered hers, and Shann hesitated.

"Shann. We can't. I want to. But not here. Someone might—"

At that moment a deep woof came from the open window of the house next door. Leigh's room, Shann recognized hazily. Tiger's nose peered at them over the windowsill.

They sprang apart. Shann's fingers were shaking so hard she

was finding it impossible to rebutton her shirt. Angie helped her and then pulled her own jacket around her.

The light flicked on, sending a bright shaft over them. Mike Callahan called the dog's name as he crossed to the window. Taking hold of the dog's collar he looked out into the darkness, his body silhouetted against the lighted room.

"It's only me, Mike," Angie said lightly. "And Shann. We've just arrived home."

"Oh. Angie. Evening, Shann. Thought it might be someone up to mischief. Come on in then or this daft dog will wake the whole neighborhood." Taking the reluctant dog with him, he crossed to the door and flicked out the light.

They were cocooned in the moonlight once more.

"Well." Shann laughed ruefully. "That certainly cooled our ardor." She pushed her tangled dark hair back with a shaky hand.

"Do you really think it did? Cool our ardor, I mean." Angie ran a finger down the length of Shann's arm and Shann felt the sear of her touch through the suede of her shirt.

Taking hold of Angie's hand, Shann checked the darkened window, and then raised Angie's hand to her lips, nibbling a slow kiss in her warm palm. Then she took one of Angie's fingers into her mouth, sucking gently.

"Shann!" Angie begged. "Do you know what you're doing to me?"

"If it's anything like what you're doing to me then I have a pretty fair idea."

"I want to stay but—" Angie drew a steadying breath. "I best go." She hesitated, holding Shann's gaze. "Shouldn't I?"

Shann was so tempted to suggest her room, but Corey was in the room next door, and Liz was an early riser. And Angie's? If by any chance Ann Callahan discovered the notorious Shann Delaney in her niece's bed, well—the last time had left scars Shann wasn't sure had healed. It would be folly to put herself into the position where those wounds could be reopened.

"Yes. I should," Angie repeated, almost to herself. She kissed her own fingers and placed them quickly on Shann's mouth before she disappeared over the fence and into the house.

Corey frowned. "Are you okay, Mum?"

They were out on the back deck. Shann had just brewed morning tea, and she was waiting for her father and Liz to join them. Gerard was studying, and Amy was visiting friends.

"I'm fine, love." Shann assured him. "I'm just a little tired from my late night. I think I'm getting old."

"Yeah, right." Corey exclaimed. "How did it go at Gina's?"

"Pretty good. I enjoyed it and, more to the point, so did the audience."

"So are you going back to sing there?" he asked and Shann nodded.

"Gina asked me to. Were you okay with it last night?"

"Of course, Mum," he said indignantly. "I'm not a baby."

"I know, but it's my job to worry about you."

Corey rolled his eyes and came over to give her a hug just as her father joined them.

"Ready for your cup of tea?" Shann got up to help him into his chair. She poured him his tea and set it in front of him. He'd been talking to Shann's stepmother on the phone.

"Ruth sends her love," he said as he added sugar to his cup. "It's the middle of the night over there, and she couldn't sleep so she rang me."

"Is she enjoying her holiday?" Shann asked.

"I think so. She's been catching up with long lost relatives." He laughed. "I can only be grateful I'm not there."

"Oh, Dad. You would have enjoyed it, too."

"Do you reckon?"

Corey passed his grandfather a plate of biscuits.

"I wouldn't have met Corey if I'd gone to England with Ruth," he finished and winked at his grandson.

Corey grinned. "We were going to come and visit you anyway next school holidays."

Shann's father glanced at Shann. "You were?"

"We'd talked about it," Shann said. "When Liz told me about your operation I thought—" She shrugged. "We came a few months early."

Liz joined them then, walking carefully but a little more freely. "I feel so much better now that I've washed my hair and, apart from that, I'm finding it's a lot less painful to move."

Shann passed Liz her tea.

"How did you go last night? I didn't hear you come in."

"That's 'cause she was very late," Corey said. "But she's going to sing there again."

"Thank you, my little PR person," Shann laughed at Corey.

"That's great, Shann." Liz sipped her tea and sighed her enjoyment.

"Do you get many jobs singing?" her father asked and Shann nodded.

"Quite a few."

"Where do you play?"

Shann hesitated. "Well, wherever I'm booked to play. Clubs. I've done some studio backup work."

Her father frowned. "Are most of these jobs at night? What about Corey?"

"He comes with me when he can. Depends on the venue, but usually I have a couple of friends who babysit for me."

"It's okay, Pop. I like staying with Pauline and Max. They have kids my age."

What would her father say if he knew Max was really Maxine? She'd better change the subject before Corey innocently elaborated.

"I've got a really good group of shows to do at the Gympie Muster in a few weeks. I'm looking forward to that."

"They get about eighty thousand people attending the Muster, don't they?" Liz asked. "Remember we saw that show on TV about it last year, Dad?"

Their father nodded. "Didn't it rain?"

Shann laughed. "They say it usually does, but maybe we'll be lucky this year."

"Mum and I went to the one at Tamworth a couple of years ago," said Corey. "We had a great time."

"I've always wanted to go to the Muster at Gympie so it will be exciting to go there as a performer," Shann said.

They talked for a few minutes about the various stars who would also be performing at Gympie, yet all through the conversation Shann's eyes kept returning to the Callahans' house. She'd seen Ann and Mike drive off after a struggle to get Tiger into the car, and she knew Angie was at work.

Had she imagined those heady, aroused moments they'd shared last night? She couldn't believe the response she'd felt to Angie's kisses and caresses. If only they'd been able to—Shann swallowed as a rush of desire arrowed down between her legs.

After Angie left her, Shann had hurried quietly inside. She'd taken a shower, letting the hot water cascade over her body, teasing her breasts that were still sensitive from Angie's caresses. Her skin had tingled as the water flowed over her and she felt her knees go weak at the memory. She'd leant against the wall of the shower until she was strong enough to climb out, towel herself dry, and slip into the oversized, long-sleeved T-shirt she wore to bed.

By the time she'd stretched out on her bed she knew sleep was going to elude her. She ached for the feel of Angie's body melded to her own.

How she wished she'd let Angie join her. Corey was a heavy sleeper. He didn't wake when storms passed over with thunder rolling. But it was her father's house. She pushed such thoughts back where they came from, telling herself that had nothing to do with the situation. But of course, to Shann it did.

On the other hand, she told herself, she wasn't a child anymore. She was an adult, a single adult. And so was Angie. If they shared a night of lovemaking what would it hurt? No one need know if they were careful. She'd never been promiscuous and, besides, Angie was hardly a one-night stand.

Shann pulled herself up. Her feelings for Angie were complex to say the least. Yet she was afraid if she tried to analyze those feelings she'd have to face even more questions.

From the moment they'd seen each other that tumult of awareness had drawn them together. It had intensified as they swayed together on the dance floor. Last night's kiss had been inevitable.

And Shann couldn't recall being as attracted to anyone. Even Leigh.

Shann paused, wondering why she'd allowed herself to compare memories of Leigh to her feelings for Angie. It made her feel just a little disloyal to Leigh. And she was hardly being fair to Angie.

There was no comparison, was there? Kissing Leigh had been exciting, too. They had barely left childhood. Their hormones had been raging. But Shann had genuinely loved Leigh. And she'd thought Leigh had loved her. She had. But not enough. Yet Shann knew her relationship with Leigh had been on Leigh's terms. Any physical contact had always been at Leigh's instigation.

After that first kiss and Leigh's decision that they couldn't do it again, it was nearly a year before they'd kissed once more. For Shann, being with Leigh had become almost bittersweet.

On that particular night, when their relationship changed again, Leigh had asked Shann to come over after dinner to help her with an overdue school assignment. Shann had found Leigh in tears. She'd been dating Evan Radford, and they'd had an argument.

"Why are guys so cruel?" Leigh sobbed.

Shann didn't think guys had the embargo on being cruel, but she suspected Leigh didn't want to hear Shann's observations. "What did he do?" she asked, feeling it was expected of her.

"He says he wants to go to the drag races with Caleb and some other guys on Saturday night, and we were supposed to go to the movies."

"You could go to the drag races, too," Shann suggested.

"I thought of that, but he said it was a guys' night out." She threw her arms around Shann's neck.

"Well, looking on the positive side, the drag races would be pretty boring," Shann said.

Leigh drew back and sniffed. "You know what I should do? I should go out with someone else. That would teach him a lesson."

"Who would you go out with?" Shann couldn't understand playing those sorts of games.

"I don't know." Leigh brushed at her damp cheeks. "I wish you were a guy, Shann."

Shann gave a laugh. "I'm glad I'm not." The advantage, Shann acknowledged wryly, would be that she could make love to Leigh without freaking anyone out.

"Remember when you kissed me?" Leigh asked, and Shann felt her breath catch in her throat.

"You kissed me back."

"I know. It was good, wasn't it? And honestly it was better than kissing Evan."

Shann felt a surge of pleasure at Leigh's words.

"Let's do it again."

"Leigh!" How Shann wanted to. "I don't think—I thought you said it was abnormal."

"No one need know."

"You're supposed to be going out with Evan." Shann reminded her.

"As of today I'm not. He can go take a hike." Leigh walked over and turned the key in the lock on her bedroom door. She turned back, leaning on the door, and smiled at Shann.

And Shann felt herself respond to that look. She'd wanted to kiss Leigh again so badly.

Leigh slowly moved back toward Shann, paused when their bodies were touching. Then she moved impossibly closer, and her lips found Shann's.

For a moment Shann resisted and then she lost herself in

Leigh's kiss and she kissed her back. Shann felt herself falling in love with Leigh all over again.

That was over ten years ago, she reminded herself. And it had nothing to do with how she felt about Angie. Did it?

It was well into the early hours of the morning when Shann finally drifted into a fitful sleep. She awoke feeling listless and not rested. And desperately wanting to continue her interrupted love-making with Angie.

"Earth to Mum," said Corey, dragging Shann back to the present.

"Oh. Sorry, love. I was miles away. What did you say?"

"I need to get some stuff for school. I just remembered." He pulled a sheet of paper from his pocket. "Mrs. Corcoran says I should get it by Monday."

"Oh, Corey. You should have said something when we were shopping yesterday. What is it you need?"

"The other kids have boxes, to keep their stuff in for art class." He held the paper out to his mother. "My teacher's put the measurements on there. She says you can get these boxes at a hardware store, and I thought we could go over to Angie's shop."

Shann hesitated, pretending she was studying the sheet of paper Corey had handed her.

"He's right, Shann," said Liz. "Why not pop over to Angie's shop. I'm not sure if they're open all day, but I think they are."

"I can't leave you and Dad alone again," Shann protested.

"Rubbish! We're fine, aren't we, Dad? I can get around now, and Gerard will be here all day studying." Liz waved Shann's protests aside. "We have your mobile number anyway."

"Why don't we go now," suggested Corey. "In case the shop closes at lunchtime."

"Well, will you be okay, Dad?" Shann looked at her father, and he pulled a face.

"I'm not planning on running a marathon," he said dryly.

"I suppose it would only take us half an hour or so."

"Great. I've been wanting to see Angie's shop," said Corey. "Don't forget the piece of paper, Mum." He headed for the stairs.

"Hold on, Corey. I have to change. I can't go like this," Shann flushed a little as she saw Liz look at her sharply. "And you need to wash your hands and face and comb your hair."

Corey gave an exaggerated sigh. "Okay," he said as he headed inside.

"You look fine, Shann," said Liz. "It's only a hardware store, and you'll probably be the best dressed customer there."

"I'll just change my sweatshirt," Shann retreated to the bedroom. But what to wear. She pulled her sweatshirt over her head and took a long sleeved tailored pale blue shirt out of the closet, slipped it on, tucking the shirttails into her jeans. She shrugged on her padded denim vest and ran her brush though her hair. She opened her door and almost ran into her son.

Corey was coming out of his room smoothing his own hair. He held up his hands. "Squeaky clean."

Shann grinned. "Looking good, too," she said indicating his slicked down hair. It was already starting to stand up in spikes.

"And you look *perfecto*," he told her.

She put her arm around his shoulders as they headed out to say good-bye to Liz and her father.

In the car Corey kept up a running conversation about anything and everything. Shann listened to her son, yet part of her was preoccupied with the chance that she might be seeing Angie again. Of course, Angie would probably be working in the office, and they could come and go without her knowing they were there. Shann knew she could seek her out but—would Angie want her to? Shann hadn't felt as uncertain in years. Where was the confident, self-assured woman she knew she was? Love had reduced her to an indecisive, ineffectual airhead.

Love? Where had that word come from? Sex, said a voice inside her. Pure sex. No, it was more than that. Angie was—

"Angie's nice, isn't she?" Corey said beside her and, disconcerted, Shann shot a quick look at him.

"Yes. Very nice," she replied.

"Do you like her?"

"Of course. Why wouldn't I? She's a lot of fun."

"No, I mean, do you really like her?" Corey persisted.

Shann turned into the car park of the hardware store, concentrating on the outgoing traffic. She found a parking spot and angled the car into it.

"So, do you?" Corey repeated as she switched off the ignition.

"Do I what?"

"You know. Do you fancy her?"

"Corey! Come on, I'm not comfortable talking about this."

"Why not?" Corey asked seriously. "If Angie was a guy we'd be able to talk about it, wouldn't we?"

"You're my son, my not-quite-ten-year-old son, and I'm, well, I'm your mother," she finished inadequately.

"If I was you I'd want to take her out. She's cute and sexy." Corey smirked.

"I think we should put this conversation into the 'things not to be discussed', don't you, Mr. Wiseguy?"

Corey giggled.

"Let's leave it that I like Angie and make that our little secret. Deal?" She held out her hand.

Corey shook it. "Deal."

Shann opened the door. "Let's get your stuff."

Angie was right. The store was busier on weekends. People were coming and going. Shann and Corey stood back as customers came through the automatic doors wheeling trolleys of all sorts of merchandise. Once inside Shann paused to get her bearings.

"Wow! This is a big place," Corey exclaimed, looking around. "Where do you think Angie is? I bet she'd know where to find my container."

"Angie will be too busy to do that, Corey. We can find it ourselves. Let's start in storage." Shann headed down an aisle on the left.

"Can I be of assistance? Oh, hello Shann." Joe Radford beamed at her. "We meet again. You must do a lot of handyman jobs." He smiled self disparagingly. "Or should that be handywoman jobs?"

Did the man work 24/7? "Hello." Shann let his struggle for political correctness go. "Could you point me in the direction of," Shann turned and took the relevant sheet of paper from Corey, "one plastic container with tray inset."

"Of course." Joe nodded importantly. "Who's this little guy?"

Shann watched as Corey drew himself up to his full height. She put her hands on his shoulders proudly. "This is my son, Corey."

"Oh. I didn't . . . I thought you said you weren't married."

"I'm not." She held his gaze, and he looked a little self-conscious.

"Oh. Well. You're single then. I was just telling my brother, Wade—remember him? He's two years older than Evan." Joe paused, apparently waiting for Shann to catch up.

Wade Radford was the school bad boy whose teasing and taunts bordered on cruelty. Shann had never been impressed by him.

She nodded. "I remember him," she said noncommittally.

"I mentioned to Wade I'd seen you, and he was wondering what you do with your spare time? I'll give you his phone number and maybe you could give him a call." Joe pulled out one of his business cards and jotted down a number. "Wade's divorced. He's had a pretty bad time of it, but he's starting to feel he should get out a bit again." He handed Shann the card.

She took it automatically. "Oh, I won't be here that long, Joe," she began.

"I don't think Wade's ready to get involved just yet," Joe said airily. "But you might both just enjoy the company. Go to the movies? For a drink?"

"I'm pretty busy at the moment looking after my father and my sister. They've both had surgery," she finished and he nodded sympathetically.

"Still. You might enjoy just a chat. I think you and Wade would have a lot in common. He has two kids about your son's age, and they spend every second weekend with him."

"Mmm." Shann murmured vaguely.

"Well, come this way, and I'll show you what we've got in stock." Joe turned, and Shann and Corey followed him.

Shann raised her eyebrows at the range of containers.

"Wow!" Corey stood with his hands on his hips. "Look at all these."

Joe started stating the pros and cons of each container, and then another staff member hovered beside him seeking his advice for a customer. "Would you excuse me, Shann? I'll only be a minute."

"Sure." Shann breathed a sigh of relief as he left them, and then she frowned at the sheet of paper.

"Did you go to school with him, too, Mum?" asked Corey.

"Yes. But he's younger than I am," she said vaguely.

Corey looked up at her. "Is everybody younger than you?"

Shann laughed delightedly. "Are you calling your mother old?" she asked him and pretended to tickle him.

Corey wrapped his arms around her waist and hugged her. "Don't worry, Mum, you look really young. And cool."

"Flatterer." She hugged him back. "Now, let's see which container fits the criteria."

"What about this blue one?" He lifted the lid. "Nope, no tray."

"We should have brought a tape measure." Shann tried to measure the box with the span of her hand.

"One tape measure coming up," said a familiar voice.

CHAPTER SEVEN

Shann spun around and Angie smiled at her. She pulled out the end of her tape. "No self-respecting hardware store assistant would be caught without one. Especially," she let the end of the tape zip back, "a retractable one."

"Hi, Angie." Corey beamed at her. "Mum and I hoped we'd get to see you."

Shann's eyes met Angie's and slid away again.

"How are you?" Angie asked softly, and Shann swallowed.

"Fine thanks. Bit tired after my late night," she added quickly and felt herself flush.

"Me, too. I almost rang my boss to say I was sick and couldn't come to work." She grinned, and Shann found herself smiling back.

"But you are the boss, aren't you?" Corey frowned.

Angie laughed then. "I guess I am so I had to come to work. So what do you need to measure?"

"I need a container for art for school," Corey told her.

"Mrs. Corcoran's class?"

Corey nodded, and Angie pointed out a stack of plastic boxes.

"This is the one then. We've supplied containers for quite a few of Mrs. Corcoran's students. Choice of red or blue."

"Red," Corey decided, and he lifted the lid. "Look, Mum, it's got a tray."

"That's it then." Shann said. "Thanks, Angie."

"Sorry I took so long, Shann." Joe Radford rounded the end of the aisle, and he stopped when he saw Angie.

"It's okay, Joe. Shann found what she was looking for." Angie told him.

"Good. I'll get on then. Maybe I'll get Wade to ring you."

Angie raised her eyebrow as Joe left them. "Wade Radford?"

"Seems he's divorced," Shann said, mindful that Corey was listening.

"He asked Mum to go out with his brother," Corey said and frowned. "You aren't going to, are you, Mum? I mean—"

"No. I don't think so, love." Shann put in quickly, concerned about what her son might say. "As I said, I don't have time."

"That's good. I don't think I liked him so I probably wouldn't like his brother."

"Corey!" Shann grimaced at Angie. "And Angie's not interested in all this. We're probably holding her up."

"No worries." She glanced at her watch. "I was about to have a break. Want to share it with me?"

"We'd love to," said Corey before Shann could reply. "What do you do on your break?"

Angie laughed. "I think perhaps refreshments. Coffee again, Shann? And maybe a fruit juice for you, Corey?"

"Are you sure you have time? We don't want to keep you if you have things to do," Shann persisted, and Angie shook her head.

"Do you know you are the most difficult customer to get to the coffee shop." Angie touched her arm, and Shann's skin tingled beneath the material of her shirt. "Come on. Relax, Shann. And I can take a break. I've passed it with the boss."

Corey laughed and walked ahead of them, carefully carrying his new container.

"So Wade Radford's my competition, is he?" Angie asked quietly so Corey wouldn't hear.

Startled, Shann looked at her, only to see the twinkle in her eyes. She laughed softly. "Not a chance."

"Not a chance for me or not a chance for Joe's apparently available brother?"

"Joe's brother, available or not. I couldn't stand him at school. And I can't see he'd change," Shann added.

"He hasn't." Angie sighed. "At the risk of being accused of undermining a potential, um, opponent, Wade Radford has a problem with alcohol."

"I'm not surprised. He always made a fool of himself getting falling down drunk back then." Shann grimaced. "So thanks, but no thanks. How does that sound?"

"Music to my ears."

"That's good. So how does," Shann looked at Corey and dropped her voice even more, "I never date guys appeal to you?"

"I do believe I hear a symphony," Angie said with mock seriousness, and Shann suppressed a laugh. "I'm so glad you don't," Angie added softly.

They walked on, and Shann felt inordinately pleased.

"How did you sleep?" Angie asked huskily.

"Not so well." Shann replied.

"Me neither." Angie gave a soft laugh. "And I've been walking around in a daze all morning." Her voice dropped even lower. "Can't seem to think past having you in my bed."

Shann's knees went weak, and she felt her heartbeat accelerate. "You're very honest."

"I suppose I am." She touched Shann's arm again. "I also can't seem to keep my hands off you. Just thinking about what I want to do to you could get me arrested."

Shann laughed breathily. "I think you're pretty safe. No witnesses except me. And I can be easily bribed."

"I'm so pleased to hear that."

"To hear what?" asked Corey, who had stopped to wait for them to catch up to him.

A blush crept over Angie's cheeks, and Shann wanted to kiss her, right there and then.

"That your mother is dying for a skinny cappuccino," Angie improvised, not looking at Shann.

"Oh, yes. She likes them. I think I'll have peach iced tea," Corey said. "Do you have that in your coffee shop?"

"I think we do."

They reached the coffee shop, but all the tables were full.

"No matter," said Angie. "We'll go to my office. It'll be quieter. Just hang on a minute, and I'll give Cindy our order." She walked to the counter spoke to one of the two young women behind the counter and rejoined them. "Cindy will bring our drinks to the office."

Shann hesitated.

"It looks busier than it is," Angie said. "I told Cindy there was no hurry." Her eyes moved over Shann's face, settled on her lips, and then she led them over to her office.

Corey put his container down and looked around. "It looks busy in here."

Angie laughed. "Well, I wouldn't like you to think I get it too easy."

"It's a really big shop. There must be stacks to do," Corey commiserated. He glanced at the computer screen on the desk. "Have you got games on your computer?"

"Only solitaire."

Corey screwed up his nose. "It's okay. I brought my own game," he said, sitting in Angie's chair and pulling out a handheld computer game.

"Corey, that's Angie's chair." Shann admonished him.

"Oh. Sorry. I thought you and Angie wanted to talk." Corey went to stand up.

"It's okay, Corey. Stay there. Your mother and I can sit over

107

here." She took some papers off an easy chair and motioned for Shann to sit before she sat in the matching chair. "These are my 'impress my business associates' chairs."

They were comfortable, and Shann sat back, trying to relax. With Angie so close that was well nigh impossible. If she reached out she could run her hand over Angie's thigh—Shann swallowed. "It must be . . . you must have to put in long hours."

"I guess I do. It's not so bad now. We've got everything in place, and I have exceptionally good staff. It's easy to delegate because I trust my staff implicitly."

"Do you—" Shann swallowed again. "Do you get days off? I mean, you don't have to work seven days a week, do you?"

Angie laughed. "No. I have been known to, but no, I don't anymore. How about you?" she asked, her gaze holding Shann's.

"Oh. I can have a break whenever I want to as long as it fits in with Dad and Liz. I usually have time to myself when Rhys is off duty. I feel better knowing Rhys is there even though Liz insists she's feeling far better than she thought she would." Shann wanted to ask Angie if she'd like to go somewhere, but her brain couldn't seem to form the words.

"So," Angie looked across at Corey before turning back to Shann. "Would you like to go somewhere one day this week? Maybe we could have lunch and be back before Corey finishes school."

"I can walk home on my own," Corey said. "Mum doesn't have to hurry back."

Shann rolled her eyes. "Corey, just concentrate on your game."

"Well, I am old enough to walk home on my own."

"I know. And you know I enjoy the walk."

"Mum hates going to the gym," Corey told Angie.

Angie's eyes moved over Shann. "You seem to be doing fine without it."

There was a knock on the door, and Corey sprang up to open it. Cindy carried a tray in and set it on the low table near Angie's chair.

"Thanks, Cindy."

"That's okay, Angie. Yell if you need anything else." The young woman left them.

Corey sat down on the floor and took the bottle of iced tea Angie handed him. "Thanks, Angie. Uncle Rhys is off on Tuesday. Are you off that day, too?"

"Tuesday? I do believe I am." She passed Shann her cappuccino and smiled at her. "That's settled then. Lunch on Tuesday?"

"I'd like that," Shann said, sipping her coffee.

Liz, Shann, and Corey were sitting on the back deck as the sun went down on Monday afternoon when the phone rang. Shann answered using the hand-held receiver.

"Shann Delaney."

"Hi, Shann Delaney." Angie's soft voice seemed to caress Shann, the low sound sending shivers over her body like a cool breeze on damp, warm skin.

"Hi, yourself. What are you up to?" she tried to keep her voice light.

Angie groaned. "Still at work for a couple more hours. So, are we on for lunch tomorrow?"

"Of course. If you still want to go."

"I do. And I know this nice little restaurant up near Montville. Do you mind driving so far?"

"No. Not at all."

"We'll be back in time to collect Corey from school, but we should leave by about ten."

"Sounds great. Is this casual as far as dress goes?"

"Yes." Angie laughed softly. "I'm just trying to imagine you in a dress. I think black, sleeveless, low neckline, straight skirt slit up one side to mid thigh. Incredible," she finished brokenly.

Shann laughed. "Very colorful description, but I don't own one."

"A dress or a black dress?"

"Neither. And I think you already know that so stop teasing me."

"Me teasing you? Can we wait a minute while I stop fantasizing over unzipping that little black number."

Shann could almost feel Angie's fingers finding the zipper, her lips languidly sliding nibbling kisses over the bare skin of Shann's shoulders. Desire clutched at her and she turned slightly, resting her hip on the table, unsure her legs would continue holding her. She heard Angie's broken sigh in her ear, and the ache between Shann's legs intensified. "Now that, Angie Callahan, is hitting below the belt."

"Below the belt? I think in deference to the proximity of my staff and your family I'd better leave that alone."

"Probably the best idea."

"I can hardly wait to get away on our own and the Montville-Maleny area is so picturesque."

"I can't remember when I was last up there. It would have to be twelve years ago."

"Then you'll notice the changes," Angie said. "It's very up-market, and even though it's a bit touristy it's still retained its quaintness. Actually, I have a couple of friends who own a gallery near the restaurant. It might be interesting to browse through there if you like that sort of thing."

"Sounds good. What sort of gallery is it?"

"They're a very talented couple. Alex is a photographer and Jo does exceptional watercolors. I haven't had a chance to see them since Christmas."

"I think I'd enjoy that." Anything or anywhere, Shann thought, as long as she spent time with Angie.

"I have a couple of urgent things to attend to here at work first thing in the morning, but how about if I pick you up at ten?"

"I'll be ready, Angie. I'm really looking forward to it."

"So am I." Angie paused as though she was about to add something and then Shann heard voices in the background. "I'll see you then. At ten."

Shann hung up the phone, the small smile on her face fading when she found Liz and Corey looking at her. For a moment she'd forgotten she wasn't alone.

"You're going out to lunch with Angie?" Liz asked her casually enough.

"Yes. We arranged it yesterday." Shann frowned. "Rhys will be here, won't he?"

"Of course. I didn't mean you shouldn't have some time to yourself." She glanced pointedly at Corey who intercepted the look and sighed loudly.

"I'll go and watch TV with Pop, shall I?" he asked with exaggerated resignation.

"Oh. No. Corey, you don't have to—" Liz began and he grinned.

"It's okay, Aunty Liz. Pop and I are going to have a game of chess." Corey gave his mother a wink and left them.

"It's easy to forget Corey's not quite ten yet," Liz remarked.

"Ten going on thirty-five," Shann agreed.

"I didn't want to say anything in front of him but does Angie know you're gay?"

"You don't have to worry about Corey. I told you he knows I'm a lesbian. He's known for years."

Liz raised her eyebrows, and Shann shrugged. "He's fine with it, Liz. Corey's a great kid, even if I do say so myself."

"He is great. And very mature for his age. But what about Angie?"

"She's pretty mature for her age, too," Shann said with a chuckle, and Liz hit her on the arm.

"I'm being serious, Shann. Does she know?"

"I'd say she has a fair idea. She saw my show the other night."

"At The Blue Moon? Angie was there?" Liz asked incredulously.

"With friends."

"Oh. Then Angie's not gay?"

Shann paused, not knowing how out Angie was.

"Is she?" Liz persisted.

"You'll have to ask her, Liz. Angie's suggested we go to a restaurant up at Montville," she added to change the subject.

"It's nice up there." Liz bit her lip. "You know Angie hasn't brought a guy home in years."

"Has she brought a girl home?" Shann tried for teasing lightness.

"Well, no. I don't think she has," Liz replied, taking her question at face value.

"Would it really matter if she was a lesbian?" she asked her sister.

"Not to me. But—"

"But?" Shann prompted.

"I was thinking about her aunt and uncle. Ann and Mike totally overreacted in my opinion with you and Leigh. I know it was ten years ago, but do you think they'd have changed their outlook?"

Shann shrugged again. "Apart from saying hello over the fence I haven't really spoken to them since I came home. I thought it would probably be best if I sort of kept a low profile where they were concerned. But Corey's talked to them about the dog."

"Basically they're good people, Shann," Liz said. "The situation was kind of sprung on them, and you and Leigh were so young. I guess we shouldn't blame them too much. I'm sure their intentions were good."

Shann made no comment.

"Is this a date tomorrow? With you and Angie?" Liz asked softly.

Shann hesitated and then made a decision. "I'd like it to be."

"Then you are interested in her? Romantically, I mean?"

"I think I am." Shann glanced at Liz when she was silent.

"Oh, Shann," she said at last. "It's so complicated."

"It doesn't have to be. In fact, it shouldn't be," Shann told her with far more confidence than she felt.

"That goes for lots of things but, unfortunately, they are."

They were silent again before Liz spoke.

"Is it serious? I mean, you know?"

"Am I in love with her?" Shann swallowed. "I'm only just getting to know her."

"What about Angie? I mean, if she's straight I can't see . . . you could get badly hurt, Shann."

Shann sighed. "Don't you think I don't know that, Liz. But what would life be worth if we played it safe all the time?"

"You have a point there," she conceded. "If I hadn't taken a chance twenty years ago and told Rhys I was in love with him we'd still probably be watching each other across the staff canteen." She looked at her younger sister. "I'm sorry things are so hard for you Shann. I so want you to meet someone, be happy."

Shann gave her a hug. "So do I," she said with feeling. "Now I'm going in to see if Dad and Corey are ready for their dessert."

"The scenery's spectacular." Shann raised her voice above the wind that whipped past the windscreen of Angie's sports car.

They were traveling along the winding road to Montville. Angie slowed the car and turned into a scenic rest area, parking and switching off the ignition.

"Sorry it's a bit difficult to talk. Would you like me to put the soft top on?"

Shann shook her head. "No. It's great fun. I've never been in an open sports car before."

It was a beautiful day. The sun warmed them, and Shann's denim jacket kept out the cool breeze. Angie had suggested Shann tuck her hair up under a cap she took from her glove box. She set one on her own head, telling Shann without the caps the wind would tangle their hair in no time.

"You look extremely cute in that cap," Angie told her.

"You look pretty cute yourself." Shann gave the brim of Angie's hat a tug.

Angie chuckled. "It makes me feel like a movie star who's going incognito." She opened her door. "Let's stretch our legs."

They walked over to the viewing shelter as a family left it.

"It's such a clear day you can see the ocean." Shann leant on her elbows on the high railing, taking in the scenery but totally aware of Angie standing so close beside her.

Angie turned, her back to the view, elbows resting on the railing. Her maroon sweatshirt molded the curve of her full breasts, and Shann could see the outline of her nipples.

"If that family leaves," Angie said under her breath, "I think I might have to kiss you."

Shann moved so that her elbow was just touching Angie's. "And I think I just might have to let you." Did Angie realize how turned on Shann was? Just being with her had her senses reeling. The breeze left her in no doubt that she was damp and aroused.

She looked at Angie's profile. "You make me feel like a kid on a first date."

Angie turned her head, a smile playing on her lips. "I know exactly what you mean."

Their eyes met, held, and Shann felt as though she was drowning in their inky green depths.

Car doors slammed, and the family in the station wagon pulled out of the rest area, leaving Shann and Angie alone. Shann turned to face her.

"Do you think it was something we said?" Angie asked with a grin. And then her smile faltered.

She took off her cap and slowly reached out and removed Shann's, dropping the caps on the nearby bench seat. Reaching out she smoothed Shann's dark hair back from her face, her fingers hesitating on the side of Shann's cheek, pausing on her lips.

Then Angie leaned slowly forward until just her lips touched Shann's. The kiss was feather-soft and fleeting. When she moved slightly away Shann followed her, the fire inside her blazing, engulfing her.

She melted into Angie, sliding her arms around her, drawing her unresisting body close. Their lips met, tongues seeking the nectar within.

Shann felt as though she was disintegrating, falling into the warmth, the softness of Angie's body. Her hands slid under Angie's sweatshirt, her fingers playing over her skin finding the indentations of Angie's spine. One hand slipped beneath the waistband of Angie's jeans, found the depression of the dimples she knew were there.

Angie's hands, inside Shann's jacket, moved up to cup Shann's breasts, and they swelled to her touch, nipples hardening as they thrust urgently against Angie's palms.

A soft moan rose in Shann's throat. She was fast losing control of herself. If this went on much longer they'd be making love right here in the open where anyone could see them.

Tires crunched in the gravel, and Angie was the first to move, stepping sideways as the car pulled into the small carpark. Angie's hands grasped the railings as she gulped calming breaths.

Shann sagged backward, her knees weak, as she tried to steady her own breathing. She picked up the two caps, passed one to Angie. Shann's hands were shaking as she fumbled to twist her hair back under her cap. Her body continued to burn, her breasts still tingling from Angie's touch, the throb of wanting raging between her legs.

The car had pulled in beside Angie's MG, the engine idling, the occupants remaining in the car pointing out landmarks.

Angie gave a soft laugh. "Do you suppose they would have rung the police and had us arrested?"

"It would have been worse if they decided to take photos."

"Ooh! I'd have ordered copies." Angie straightened. "You know I can't believe we almost made love hanging over a precipice." She indicated the drop below the viewing shed, and Shann stepped back a little.

"And I'm not too fond of heights," Shann told her, and then flushed. "I must have been distracted."

Angie's gaze ran over her as she smiled ruefully. "It's a pity it's so public." She glanced at the car. "Perhaps we should go. At this rate we'll be late for lunch."

They returned to the car and continued on their way. Once the road became less winding Angie reached over and lifted Shann's hand, resting it on her thigh, covering Shann's hand with her own.

The restaurant was small and boasted panoramic views over the sweep of picturesque rural country to the deep blue of the sea. They ate at a small table, and Shann was sure the meal was delicious. She knew she ate it but later couldn't have repeated the menu. The view, the food, faded into obscurity compared to Angie, to watching her eyes crinkle at the corners when she laughed, to the curve of her lips when she smiled.

"If you keep looking at me like that I won't be responsible for my actions," Angie said huskily.

Shann gave a small smile. "What did you have in mind?"

"I could surprise you perhaps?" She took a mouthful of pavlova, swallowing, her tongue tip licking her lips.

"Tell me, would it involve another threat of arrest?" Shann asked lightly and a slow, knowing smile lifted the corners of Angie's mouth.

"Oh, I think we can safely say they'd probably throw away the key."

Shann laughed. "I can hardly wait." She sobered, and played with her unused cutlery. "You know this is pure torture, don't you?" she asked softly.

Angie nodded. "Would I be forward if I suggested we need privacy."

Shann glanced at her wristwatch. "And more time than we have this afternoon," she added regretfully.

"I suppose we do." Angie looked into the small amount of coffee left in her cup. "I have a unit—" She glanced up at Shann and away again. "I bought it last year and it's being renovated. That's why I'm temporarily back with Ann and Mike. The unit just needs painting now, and then I plan on moving back in. It's not far from Ann and Mike's and it has great views of the river to the city. It's very spacious and—" she paused "—and I'm babbling."

"I'd love to see it," Shann said, and her heartbeat accelerated at the thought of being alone with the other woman.

"I'd love to show it to you, anytime you want."

"Well, maybe one evening? Corey's in bed before eight, eight-thirty," Shann told her.

"I don't mind if you bring Corey, but maybe one night we can go down later, to see the city lights, that sort of thing." Angie held Shann's gaze. "I thought I might, well, try a big seduction scene. What do you think?"

Shann feigned giving the idea deep thought. "Would this involve wine, some of your fantastic kisses, and the arresting stuff?"

"I think it could be arranged without a lot of trouble." Angie sipped her coffee.

"What if we find we aren't interested if there isn't any chance of being arrested?" Shann asked with mock seriousness.

Angie laughed again. "I could leave the curtains open."

"That might work."

"If it doesn't there's a very nice balcony."

"Sounds perfect." Shann met Angie's gaze again, and they laughed a little nervously.

Angie reached out, covered Shann's hand with her own, gave it a light squeeze. "You know, I don't think I've wanted anyone as much as I want you," she said huskily.

Shann turned her hand beneath Angie's, squeezed it back, releasing her when the waiter reappeared.

They paid the bill and then walked next door to the gallery belonging to Angie's friends.

"I met Alex and Jo through some mutual friends," Angie told Shann before they went inside. "They're a fantastic couple. Meant for each other. They both had bad relationships then they found each other. It's a romantic story."

As they entered the gallery Angie took Shann's hand and held it. A tall, dark-haired woman looked up from her desk. She glanced over the top of half glasses and when she recognized Angie, her face lit up with a welcoming smile. She put her glasses on the desk-top, stood up and walked toward them.

The woman was striking, not quite as tall as Shann was, with broad shoulders and full breasts. She wore dark jeans, and her white T-shirt advertised the gallery.

If Shann had been asked to describe Alex Farmer she knew it would have been impossible not to add the word *Amazon*.

Alex enveloped Angie in a hug, and Shann knew her sharp eyes hadn't missed Shann's and Angie's clasped hands.

"Angie. How have you been? We haven't seen you for months. I suppose you've been working yourself into the ground."

"Pretty much." Angie returned Alex's hug and laughed. "Same old boring stuff." Then she turned and drew Shann forward. "This is an old friend. Alex Farmer, meet Shann Delaney. Shann's family lived next to mine when we were growing up."

Alex reached out and shook Shann's hand. "Pleased to meet you." She frowned. "Shann Delaney? Where have I heard that name?"

Angie grinned at Shann. "See, I told you you were famous."

Alex looked from one to the other.

"Shann's a songwriter," Angie said. "She wrote the theme for *The Kelly Boys*."

"Oh. Yes. Now I remember. You're going to be performing at the Gympie Muster. I read an article about it in our local paper last week."

"Yes. The weekend after next."

"Jo and I have been talking about going up to the Muster for a couple of years. Have you been there before, Shann?"

Shann shook her head. "Not to Gympie, no. I've been to Tamworth, but this will be my first time at Gympie. It's supposed to be a fantastic week."

"So we've heard," Alex agreed. "I'll have to see if we can get someone to mind the gallery so we can come along. When are you performing?"

"I'm doing three shows, two during the lead-up week and then

118

one on Friday night. There'll be a great lineup of Aussie talent performing."

"Angie Callahan!"

They turned at the sound of the voice to see a slim, blond-haired woman striding toward them. She'd come through a staff door from the back of the gallery, and she hugged Angie. When the woman released her, Angie introduced Shann.

"Jo Creighton, meet Shann Delaney, an old friend of mine. Jo does these wonderful watercolors. The photos are Alex's."

They shook hands, and then the four of them walked around the gallery, looking at the photos and paintings. Shann thought the photos were striking, like the photographer, while the watercolors were wonderfully delicate.

Shann stopped in front of one exquisite watercolor. "Isn't that the view from that lookout we stopped at?" she asked Angie.

"Oh, yes. I think it is." Angie's cheeks colored a little.

Shann wanted desperately to kiss her. Her mind threw up a picture of the two of them, bodies straining together, hands moving to tease, to tantalize, and her own face felt warm.

They moved on, Alex and Jo telling them that the gallery had started making a name for itself and business was gradually improving. They spent an hour with Angie's friends, and eventually they had to leave so that Shann could get back in time to collect Corey. To save time rushing back, Angie suggested they go straight to the school and collect Corey together on their way home. They were a few minutes early so they sat in the car waiting.

"I've had a great day," Shann said to Angie.

"Me, too." Angie took her sunglasses off and sat them on the dashboard. "We'll have to do it again."

Angie nodded. "Shann, about, well, visiting my unit." A slight flush touched her cheeks. "I . . . do you still want to," she swallowed, "come and see my unit?"

"Of course. I'm looking forward to it." Shann smiled crookedly. "Make that desperately looking forward to it."

Angie chuckled. "Desperate is the word." She grimaced. "I'm

having one of those weeks this week. I have to fly to Sydney tomorrow to check out some of my distributors. I have meetings all day and Thursday morning. I fly back midafternoon to a staff meeting and a couple of interviews for prospective staff members. So, I was thinking Friday." She raised her eyebrows inquiringly. "Tell me you aren't booked at The Blue Moon on Friday night."

Shann laughed. "No. Saturday night after the Muster, so Friday would be perfect."

"Perfect," Angie said huskily. "Roll on Friday night."

They turned in their seats as the sound of little voices rose. Shann climbed out of the car so that Corey would be able to see her. The Lollipop Lady came out with her flag and whistle, and children streamed out of the school gate. Before long Corey walked out deep in conversation with two mates. He looked up and caught sight of Shann. He waved and then saw Angie and the MG and his face lit up. He turned to say good-bye to his friends before running up to Shann and Angie.

"Am I getting to ride in the MG?" he asked excitedly after he'd greeted them.

"This should do great things for your image," Shann said, slipping the passenger seat forward so he could climb into the narrow back seat. She helped him buckle his seatbelt before she slid back in beside Angie.

They were home in a few minutes and when Angie drew up in front of their house, Shann turned and thanked her again. She wanted to pull Angie to her but of course that was impossible.

Corey unbuckled his seatbelt and leaned over between his mother and Angie. He put an arm around each of them and kissed his mother's cheek and then Angie's. "That was excellent. Just excellent. It's a fantastic car, Angie. How long have you had it?"

"A couple of years. It needed stacks of work when I bought it, but it's been worth it."

Shann reluctantly climbed out of the car, and Corey followed her. "Thanks, Angie," she said sincerely. "Until Friday then?"

Angie nodded. "Until Friday," she said softly.

Angie rang Shann from work on Thursday. "Hi! I just got back. How are you?"

"Hi to you, too! And I'm fine." Shann put her guitar down and stretched herself out on her bed, booted feet crossed, her hand behind her head. She was glad she was alone as she felt a silly smile light her face. Her body responded to the sound of Angie's voice. "I'm all the better for hearing your voice."

Angie laughed softly. "I was depending on the old 'absence making the heart grow fonder' adage. Has it worked?"

"Very much so." Shann swallowed. "I can't seem to get Friday night off my mind." If Angie only knew how true that was. She'd been so vague and restless that Liz had commented on it. Even Corey had raised his eyebrows at her a couple of times.

"Is there any chance you can get away, say, this evening?" Angie asked.

A spiral of desire surged inside Shann, ricocheting about, making her burn. "Tonight?" she repeated, her mouth suddenly dry, and she was glad she was lying down.

"Mmm. But if you can't get away, well, that's okay, too. I just thought, well, I thought I'd be tied up interviewing, but three of the five candidates have cried off so, well, I'll be finished early."

"But won't you be tired with the plane trip and everything?" Shann asked, her elation swelling inside her.

"When you compare the way I'm not sleeping thinking about you, then a round of interviews and an interstate flight are a piece of cake. So, what do you think? Will I see you tonight?" she asked softly.

"I've consulted my social calendar, and I do believe I'm free," Shann said with mock seriousness. "But even if I hadn't been I'd have made myself free," she added quickly and Angie laughed.

"Fantastic. I'll pick you up between eight and eight-thirty, hmm?"

"What shall I bring?"

"Just yourself."

"How about some wine?" Shann suggested.

"All taken care of." Angie paused. "Well, I guess I should get going to my staff meeting. Let's hope I can keep my mind on it or else I might inadvertently agree to massive staff pay raises and double holiday time."

Shann chuckled. "Not the astute Ms. Callahan. I can't see that. You're too, well, together."

"Do you think so? Then who's this person talking to you, the one with the shaking hands and sweaty palms, the one who can't keep a coherent thought in her mind for more than a second?"

"It's such a relief to know I'm not the only one," Shann said.

"I do have to go, Shann. If I could I'd be over there right now but . . . I'll see you tonight."

"Yes. Tonight." Shann hung up the receiver and stretched languidly on her bed.

She felt like the Cheshire cat, grinning from ear to ear. She would be seeing Angie tonight, in mere hours. She sat up and lifted her guitar onto her lap. This was the moment for a love song or two. She began picking out the melody of the song she was working on.

Was she making a huge mistake? As she absently strummed her guitar a little later, her rational mind turned that question over and over. Wasn't getting involved with Angie Callahan putting herself slam-bang in the middle of an emotional minefield? That she was attracted to the other woman was an understatement. Shann knew she'd never felt this drawn to anyone. Even Leigh.

Shann paused, knowing this was the source of her disquiet. Angie was Leigh's cousin. They'd been raised in the same house, almost sisters. And Angie knew the history, or part of it, that Shann shared with Leigh.

She wasn't still in love with Leigh, she reminded herself. She had betrayed Shann when Shann needed her the most. Leigh had professed her love, when all the while that love had been conditional, always on Leigh's terms. And now Leigh was married, had a life of her own.

Shann couldn't think about that afternoon all those years ago without feeling the pain and despair. They had loved each other, and yet when Shann had needed Leigh's support and understanding, Leigh had broken her heart.

After the Callahans' twenty-fifth wedding anniversary party Shann had walked around in a daze. As she saw it she had no one to talk to about her fear. Leigh certainly wouldn't believe her, being convinced Shann had had too much to drink. Her father would never take her side against Ruth. Pat was working in Canberra and Liz was married and living in the north of the state.

Shann had desperately wanted to confide in Leigh, but Leigh was training for the school swimming carnival and was spending most afternoons at the pool. The fact that Evan Radford was on the swimming team was not lost on Shann.

And Shann wasn't sure she could reveal to Leigh what had happened that night in the garden behind the hall. Even when Leigh had sought Shann out, Shann had barely been able to respond when Leigh spoke to her.

The afternoon Shann came home from a terror-filled visit to their family doctor she had sat in a deck chair on the front veranda in a state of shock. She was pregnant. The nausea, her missed period, told the doctor all he needed to know.

Who was the baby's father, Dr. Fleming had asked her kindly. Shann had sat with tears rolling down her face, unable to talk about it. The doctor had discussed her options with her, and he'd been reluctant to let her leave until she assured him that her parents would be home. It hadn't been a lie, Shann justified. Her parents would be home. In a couple of hours.

So she sat on the veranda wishing Leigh was home. And that she could turn back the clock, be forewarned about that dreadful night. Part of Shann was in total panic while the other part was completely numb.

Then she caught sight of Leigh riding along the street and turning into her driveway. Shann stood up and ran down the steps and over to the Callahans'.

123

"Leigh, I need to see you. Thank heavens you're home."

"So you're talking to me now." Leigh propped her bike against the garage wall.

Her parents' cars were both gone, Shann noticed with relief, so they were on their own. "I can't—I don't know what's happened to us, Leigh. And I need to talk to you."

"You know what happened, Shann. We got caught out, and now everyone thinks we're lesbians."

"I don't care about that." Shann bit down on her lip as a hysterical laugh bubbled inside her.

"I'm glad you find it funny, Shann." Leigh crossed her arms. "Because I *do* care, and I can't believe you don't as well."

"I do care, but—that's not that I want to talk to you about. Can we go upstairs?"

"Shann, I can't. I can't take the chance Mum will come home. She'll freak out if we're on our own."

"Come over to my place. Dad and Ruth are still at work. You can put your bike behind the fence. No one will know you're there."

Leigh nodded reluctantly, wheeled her bicycle next door and followed Shann up the steps, and down the hall to Shann's bedroom. Shann sank down on the side of the bed, and Leigh sat on the chair near Shann's desk.

"Look, Shann, we have to stop all this torturing each other," Leigh said immediately. "If we hadn't, well, let things get out of hand we wouldn't be in this mess."

"We were kissing each other. That's all. It wasn't as though we were naked," Shann appealed.

"We might as well have been the way our parents totally lost it. And, if you remember, I said that would happen all along, Shann. People don't like gays."

"Not all people are like that. Leigh, I haven't told you but I've been to a club, I've met lots of other lesbians, and it was wonderful. None of them had two heads. They were nice normal women. Some were doctors and nurses and even teachers."

"One of our teachers?" Leigh exclaimed.

124

"No. Not from our school. Why don't you come with me one night."

"Shann, I'm not a lesbian," Leigh said forcefully.

"You just like kissing women?" Shann threw back at her, and Leigh sighed.

"I'll admit I like kissing you Shann, but it's, well, it's just part of growing up.

"We're growing up, and we have to put all that behind us. Mum says that a lot of gay people just haven't grown up emotionally."

"That's a lot of crap, and you know it. What about love? You said you loved me."

"I do, Shann. But not, well, sexually."

Shann stared at her impotently. How could she have been so wrong about Leigh? They'd been friends since childhood. And now—

"Apart from all that," Leigh was continuing, "it's far too hard to be gay. I don't want that for my life. Sneaking around. Keeping secrets. I want a husband and children."

"You don't need a husband to have children," Shann said flatly and her stomach churned.

"I know what's expected of me, Shann, and it's easier for me to go along with that."

"Even if it's not what you want?" Shann said bitterly.

Leigh shrugged. "Maybe I don't want anything else badly enough to fight the world for it."

Shann felt as though Leigh had twisted a knife inside her.

"I'm going out with Evan and that suits me."

"But you can't love him," Shann appealed, and Leigh stood up, paced across the room and back again.

"I'm seventeen years old. I don't want to get married for at least two years. As I said, Evan suits me at the moment. I just want to have fun."

"Like we had fun at your parents' party?"

"I did have fun that night. And you could have, too. Remember I wasn't the one who had too much to drink."

"I didn't either," Shann said quietly. "There must have been something in the drink I had. It made me sick. I only had one mouthful."

"You weren't used to drinking, that's all it was."

"I passed out. I was in the garden." Shann paused, trying once again to sort out her fragments of memories. "Someone took me there."

"Who?"

"I don't remember exactly. Evan was there—"

"Evan? You think Evan put something in your drink. That's ridiculous. Why would he do that?" Leigh's eyes narrowed. "Are you sure you're not just jealous because he's going out with me?"

"I'm not jealous." But Shann knew she was. Burningly jealous. "And it wasn't just Evan. Caleb was there and the twins, your mother's boss's sons. I know it was the drink, but I didn't see—I just can't remember."

"For heaven's sake, Shann. You're so naive. You have to be careful. Not all guys are, well, they don't care as long as you have sex with them."

Shann burst into tears, gulping huge sobs.

Leigh walked across and sat beside her, not touching her. "Shann, you didn't—did you?"

"I'm pregnant," Shann got out between gulps.

"Pregnant? Oh, my God, Shann! What were you thinking? Aren't you taking contraceptives? Or at least insisting the guy uses a condom."

Shann rubbed her hand across her eyes. "Why would I need to? I was in love with you. I didn't want anyone else."

"Well, I didn't get you pregnant so you must have wanted someone else," Leigh said dryly, and Shann looked at her incredulously.

"Someone raped me," she said.

CHAPTER EIGHT

Shann's revelation hung in the air about them like a heavy, pungent fog. Leigh stood up again, put space between them when Shann desperately wanted Leigh to just hold her.

"Raped you? Shann you can't go around accusing someone of doing that when you don't even know who did it. If you were so drunk—"

"Leigh, I told you. I think someone drugged me, and it had to be Evan, Caleb, or one of the Kingsley twins. They were the only ones there."

"No one will believe you, Shann. Two separate people told me they'd seen you leaving the hall drunk. I heard Angelina tell my mother that Ruth had taken you home." Leigh looked at her. "Do your parents know? About the night of the party? Or—"

"No one knows." Ruth was convinced Shann had been drunk that night and so was her father. They'd grounded her for a month. Little did they know she had no desire to so much as leave her room. She'd have stayed there if she hadn't had to go to school. She bit her lip and looked at Leigh. "You believe me, don't you? About being raped?"

"Well, yes. If you say it's true," Leigh replied without meeting Shann's gaze.

A sharp pain stabbed the region of Shann's heart. If Leigh didn't believe her—

"What are you going to do?" Leigh asked. "You'll have to have an abortion."

Shann couldn't seem to compute the word. Abortion. Contraceptives. Condoms. Pregnancy. They'd only been words until now. Words that had had nothing to do with her or her life. They were way out of her league.

"You are going to have an abortion, aren't you?" Leigh asked.

"I don't know," she said flatly.

"Shann, you can't have this baby. You're too young. It will ruin your life."

"I just don't know what to do."

"If, as you say, you don't even know who the father is, well, how can you even consider it?"

Shann looked at Leigh and swallowed. "You don't believe me, do you? That I was raped?"

Leigh's gaze fell. "I don't know what to believe, Shann. It's such an improbable story. I mean, how would you not know if someone was doing that to you?"

Pain clutched inside Shann again, and she fancied she felt her heart actually break. "Oh, I remember *that*, Leigh. Believe me I won't ever be able to forget it. I just don't remember who it was or if I actually saw him. It was dark and—" She made a dispirited gesture with her hand. "It was too dark."

Leigh made no comment, and Shann pushed herself to her feet. "I can't stay here. I do know that. Dad and Ruth will—" Shann shook her head. "I've decided I'm going to run away."

"Where will you go?" Leigh asked.

"I don't know yet." She looked at Leigh. "I was going to ask you to come with me."

The words hung in the air between them.

"We could get a flat together," Shann said quickly. "Maybe Sydney. We could get jobs."

"I can't do that, Shann."

"Why not? We said we were going to move out of home together, share a flat."

"That was after we'd finished school," Leigh reminded her. "We need to do well this year. You know how important it is."

"Do you think they'll let me sit for final exams if I'm pregnant?" Shann asked, looking at Leigh as though she'd never seen her before.

"Don't you see, Shann. That's why you have to get an abortion. You said you'd saved money from your job at that place." Leigh crossed the room and took hold of Shann's shoulders. "We could find out where to go. I could come with you. Your parents need never know about it. I wouldn't tell. No one would ever know."

"Did you ever really love me, Leigh?"

Leigh let her hands fall, and she put space between them again. "Love hasn't got anything to do with it, Shann. I can't live my life so, well, so—"

"Honestly," Shann finished, and Leigh gave an exclamation of irritation.

"I told you, Shann. I'm not a lesbian."

They regarded each other in silence.

A car door slammed and Leigh moved then. "That's Mum. I have to go, Shann." She paused at the door. "I meant what I said. If you need someone to come with you I will."

Shann had left the house then and just kept walking. She ended up at the shopping center with no conscious idea about where she wanted to go. She had no money with her either so she sat and watched other shoppers coming and going. Her brother found her there three hours later and brought her home.

Ruth gave her her dinner, food she couldn't eat, and then they'd cross-examined her. After she'd answered in monosyllables or not at all, her father grew angry. One thing led to another, and Shann had blurted out that she was pregnant. Her parents were flabbergasted. And then came the demands to know who the father of the child was. Shann refused to say. And the arguments continued until Shann left home again. This time she planned what she saw as her escape. She flew down to her only aunt who lived in suburban Sydney.

After dinner that evening Shann sat on Corey's bed with him, and they read the next chapter of the Harry Potter book they were reading. At least having to concentrate on the words gave Shann some respite from the pendulum swings of feelings she had been experiencing all afternoon.

"Where are you and Angie going?" Corey asked as Shann tucked him in.

"We thought we might have some supper," she replied vaguely.

"Well, don't have too much coffee. It's not good for you late at night," he said, looking up at her seriously.

Shann bent over and gave him a hug and a smooch on the cheek. "Wouldn't think of it, Doctor Delaney."

Corey grinned.

"Now," Shann glanced at the time. Five to eight. Her tummy fluttered with nervous anticipation. "Do you want to read for a while?" she asked her son.

"I think I'll do some puzzles in my puzzle book." Corey took a paperback off his bedside table.

"Okay. Aunty Liz will be in to say good night, and I'll see you in the morning."

"Tell Angie I said hello."

"I will." Shann headed for the door.

"And Mum . . ."

She stopped and looked back at Corey.

"You look excellent."

Shann felt her cheeks warm. She wore a pair of dark green gabardine slacks and a lighter green thick knit sweater. It was a cool evening, and Shann wasn't sure if Angie's unit was air-conditioned.

"And Mum," Corey continued, "you smell delicious."

"I'm glad about that," Shann chuckled. "The alternative doesn't bear thinking about."

Corey giggled. "Have a nice night, Mum."

Shann blew him a kiss and went to her room. She took a steadying breath and picked up her brush, running it through her dark hair. She looked at herself in the mirror. Her face was slightly flushed, her eyes bright. She looked like a woman who was about to meet her lover.

Or like a woman who was coming down with something, she chided herself derisively, and bit off a nervous giggle.

Pulling back her sleeve she glanced at the time again. Angie should be here anytime now. She decided to go out onto the veranda to wait for her so she wouldn't have to get out of the car. Or so she wouldn't come in because the astute Liz would surely see their plans written in their eyes.

She popped her head into the living room where Liz and Amy were watching television. Her father had decided to have an early night as that morning Shann had taken him to his specialist for a checkup, and he was tired. Shann told Liz she'd wait for Angie outside.

"Say hi to her," Liz said, looking up from her knitting. "Have you got your key?"

Shann laughed. "Yes, and I'll try not to be too late."

Amy laughed. "Don't worry, Shann. Mum can't help herself."

"I know. I'll see you then." Shann went out onto the veranda, closing the door behind her.

She sat on the veranda railing and drew in the smell of the shrubs, the residue of a barbecue wafting on the air. Her eyes were drawn to the house next door. It had been a second home to her.

That was until Ann Callahan had discovered Shann and Leigh kissing. Eventually both sets of parents had sat with Shann and Leigh and spoken to them at length about accepted behavior. They were told it would be better if they didn't see as much of each other. They reluctantly agreed in the face of the combined parental front.

Afterward, the families decided that pretending the incident had never happened was the way to go.

Shann wrapped her arms around her body as the breeze picked up, scooting fallen leaves across the bitumen.

A couple of minutes later Angie drew the MG to a halt in front of the house. Shann's knees went weak, and she took a deep breath before walking down the steps.

In the glow from the streetlight Angie's fair hair gleamed like shot silver. Something caught in Shann's chest, and her mouth went dry. She walked through the gate, loped across the footpath and swung herself into the passenger seat without opening the door.

"Very cool," laughed Angie.

"Do you think so?" Shann smiled back. "It just occurred to me I could have ended up on my face and totally embarrassed myself."

"Not the famous Shannon Delaney. No way."

Their eyes met and Shann couldn't seem to find her voice. She could only drown in Angie's smile, in the dark pools of her eyes. She saw Angie swallow.

"You know, I think we should go. Otherwise I might have to kiss you right here, with old Mrs. Jones peeking through her curtains."

Shann resisted the urge to turn and look at the house across the street. "And I just might kiss you back, no matter who's watching," she said softly.

"Word would spread like wildfire," Angie said as she put the car into gear. "Mrs. Jones could dine out on that story at the Senior Citizens Club for years."

"Mrs. Jones is ninety-seven. Are you sure she'd recognize us in the dark?"

"Streetlight." Angie pointed to the light almost directly above them. "And Mrs. Jones is as sharp as a tack and probably has better eyesight than the two of us put together."

Shann laughed as Angie put the car into gear and pulled away from the curb. In minutes she'd turned the car into an underground garage. She inserted a key in the wall-mounted box, and the door rumbled upward. Driving in, she parked and turned off the ignition.

"Shall we go on up?" She raised a fine brow and Shann smiled. "Oh, yes. I think we should."

They climbed out of the car, and Angie unlocked the boot. She passed a wine cooler to Shann and took a small icebox and a colorful cotton blanket out of the back of the car. They stepped into the elevator and as the door slid closed, Shann felt herself flush. She glanced at Angie to find Angie looking at her.

"Top floor?" Shann said breathily.

"Mmm." Angie swiped her keycard. "I can't wait for you to see it. I think the previous owners merged two smaller units. Anyway, it's really quite big. Three bedrooms and a small study."

They fell silent, and the air in the elevator seemed to grow thick with tension. Shann passed the wine cooler from one hand to the other and when the elevator dinged at their floor, she almost jumped with fright. The doors opened into a small foyer, and Angie stepped across and unlocked the ornate door. She reached inside and flicked the light switch, turning and stepping back. "Welcome. You're my first guest."

Shann walked into the unit and whistled softly. "Angie, this is great."

The kitchen was off to the right and a small study to the left. In front of her was the living-dining room. The floor was polished timber and although the unit was unpainted, the potential was obvious. Leaving everything on the kitchen bench, Angie showed Shann the rest of the apartment. Then she slid the glass doors open and they stepped out onto the balcony.

Shann made a point of not looking directly down and she took hold of the railings to steady herself.

The breeze whipped Shann's hair across her face, and she brushed it back. The view was spectacular. The lights of the city a couple of miles away hung in the darkness.

"Wonderful," Shann said and turned to find Angie's eyes regarding her again, a small smile lifting the corners of her mouth.

"Wonderful," she repeated, and Shann felt heat radiate to every corner of her body.

Angie reached out, her fingers running over the back of Shann's hand where she clutched the railing. The caress was so light, but it seemed to burn where it touched, fired Shann's blood, and she shivered.

"Are you cold?" Angie asked, concerned.

"No. Not really." Shann shook her head, and Angie held her gaze for long moments.

"Come on inside. It's warmer in there."

They crossed the balcony and stepped back into the unit. Angie closed the sliding glass doors and crossed to the kitchen. The living room was empty apart from a large old couch and a cardboard carton upturned as a coffee table.

"Not much furniture," Angie said ruefully. "But—" She smiled at Shann and held up her hand. "I come prepared." She reached across and lifted the lid of the wine cooler, removing a bottle of red.

And Shann's eyes watched as she reached over, followed the curve of her jean-clad hip, the swell of her rounded buttock, the lines of her body. She shivered again, knowing it had nothing to do with the room temperature. Her whole body was tuned to the other woman, the nuances of her movements, the sound of her voice. Her body was damp and so ready for Angie's touch.

Shann took herself impatiently to task. It had been a long time since she'd had a relationship, she acknowledged, but that didn't mean she had to fall on Angie like some sex-starved teenager. They were both adults, and Angie would expect Shann to act like one. But Shann didn't feel like a mature, in-command-of-herself adult. She wanted to kiss Angie, make love to her, right here in the middle of this empty, wonderful unit.

"I hope you like red wine?" Angie asked, looking over her shoulder at Shann, and Shann nodded.

"Red's fine."

Angie stepped around behind the breakfast bar and opened the wine cooler again.

"Can I help?" Shann moved forward and then stopped, the narrow expanse of the breakfast bar between them.

Angie smiled and shook her head. And that smile almost undid Shann's hard-fought composure.

"It's okay. I opened the bottle before I came out and," she held up two narrow, long-stemmed wineglasses, "I remembered the glasses, too." She poured some wine into each glass and slid one glass closer to Shann.

Shann's eyes were locked on Angie's smile, and she couldn't look away. Did Angie know the incredible effect of that smile? How could she not know?

Angie raised her eyebrows inquiringly, her smile fading a little when Shann didn't move to pick up the glass.

"Do you know just how beautiful you are?" Shann asked huskily, and Angie looked a little disconcerted.

"Beautiful? That's stretching it," she said, a flush coloring her cheeks.

Holding Angie's gaze, Shann shook her head. "No. It's no stretch. I don't think I've seen anyone with eyes that shade of green. I feel like I could drown in them."

Angie looked down, then back at Shann, and Shann saw the erratic flutter of the pulse at the base of Angie's throat. That sign of Angie's arousal only set Shann's already sensitive nerve endings on another wild erotic surge through her body. She felt fragile and yet capable of anything.

"Oh, dear. No drowning," Angie said thickly. "I'd have to save you."

What would Angie say if Shann told her she suspected Angie already had done just that? Her mouth went dry, and as she watched, Angie's eyes darkened, and Shann was drawn into that same swirling vortex. Her body tensed. She had to stop herself walking around the breakfast bar and making love to Angie right there and right then.

Angie gave a soft laugh that played over Shann like a mellow melody on a steel guitar. "Well, at least I can save you from hunger," she said and took a paper plate and a molded plastic box out of the cooler. She proceeded to arrange large, juicy, chocolate-dipped strawberries on the plate.

"Wow! Now that's decadent," Shann laughed.

Angie chose a strawberry and reached across the breakfast bar to pop it into Shann's mouth. Then she licked the chocolate from her fingers as Shann swallowed the delicious berry. "Oh, I think tonight's the right night for decadence," she said, picking up Shann's wineglass and holding it out to her.

Heat suffused Shann's body again, and she thought she was about to combust. She took the glass and their fingers touched for long, electrifying moments.

"A toast." Angie raised her glass. "To tonight."

Shann swallowed quickly. "To tonight," she repeated, and her voice sounded unlike her own.

Tucking the blanket under her arm, Angie picked up the plate of strawberries and walked around the counter. "Shall we sit on the couch?"

Shann followed Angie, waiting while she set the plate of strawberries and her glass of wine on the upturned carton and spread the cotton blanket out over the couch, the bright colors adding a vibrant touch to the room. Shann sank down on the couch before her shaky legs gave way beneath her. Angie didn't join her but walked over to the balcony doors.

"These are the old curtains. They'll remove them before they start painting, and I'll replace them." She pulled a cord, and the heavy curtains slid over the doors and floor-to-ceiling windows, then she turned to grin at Shann. "In deference to any zealous arresting officers who might be passing by when we may not want them to, and we don't hear the helicopter," she added dryly.

"Is this before or after Spiderman trips across the balcony?" Shann remarked with a laugh.

"Very droll." Angie returned to sit down beside Shann. She picked up her wine and took a sip. She turned to look at Shann, resting her head on her hand, her elbow on the back of the couch.

"You know, I didn't think tonight would come. It's been the longest afternoon of my life," she said softly.

"And mine." Shann twisted her wineglass in her fingers. "I've been totally useless all afternoon."

"Me, too." Angie sighed. "I'm sure my staff wondered what was going on with me today. Sitting in the meeting I kept thinking about you, and I'd have to move in my seat. I don't think I've ever been so tuned out. Or so turned on."

Shann laughed in sympathy. "Liz was giving me some very strange looks at dinner. I didn't hear a word anyone said, and I'd have to keep reminding myself to eat another mouthful." Her gaze dropped to the curve of Angie's lips.

"So," Angie gave a quick smile. "And now it's here," she said, her voice enticingly low.

CHAPTER NINE

Angie leaned across and put her lips on Shann's. Touched softly. Drew back. Touched again. Nibbled gently on Shann's lower lip. Pulled back again.

Pure desire clamored inside Shann and arrowed down to her center. Angie kissed her again, and she murmured against Angie's lips, deepening the kiss. When they parted they both drew shaky breaths.

Lifting her hand Shann ran her finger lightly along the line of Angie's jaw, gently touching the exquisite softness of her lips. Angie took Shann's fingertip into her mouth and sucked sensually. Shann leaned in to kiss her again only drawing back when she spilled some wine on her slacks.

She gave a hiccuping laugh. "Oops! What a waste." She took a sip and placed her glass carefully on the box beside Angie's. Then she chose a strawberry and fed it to Angie before reaching over and licking the chocolate from Angie's lips. "Mmm. Delicious."

Angie rested her hand on Shann's thigh, moved her hand upward over Shann's stomach, paused on her midriff, and Shann groaned. She relaxed back against the couch, pulling Angie with her until Angie was half lying across her.

Shann moved her hands over Angie's firm jean-clad buttocks, continued upward over her hips, slid beneath her sweatshirt, luxuriating in the feel of her firm skin. She paused and then cupped Angie's lace-covered breasts in her hands.

Angie made a soft, so aroused sound that reached inside Shann and found an answering fire.

Shann peeled Angie's sweatshirt up and over her head, discarding it on the floor, before reaching around to unclasp and remove her bra. Angie arched over her and Shann slid down and buried her face between Angie's firm naked breasts.

Her fingers found the puckering nipples, her thumbs gently caressing until Angie slumped forward, her body melding with Shann's. Angie drew a deep breath then raised her head, her gaze moving over every facet of Shann's face before she slowly lowered her head so she could kiss Shann again. The lingering kiss shuddered through Shann and as it grew more urgent, their bodies strained together. The exciting, drugging kisses continued until eventually Angie pushed herself up on her elbows, looking down at Shann through heavy-lidded eyes, the corners of her mouth curved up in a smile of arousal.

"Aren't you just a little overdressed?" she asked huskily. She sat up, pulling Shann with her. In no time she'd dispensed with Shann's sweater. She traced the edge of Shann's lacy bra with her finger, then her lips, before unclasping it and sliding her fingers inside to cup Shann's breasts.

Shann's breasts swelled to fill Angie's hands. She slipped the bra straps off her arms and dropped the bra on the floor.

Angie's eyes drank in the mound of Shann's breasts as she cupped them. Then she lowered her head and took one rosy peak into her mouth, gently sucking, her tongue rasping, and Shann arched toward her, desire exquisitely setting her aflame.

139

"Angie, I can't . . . I can't stand it," Shann breathed brokenly, her hands twisting the blanket where she clasped it. "I need you . . . I need you to touch me." Her voice caught on a sob, and Angie slid her hand down and cupped Shann through her slacks.

Shann groaned unevenly, and with shaky hands she fumbled for the press-stud on her pants. The sound of it opening seemed to vibrate around the empty room and their eyes met, held for long moments before Angie gently moved Shann's fingers aside and slid Shann's zipper down. She went to peel Shann's pants down, too, but Shann struggled up, pulling off her boots before helping Angie remove the rest of her clothes.

Shann felt coolness on her heated dampness, and when she saw Angie's gaze move slowly over her completely naked body, a powerful surge of desire had her falling back against the couch.

Gentle fingers cupped Shann's mound and settled there. Shann moved, covering Angie's hand with her own, halting her. She reached up and undid Angie's jeans, peeling them over her hips. Angie stood up and disposed of her own jeans and undies.

With a shaky smile Shann feasted on the beauty of Angie's slim body, her full breasts, curving hips, the tantalizing tangle of fair curls between her legs. Shann sat forward and put her face against the soft, damp curls. She looked up at Angie and Angie smiled.

Reaching out, Shann put her finger on the silver charm hanging from Angie's pierced navel. It was a tiny ax, a labrys. "So that's what I saw glistening the other night at the club," she murmured.

"I had it done for my twenty-fifth birthday. I chose the belly button piercing because it was, well, reasonably unintrusive. It was simple to conceal, and I thought if I got sick of it, it would be easier to remove than a tattoo."

"It's very erotic," Shann said thickly, and let her finger slowly circle the tiny charm. She looked up at Angie through narrowed lids, and she heard Angie murmur deep in her throat before she slowly stretched out over Shann until they were thigh to thigh, stomach to stomach, breast to breast. Her nipples grazed against Shann's and Shann instinctively thrust her pelvis against Angie's, moving provocatively.

Angie slipped her hand between them, slid her fingers into the wetness, and Shann shuddered. She reached up and caressed Angie's breasts, heard her catch her breath again and moan softly. Then Angie was moving so that she was kneeling over Shann, her legs on each side of Shann's hips.

Moving one hand between them, Shann touched the soft curls, cupped Angie's mound, her fingers sliding inside her. And they both moved in time, fingers circling, sliding slickly.

In no time Shann's muscles tensed and she orgasmed, clutching Angie to her as Angie followed just seconds later. They lay together, entwined, hearts beating fast, breathing ragged, until eventually Angie stirred, raised her head and slowly kissed Shann's lips.

"That was fantastic," she whispered against Shann's cheek, her breath feathering Shann's skin.

And Shann smiled languidly. "Absolutely fantastic. I didn't mean to be so quick but I've wanted you for so long I . . . I couldn't . . ."

"I know. Me, too." Angie smiled crookedly. She let her gaze fall to Shann's breast again, and she moved her hand, fingers teasing, and Shann's nipple jumped to attention, her clitoris throbbing, and she knew she was ready again.

Reaching up she cupped the side of Angie's head so that her fingers slid into Angie's short hair, and she gently pulled her down so she could kiss her soft lips. Her other hand found the indentation of Angie's spine, gently caressing.

Shifting slightly, Shann moved Angie, pressing her back onto the bright cotton blanket. She slid to the floor beside her and reached for a strawberry. Flicking light glances at Angie's face to watch her change of expression, Shann slowly smeared chocolate over Angie's breasts, across her nipples, then she popped the strawberry into Angie's mouth.

Choosing another strawberry she left a trail of chocolate around the indentation of Angie's navel and the small silver ax, down over the soft mat of fair curls, the inside of her thigh, and Angie gave a low chuckle, her body arching.

Shann put the strawberry into her mouth, chewed and swallowed.

Angie's eyes were dark pools, and her lips parted in a low moan. "Mmmm. I hope you're a chocoholic."

"Guilty," Shann replied huskily, and she leaned slowly forward, leisurely licking at the smudges of chocolate on Angie's smooth skin, unhurriedly heading toward the hard peaks of her nipples. She paused and then covered one chocolate-smeared nipple with her mouth, sucked, licked, teased, until Angie moaned, her body writhing.

Continuing her quest, Shann's mouth meandered downward, lapping the smears of chocolate that encircled Angie's navel. She raised her eyes to see Angie's softened, so aroused expression.

"Shann," she begged thickly, her fingers twining in Shann's dark hair, and Shann moved lower.

Her lips slipped into the dampness and Angie's legs parted, her hips lifting, thrusting toward Shann's questing tongue. Shann matched her rhythm to Angie's movements, hands holding her thighs as Angie's tension rose to finally reach its peak. And Shann held her tenderly as she cascaded downward.

After a few moments Shann moved up and kissed Angie slowly, gently. The kiss deepened and she felt Angie's hands seeking, finding her secret erotic places, and she was so ready again. Shann clutched Angie's fingers inside her, and she cried out as she fell into her climax.

Angie's fingers continued to tantalize, her tongue teasing Shann's breasts and amazingly, Shann came again. She collapsed onto the couch beside Angie, completely sated.

They pulled the cotton blanket over their damp bodies, legs entwined, arms wrapped around each other. Shann settled Angie's head onto her shoulder, and they fell into a light sleep.

Some time later, Shann reluctantly stirred. She felt the soft flutter of Angie's breath against her neck, the warmth of the other woman's beautiful body molded to her own, and she smiled. Opening her eyes she found Angie watching her, a small, answering, oh-so-satisfied smile lifting the corners of her mouth.

"Hi." Angie said softly.

"Hi, yourself," Shann murmured. "I hope you feel as wonderful as I do."

"Oh, I rather think I do." Angie laughed softly. "Don't try this at home, folks, unless you disconnect the phone, lock all the windows and doors and pulls the curtains."

"And make sure the police are otherwise engaged." Shann chuckled. "The taste of chocolate and strawberries has taken on a new meaning for me."

Angie lifted her hand, brushed a strand of Shann's dark hair back, ran her finger lightly over Shann's forehead, down her cheek, across her lips, her chin, and down to encircle one breast.

Arousal gathered in the pit of Shann's stomach, shivered down between her legs. She placed a soft kiss on Angie's nose.

"Did I mention that you were a fantastic lover?" Angie asked, her gaze holding Shann's.

"Aw, shucks. You're putting me to the blush." Shann's cheeks warmed with pleasure.

Angie chuckled. Her eyes moved over Shann's body, and Shann felt her nipples tighten under Angie's gaze. "Oh, and did you know you blush all over?" she asked, her eyes twinkling with amusement.

Shann laughed ruefully. "It appears I can't disguise what you do to me." She sobered. "And if we're talking about fantastic lovers, well, it takes two, you know."

Angie kissed her. "I'm glad you think so. I . . . it was incredible."

They kissed slowly, lingeringly, and when they drew apart Shann sighed.

"I suspect it's rather late." She glanced at Angie's wristwatch and groaned. "One thirty. Where did the time go?"

"I don't know, but it went beautifully." Angie sat up and reached for her wineglass, took a sip and passed it to Shann. She gazed down into Shann's eyes and then carefully took the wineglass and replaced it on the box. She lowered herself onto Shann with a self-derisive laugh. "I can't believe it. I'm—" She took Shann's hand, moved it between them, straining against Shann's seeking fingers. Angie murmured her pleasure and then cried out Shann's name, collapsing into her arms.

When Angie's breathing quieted she raised her eyebrows at Shann. "You have magic fingers," she whispered and put her lips to Shann's breast.

Afterward they reluctantly sat up, and suddenly famished, they finished the strawberries, pausing for soft, slow kisses between bites.

"We should go," suggested Shann halfheartedly. "You have to go to work tomorrow."

"And you have to get Corey off to school." She took hold of Shann's hand. "I'd like to stay forever but—" She kissed the back of Shann's hand and resolutely stood up, bent to collect their strewn clothes. She turned to hand Shann her slacks and sweater, pausing as she caught Shann's grin. "What's so amusing?"

"Oh, this isn't an amused smile," Shann told her. "It's more of a oh-my-God-what-a-spectacular-view sort of smile."

Angie giggled, pulled Shann to her feet and into her arms. Their naked bodies merged, and Shann wrapped her arms around the other woman, delighting again in the way they seemed to fit each other. She realized she never wanted to let Angie go. Her arms tightened and she rained soft kisses over her shoulder, the line of her jaw to her pliant mouth. She sighed against Angie's lips and drew away to look at her.

A tear trickled down Angie's cheek, and Shann stiffened, immediately concerned.

"Angie? What is it? I'm sorry. Did I hurt you?"

Angie shook her head. "No. Never. I'm fine." She dashed at her damp cheek with her hand. "I'm being silly. I just . . . I feel like I don't want to let you go in case . . ."

"In case what?"

"Maybe in the cold light of day you might, well . . ." Angie shrugged. "I'm sorry. I'm being foolish. Let's get dressed."

Shann kept Angie in the circle of her arms. "The cold light of day isn't going to change this wonderful night," she said sincerely.

"Oh, Shann." Angie clung to her. "I want to say so much, but I don't know where to start. And it's so late."

"We can talk tomorrow," Shann assured her. "I promised I'd play board games with Corey after dinner, but you're welcome to join us if you don't mind that sort of thing. And after Corey goes to bed, we could have some time alone."

"That would be great."

"Are you sure? I mean, you can wait till after Corey goes to bed if you like."

"I'm positive. I'd love to spend time with you and Corey. I should warn you though, I take no prisoners when it comes to board games."

Shann groaned. "Oh, no. Neither does Corey. He'll appreciate a better opponent than me." Shann shivered as a cool breeze moved the curtains on the window nearest them.

"You're getting goosebumps." Angie rubbed Shann's arm. "We'd better get dressed before we catch cold." She shot a teasing look at Shann. "Or we could find a far more exciting way to warm up, hmmm?"

Shann gave a regretful laugh. "I wouldn't take much tempting, but if we do we'll be here all night. The one drawback is that Liz is an early riser. She'd be sure to catch us sneaking in, and then she'd give us the third degree."

"Good point," said Angie. "And I always look so guilty. Especially when I'm really guilty."

They started to dress. Shann pulled on her underpants and slacks and was reaching for her bra.

"Shann?"

She turned back to Angie and when Angie paused Shann raised an inquiring eyebrow.

"I just—" Angie shook her head. "Just thank you for tonight."

Shann grinned. "Thank you," she said with feeling.

"It wasn't too, well, staged, was it?" Angie asked. "I mean, we came here to . . . it wasn't unromantic, was it?"

"Unromantic?" Shann laughed delightedly. "Fine wine. Succulent strawberries. Absolutely delicious chocolate. And you. Especially you. It was the most romantic night of my life."

"It was?"

"Oh, absolutely." Shann gave her a quick kiss.

"I'm glad," said Angie, a smile lighting her face.

The next morning Shann had to strive desperately to put on an outward show of normality. Only she knew what a complete facade that was. The few hours sleep she'd had kept her functioning just half a beat behind everyone and everything else. And the fantastic time she'd had with Angie had her replaying moments at totally inopportune moments.

She barely went through the motions of assisting her father, preparing breakfasts, organizing lunches, and getting Corey off to school. At ten o'clock Shann and Liz were sitting on the back veranda waiting for their father's physiotherapist to arrive when she couldn't prevent a yawn.

Liz raised her eyebrows. "You look like you're auditioning for the lead role in a zombie movie," she said without preamble. "Exactly what time did you get to bed last night anyway?"

Shann shrugged vaguely. "Pretty late. Angie and I were talking, and we forgot the time."

"Where did you end up going? I didn't know there was anywhere around here that stayed open particularly late."

"Actually, Angie showed me her unit. It's only a couple of streets away."

"Oh, yes, that's right. That's why Angie's staying with Ann and Mike. And I know how much Ann's enjoying having Angie back home while the renovations are being done. Ann says the unit's magnificent."

"It is that. It has great views of the city."

"How's the renovation going?"

"It's ready to be painted, and she's getting new curtains."

"When does she plan on moving back in to the unit?"

"I'm not sure." Shann shrugged. "As long as it takes the painters and decorators to finish I guess."

"So what about supper?" Liz persisted, and Shann rolled her eyes.

"We had supper at the unit. And before you ask, it was red wine and some fruit."

"Oh. I see." Liz raised her eyebrows. "Then maybe the wine has more to do with your spaced out look."

"I wasn't drunk, Liz. I don't think we even finished a bottle," she said defensively.

Liz gave Shann a probing look. "Shann, you will be careful, won't you?"

Shann shuffled the pages of the newspaper she'd been pretending to read. "Careful of what? I don't know what you mean."

"Yes, you do. I mean, you and Angie."

Shann swallowed. "What about us?"

"Oh, Shann." Liz leaned across the table, her expression all concern. "I don't think Ann and Mike are going to be pleased if you, well, you know."

"What are you implying, Liz?" Shann asked, valiantly trying to brazen it out.

"You're my sister, Shann, and I care about you." She checked to ensure their father wasn't coming down the hallway. "I'd have to be blind not to see there's something going on with you two. You don't seem to be able to take your eyes off each other."

Shann ran her fingers over a knot in the pine wood table. "We're both adults, Liz," she said quietly.

"So there is something between you?"

"I didn't say that."

Liz sighed. "I don't think you have to, love. As I think I said, I have wondered about Angie, not having any young guys in tow. She's far too attractive not to have unless she's not interested in men." Liz paused. "I take it Ann doesn't know about her."

"I don't know what Ann Callahan knows," Shann said tersely. "Can we change the subject?"

Liz sighed again, louder this time. "I wish things weren't so complicated for you, that's all."

"It's only complicated sometimes," Shann acknowledged. "And it's more to do with other people's problems."

Liz nodded. "It's sad really. We all profess to love our children unconditionally, but if we're put to the test not all of us pass with flying colors. Dad and Ruth surely didn't all those years ago. Neither did the Callahans."

"I *am* going to have to tell Dad. You know that, don't you, Liz?" Shann asked her sister, and Liz nodded.

"Yes. I know. And Rhys and I will be here this time to support you whenever you decide to tell him."

Shann lifted Liz's hand and kissed it before returning it to the table. "You're a great sister, Liz. Even if your interrogation techniques would do *ASIO* proud," she added with a grin.

Liz smiled too, and then sobered. "Angie Callahan is one of the nicest people I know," she said. "I just wanted to tell you that. She always was, even as a kid."

"Yes. I know." Shann said, unaware that her voice, her expression, had softened for one unguarded moment.

Liz regarded her through narrowed eyes. "You're in love with her, aren't you?" she said, her voice almost a whisper.

"Liz!" Shann suspected the warmth that rose in her cheeks was clearly visible.

Liz smiled crookedly. "On the bright side, love. You won't get pregnant this time."

Shann shook her head exasperatedly and then laughed reluctantly. "I suppose I won't. But the big letter *L* glowing in the middle of my forehead might be a trifle difficult to explain."

Liz laughed delightedly and then glanced at her wristwatch. "You know, I think I feel like coffee and cake."

Shann went to stand up. "I'll boil the kettle."

"No, stay there, Shann." Liz held out her hand. "I mean real coffee. Dad's physiotherapist will be here in a minute. When he arrives, let's go out. Gerard will be here if Dad and Derek need anything."

"Are you sure you feel up to getting in the car?"

"I'm fine." Liz waved her hand dismissively. "I just won't break into a sprint or anything."

A few minutes later, the physio was with their father, they'd promised they'd be back within the hour, and Shann had settled Liz into the passenger seat of her car. She switched on the ignition and turned to her sister. "Where to?"

"Let's go to Angie's. That's the closest," Liz said casually.

"Liz! We could go to that well-known coffee shop over in Paddington."

"Angie's is just around the corner. They have a new coffee shop there now and the coffee's superb."

Shann's heartbeats were falling over themselves at the thought of seeing Angie again, but being in Angie's company under her sister's eagle eye, well, Shann didn't think that was wise. And yet— "Angie will probably be busy," she said offering little to no resistance.

"So? We don't need to talk to her, do we?" Liz chuckled and nudged Shann playfully. "I just like the coffee they serve there."

"To quote Corey, yeah right!" Shann drove the short distance to the hardware store, and she was a jumble of mixed emotions. Yet she had to admit the thought that she might see Angie again surely won out.

They found a park close to the entry, and Shann helped Liz climb from the car. The automatic doors swung open and Shann felt her senses quicken as her heartbeats thudded in her chest.

As they passed the tool section Shann noticed with relief that Joe Radford was busy helping a couple of tradesmen. Angie was nowhere in sight, and they reached the coffee shop without seeing her. They made their way up to the counter and when Cindy saw Shann she smiled broadly.

"Hi there! What would you like today? Weak skinny cap, wasn't it?"

Impressed, Shann smiled. "Right. And one straight cappuccino for my sister."

"Angie anywhere about?" Liz asked lightly.

Shann stiffened and frowned a warning at her sister.

"She was here a minute ago," replied Cindy. "You just missed her."

"Oh, well, we might catch her before we go," Shann put in quickly.

"I can give her a call," offered Cindy.

"No. That's okay," Shann began.

"Would it be any trouble?" Liz asked with a smile.

"None at all." Cindy picked up the phone on the counter behind her and turned back to them. She smiled over Shann's shoulder. "No need to call. Here she comes." She indicated with the handheld receiver before she replaced it.

Shann turned slowly and saw Angie striding toward them. And everything else simply dissolved into the background. She took in the faint movement of Angie's short fair hair, her well-defined brows, the way her lips curved upward in that ready smile. She was wearing her uniform of dark pants and blue short-sleeved tailored shirt and Shann's gaze drank in the rise of her breasts, the sway of her rounded hips, her long, slim legs.

And Shann had touched every wonderful, desirable inch of her.

The now familiar surge of sybaritic hunger caught Shann unawares. It burned inside her to settle at her center and she was hard pressed to catch her breath.

She wanted to narrow the distance between them, draw Angie into her arms, kiss her feverishly, make love to her again the way they had last night. And she knew for better or worse she *had* fallen in love with Angie Callahan. Desperately in love.

CHAPTER TEN

She loved everything about her. Her vivid green eyes. Her smile. Her ready sense of humor. The way she felt in Shann's arms. The low, sensual sounds she made when they made love.

Angie had reached them and although her smile encompassed them both, her eyes found Shann's. "Hi."

Shann smiled, but her voice totally deserted her.

"Hello, Angie." Liz greeted her brightly. "We were hoping we'd see you. Would you like to join us for coffee?"

"I'd love to." Angie's smile broadened.

"Then I'll go and save that table over there," Liz said. "And get some goodies, Shann," she added as she left them.

Angie continued to gaze at Shann. Her eyes moved down, focusing on Shann's lips, and after long moments her eyes met Shann's again. "How are you?" she asked huskily.

"Fine. And you?" Shann could almost cringe at her inanity.

"A little spaced out but," she drew a shaky breath, "wonderful."

Shann found herself drowning in the depths of Angie's eyes again, and then someone said something over the loudspeakers, reminding Shann of where she was. "I have to get something to have with our coffees," she said and made herself turn back to the glass-fronted display beneath the counter. At the sight of a plate of chocolate-dipped strawberries, Shann's knees nearly gave way beneath her. "They all look so delicious," she got out thickly.

Angie leaned forward. "I can indubitably recommend the strawberries," she said softly.

Shann coughed, her mouth dry. "Maybe some ginger sticky date cookies," she told the waiting Cindy. "Oh, and coffee and cookies for Angie."

"Put the bill on my tab," Angie told Cindy but Shann protested, taking out her wallet and paying Cindy.

"My shout this time," she told Angie, and Angie acquiesced reluctantly.

"Sit down and I'll bring it over," Cindy said, and Shann followed Angie over to the table where Liz waited for them.

"I was just telling Shann how superb your coffee is here," Liz said as they sat down.

Shann slowly moved her leg so that her knee rested against Angie's.

Angie shot Shann a startled glance and then looked back at Liz. "Thanks, Liz. We started the coffee shop as an experiment and it's been highly successful. We're thinking we might expand to light lunches, like salads and gourmet sandwiches."

"That should go well, too. Sure beats a sausage sizzle." Liz laughed.

Cindy came over with a tray and distributed the drinks. She set the plate of cookies in the middle of the table and left them.

"So you and Shann had a late night last night," Liz said, cutting to the chase without warning.

Angie slid a quick look at Shann, and a flush washed her cheeks.

"I told Liz we were talking and forgot the time," Shann said quickly.

"Yes. We did." Angie laughed. "You know me, Liz. Once I get started I can talk the leg off an iron pot."

"True." Liz laughed with her. "Shann also tells me your unit is almost finished. Are you looking forward to moving back on your own?"

"I am. It's taken longer than I hoped it would, but I can't say I haven't enjoyed being back and having Ann spoil me."

Shann passed the plate of biscuits around.

"Have Gerard and Amy finished their exams?" Angie asked politely before taking a bite of her cookie.

Shann drew her eyes away, concentrated on her own biscuit.

"They both finish next week. Amy on Tuesday and Gerard on Thursday, which is good," Liz continued, "because they'll be at home so Shann's free to go up to Gympie to the Muster."

"That's next week?" Angie glanced at Shann and she nodded.

"I've planned to go up on Tuesday morning to get settled in. My first show is on Tuesday afternoon."

"How long will you be up there?" she asked.

"For the week. I'll probably come back on Sunday afternoon or if I'm too tired early Monday morning. From all accounts it's a week of continuous music if you camp on the site."

"You're camping?" Angie raised her eyebrows, and Liz chuckled.

"You know you didn't do camping very well when you were a kid," Liz said. "If I remember rightly you always drove us mad wanting to go to the toilet in the middle of the night."

Shann grimaced. "I don't remember that."

"Selective memory?" suggested her sister.

"Well, everyone can rest easy," Shann said dryly. "I suppose for me to call it camping would be stretching it a bit because I've been provided with a trailer or a campervan. So I'll have a bed, a shower, all mod cons."

"Now that's what I call camping," Angie patted Shann's hand.

And Shann's skin burned where Angie had touched her.

"If I hadn't had my surgery we'd have all gone up to see Shann's shows," Liz said regretfully. "You know I've yet to see Shann perform on stage."

"Really?" Angie raised her eyebrows in disbelief. "You'll have to come down to The Blue Moon next time Shann's playing."

"I told Liz you called in with some friends," Shann put in quickly, and Angie smiled crookedly.

"I think Liz knows why I was there, Shann." She turned to Liz. "Maybe you can come along with me because I don't intend to miss any of Shann's performances."

"I might just do that." Liz smiled at Angie. "Who knows, I could have hordes of women vying for my attention."

Angie laughed delightedly at the expression of horror on Shann's face, and Liz joined in. "You always were easy to tease, Shann." Angie took a sip of her coffee and winked at Shann over the top of her cup.

"Now that's the truth," agreed Liz. She paused and looked at Angie. "About The Blue Moon, Angie. Does Ann know?"

"About my sexual preference? Not in so many words."

"Do you intend to tell her?" Liz asked.

Angie shrugged. "When I said not exactly, I meant I think she suspects. We just haven't brought it out in the open. The right time will come up."

"What if," Liz glanced at Shann, "you meet someone? Someone special?"

Shann shifted in her seat. "Liz, maybe Angie doesn't want to talk about this."

"It's all right, Shann. And I know why Liz is asking me these questions. She's your sister, and she's worried about you." Angie looked directly at Liz. "Hmmm?"

Liz gave a soft laugh. "Something like that."

"I do intend to tell her as soon as I can." Angie held Shann's gaze.

Shann swallowed. Her memories of Ann Callahan's anger could still churn inside her. She had to admit she was hard-pressed to see Angie's aunt accepting the fact that Angie was a lesbian. When

Angie put Shann herself into the equation, well, Shann's reservations only deepened.

Liz sighed. "Have you considered that it may not go as well as you hope Angie?"

Angie nodded. "I think perhaps Ann and Mike are a little more open-minded than they used to be."

"Are you absolutely sure?" Liz frowned. "What if they're not?"

Angie shrugged slightly. "You're right, I suppose. Maybe we can't ever be sure about anyone. But how Ann and Mike react to the fact that I'm a lesbian is something that's out of my control. I don't want to hurt them, but I can't change what I know's right for me to suit anyone else."

Liz nodded. "And I'm sure Shann feels the same way. It's just so difficult for you both." She patted Angie's hand. "I do hope it does go well. Now I'll leave you two alone for a minute." She drained her coffee cup. "I need to get a replacement bulb for my reading light."

Shann stood up. "I can get that for you, Liz."

"There's no need, love. Stay there. I'm quite capable of performing this little chore otherwise I wouldn't consider it. I'll be back in a few minutes. Unless I run into Joe Radford. In that case I'll probably need you both to carry the boxes of new lamps for the entire house that he'll talk me into buying."

Shann watched Liz go, and suddenly she felt gauche and tongue-tied.

"Liz seems to be recovering well," Angie remarked.

"Yes. I—" Shann met Angie's beautiful green eyes. "I'm sorry she's so nosy. She doesn't leave any stone unturned when she's seeking information."

Angie grinned. "I'll bet Amy and Gerard have absolutely no secrets."

"Probably not," Shann agreed.

Angie's smile faded. "You know Liz all but put me under a bright light after you left ten years ago. Luckily I couldn't tell her much."

"Angie, I'm sorry Liz dragged you into it—" Shann began to apologize.

"It's okay, Shann. I wanted to help. I was worried, too. We all were. And Liz would have interrogated the entire suburb if she'd thought it would have found you. She loves you."

"Once a big sister always a big sister." Shann tried to lighten the conversation.

"Very much so. That's why she wants to make sure you don't get hurt again." Angie replaced her cup carefully on its saucer. "She has no need to worry on that score," she said softly.

Her tone, her words, trickled over Shann like sweet, warm honey.

"But I guess this is too public for that conversation," Angie said regretfully. "And I suspect we're both borderline sleepwalkers, hmmm?"

"Good description." Shann smiled. "But I'm also elated at the same time."

"Me, too."

Shann shook her head. "I was trying to work out how I was going to escape for a while so I could come over here to see you when Liz suggested coffee. I all but drove over here as the crow flies."

Angie laughed. "I'm glad you came. I was going to phone, but I thought you might think I was too needy or something."

"Well, I needed to see you," Shann told her, and Angie grinned.

"I feel like the cat with the cream. Lucky darn cat."

They laughed together.

"Angie, about Ann and Mike," Shann said seriously. "You know you don't have to tell them anything on my account."

"Don't worry, Shann. I've been pretty much preparing the way since I came home. I do think they already know, and I get the feeling Ann's ready to discuss it."

"In a positive way?" Shann couldn't help being skeptical.

"I hope so."

Shann pulled a face. "It probably might not be the best idea to mention me specifically in that conversation."

Angie laughed. "You mean the notorious Shannon Delaney?"

"That might not be far from the truth where your aunt's concerned. I wasn't exactly the flavor of the month back then with both sets of parents but especially with Ann."

"I know." Angie sighed. "But I do think she's quite aware she overreacted. She's mellowed and apart from that, she's been raving about what a wonderful boy Corey is and what a marvelous job you've done bringing him up on your own."

"I was on such tenterhooks the day she first came over I have no idea what transpired. I was too busy trying to walk on eggshells. But I do know I don't have to worry about Corey. I'm a little biased, but I think he's wonderful, too."

"He's so very much like you. He is," Angie repeated at Shann's doubtful look. "And Ann and Mike are totally impressed about Corey getting that lump of a dog to actually take some notice."

Shann laughed. "It's amazed all of us."

"Not that any of us will be sorry to see Tiger go next week."

Shann stilled and her gaze fell to her empty coffee cup.

"Leigh and Evan and the kids are back from New Zealand," Angie continued. "They're in Melbourne at the moment, then they go on to Sydney. They'll be coming home as soon as Evan finishes his business down there. The last Ann heard was it was supposed to be in the next week or so."

Hopefully when she was at the Muster, Shann thought. And she knew she felt a certain amount of relief knowing she wouldn't have to face Leigh at the moment. "Well, no doubt I'll catch up with them some time or other," Shann said vaguely.

Angie hesitated. "Will it be a problem?" she asked, sounding far more casual than Shann suspected she was.

Shann considered the question. When she'd agreed to come home she was aware there was a chance she might see Leigh. Leigh who'd caused her so much pleasure and pain. She knew at first she'd felt a certain anticipation and that perhaps a small part of her had still clung to the faint hope that Leigh might admit she'd made a bad choice all those years ago. But would that change anything?

"I don't think so," Shann replied cautiously.

Angie looked down at the tabletop so Shann was unable to read the expression in her eyes. The silence grew, an uneasiness swelling between them. Shann searched for something to break the heavy weight of disquiet that seemed to have encompassed them, but eventually it was Angie who broke the silence. She raised her eyes to Shann's.

"Are you looking forward to performing at the Muster next week?"

"Yes." Shann relaxed, grateful that Angie had changed the subject. "I had hoped to go to the last one, but I couldn't get away. It's a definite highlight of the country music year."

"I wish I could see your show at the Muster," Angie said. "I know you'll be fantastic."

"Thank you." Shann grinned. "And I wish you could come to my shows, too. Can you get away?"

"You'd like me to come?"

"Well, yes. I'd love you to," Shann told her honestly.

"But would I be able to find accommodation this late? Or perhaps I could just come up for the day."

"I have a trailer to myself. Sleeps six, I think."

Angie flushed. "You can have," she paused and swallowed, "guests?"

"Sure. I can check, but I can't see why I can't. Originally Corey was coming with me, but I didn't want him missing any more school, not when he's only just started at his new one. And he has exams next week, too. He's so disappointed, and I've had to steel myself not to back down and say to hell with exams; of course you can come with me."

"I'd have to check my diary. I think I have a pretty full week, but maybe I could bring Corey up with me on Friday."

"Would you? Oh, Angie, he'd be dead chuffed." Shann paused and swallowed. "Would you mind Corey being with us?"

"No, of course not." Angie smiled derisively. "I'll take being with you whenever, however I can."

Shann smiled and gave Angie's hand a squeeze. "I feel the

same." She lowered her voice. "Even if I'll probably go crazy not being able to have an action replay of last night. I'm not sure about the sleeping arrangements in the trailer."

Angie reached out and took Shann's hand, twined her fingers with Shann's for long moments. "I wish . . . I want to kiss you so much," she said thickly.

Shann moved her knee slowly against Angie's thigh, fancied she could hear the rasp of denim and garbadine. Her gaze dropped to Angie's lips, fascinated by their shape, the way her tongue tip dampened their sudden dryness. Then Angie's lips parted slightly, and Shann heard her catch a steadying breath.

"Is that a police siren I hear?" she asked huskily, and Shann laughed softly.

"If it isn't it should be."

Angie reluctantly released Shann's hand, and Shann saw Angie's hand was unsteady as she ran it through her short fair hair.

"We should—" Angie swallowed. "Liz will be back any minute and we don't want to—"

"Invite another interrogation?" Shann finished, and Angie nodded.

"I'll see what I've got in my diary for next week. I know I have to speak at a conference in Melbourne on Tuesday, and I also have some appointments down there at the same time, but I'll let you know tonight. Okay?"

"Sure. I hope you can manage to come." Shann leaned back in her chair. "I won't say anything to Corey until you know for sure. He'll be really excited." Shann grinned. "So will I."

Liz rejoined them then, and they chatted for a few minutes more before Liz looked at the time and said reluctantly that they should be getting back to their father.

Just before four Shann left to collect Corey from soccer practice at school. Because Angie was coming over she decided to drive, and she waited in the car, watching the last quarter of an hour of the team's ball-handling skills.

As she watched Corey dribble the ball up the field, Shann stretched languidly, thinking of Angie, and she felt herself smile. It had only been hours since she'd seen the other woman, and she could barely wait to see her again. She had had no idea when she returned to Brisbane those few short weeks ago that her life would take such a turn and that she'd fall in love.

And she had fallen in love. And it was wonderful. Her rational mind warned her to be wary, but her heart soared, spinning way out of control. She could only hope that Angie felt the same way.

Corey climbed in the car and planted a wet sweaty kiss on Shann's cheek. He chattered on about school and soccer as they headed for home.

"And what sort of day did you have, Mum?" he asked solemnly as Shann turned the four-wheel drive into their street.

"Pretty good," Shann hid her smile. "Nice of you to ask, love."

"That's okay. I am interested you know, Mum."

"Well, I went out for coffee with Aunty Liz this morning. That was nice. We went to Angie's store."

"Did you see Angie?" Corey asked.

"For a while." Shann parked the car in front of the house. "She had coffee with us."

"Cool. Angie's nice, isn't she?"

"Yes, she is." Shann smiled. Angie was more than nice.

"You knew Angie before I was born, didn't you?" Corey asked.

"Yes. Why?" Shann reached out and turned off the ignition.

"Did Angie know my father, too?"

Shann turned to look at her son. "Corey, please don't ask Angie about your father. I told you Angie was younger than I was, and she didn't go about with us. Do you understand, love?"

"I guess." Corey sighed. "I wouldn't have asked her, actually, but . . . I'm sorry I upset you, Mum."

"You haven't upset me. I want you to feel you can talk to me about anything, and I'll try my best to answer any questions you have. I'd just prefer it if we kept any conversations about your father private, between you and me. Okay?"

"Because it's too painful for you?"

160

"Partly," Shann replied carefully.

"Did my father break your heart?"

"Not exactly. But you, Corey Delaney, can be sure you're the very best of your father and me. And I love you."

Corey flushed a little. "Thanks, Mum. And if you ever wanted to fall in love with someone besides me I wouldn't mind."

Shann suppressed a smile. "Thank you for that. And I promise you'll be the first to know if I do. Okay?"

Corey nodded. "Talking about that, I just wanted to say I wouldn't mind if it was Angie. In fact, I reckon you should marry her," Corey said, looking across at his mother.

Shann laughed. "Marry her? You know I can't do that."

"You can if you want to. People who love each other get married all the time."

"Corey! We've spoken about this before," Shann began.

"I know. It's not legal when it's not a man and a woman. But I think that's weird. You should be able to marry who you like."

Shann laughed and patted him on the leg. "I love you, do you know that?"

"Yeah, I know. I love you, too." Corey grinned at her. "What time do you think Angie will come over tonight?"

"After dinner. And, Corey, no talk about marriage. All right?" Shann warned. "We don't want to embarrass Angie."

"Okay." Corey sighed loudly. "Hey, Mum!" He slapped the side of his head. "I'm really dumb. I'm a guy. I could marry Angie then she could live with us."

"Corey, please. Knock it off with the marrying bit. We're going to have a nice night playing board games."

They had a wonderful evening sitting around the dining room table playing Balderdash, RapiDoh and Upwords. Liz, Amy, and Shann's father joined in, and they seemed to laugh all night.

Eventually Shann persuaded Corey to go to bed as his eyelids began to droop. Her father had retired earlier, and Amy also decided to call it a night. Liz, Shann, and Angie sat out on the deck

161

for a final cup of tea. When she finished hers Liz left them, too, and Shann and Angie grinned at each other.

"Alone at last," Angie whispered, and Shann laughed softly.

"Well, if you can call sitting in this circle of bright light on show for all the neighbors being on our own."

"We could take a walk down the backyard. There's a bench under the mango tree that's relatively secluded." Angie raised her eyebrows suggestively.

Warmth radiated through Shann's body. "If it means I can kiss you what are we waiting for?"

They walked sedately down the stairs and along the short path between Liz's vegetable and herb gardens. When they were sitting down side by side on the bench, Angie looked up and stifled a giggle.

"Lucky it's not mango season or we'd be dodging falling fruit and the prying eyes of numerous possums."

"They can't hide their prying eyes," Shann sang softly, and they laughed together. Then their arms were around each other, their lips meeting in a kiss that left them both breathless.

"I love your kisses," Shann murmured against Angie's so soft lips.

"Then you don't mind if I keep kissing you, hmmm?" She kissed Shann. "And kissing you." She kissed her again.

"I'll give you all night to stop doing that," Shann said breathily and groaned. "I wish we had all night. Do you think anyone can see us down here?"

"What if they can? Just at the moment, my need to kiss you far outweighs my concern about scaring the neighbors. At least Mrs. Nosy Parker Jones out the front can't see us. That might have been a problem."

Shann stilled. "You did say Ann and Mike were at the movies, didn't you? Would they be home yet?"

"Probably not. They usually go for coffee and a chat afterward with their friends. Don't worry about Ann and Mike, Shann. How they feel about us is, well, their problem."

"I know, but—"

Angie sighed and slid her arms from around Shann's shoulders. "We'll behave. Probably best anyway. Kissing you only makes me want to do more than kiss you." She ran her hand slowly along Shann's thigh. "And not just on the lips, " she added thickly.

Shann shivered and covered Angie's hand with her own. "And this is behaving?" she asked with a broken laugh, her body responding to Angie's touch.

Angie lifted Shann's hand and kissed it before resting their clasped hands on her lap. "It's your fault for being such a turn on, Shann Delaney."

"I am?"

"You are. I could barely keep my hands to myself all evening. Not easy with your family looking on."

"Especially Liz, of the eagle eyes."

They laughed together.

"It was a great evening, wasn't it?" Shann said. "Corey really enjoyed it. He loves playing board games. Thanks for, well, for being so nice to him, even when he asked you to marry him."

Angie laughed. "It's the very best marriage proposal I've ever had. Actually it's the only one I've had."

"Really?"

"I've never let guys get close enough to talk marriage."

Shann swallowed. "What about women?"

"There's never been anyone I cared enough about to want to make that kind of commitment." She played absently with Shann's fingers. "I want to be sure. It has to be always and forever for me. But I have to admit Corey's cute enough for me to consider him very seriously."

Shann suddenly wanted to ask Angie to consider her. Yet while her nerve endings clamored for her to say the words, her head reminded her that she could get badly hurt again.

"Corey's so cute," Angie was continuing. "Just like his mother."

"So you think so?" Shann's heartbeats accelerated.

"Oh, definitely. Pity Corey got in first," she said with a grin. "However, I'm open to all offers."

Was Angie joking or—? Shann swallowed. "I'll remember that."

Angie's gaze held hers for long moments. "If you don't I'll remind you. So, have you decided what you'll be singing up at the Muster?"

"All set. And I've worked with the backing band before as well so that's a relief. That's one thing I won't have to be nervous about."

"I'm really looking forward to it. Especially since I saw you at The Blue Moon. You were fantastic."

"I think you're as biased as Corey is." Shann couldn't hide how pleased she was. "And thanks for getting time off work next week. Corey was pretty ecstatic that he's going to the Muster. I was pretty ecstatic, too. I'm not sure how I'm going to cope with waiting for three days for you both to arrive."

"It'll be the same for me waiting till I can get up there. If I didn't have those appointments, and that conference I'm committed to in Melbourne, I'd come up for the whole week." Angie laughed ruefully. "While you're away I might come over just to look at Corey to feel close to you. He has your eyes and your incredible smile."

"Liz says that, too."

"What about Corey's father? Does Corey look anything like him?"

"I don't talk about that, Angie. As far as I'm concerned Corey's my son. He doesn't have a father."

"Corey doesn't know who his father is?"

"No."

She was silent for a moment. "What about your parents? And Liz?"

"No one knows."

"But why? Was he married or something?"

"Angie—"

"He would have had to have been someone we knew," she said, almost to herself, and then she stiffened. "Oh, my God. Shann." Angie put her hand over her mouth. "I think I know who he is."

"How do you know?" Shann frowned, and her stomach tightened as memories of that night threatened to flood back. "You couldn't possibly know," she added flatly.

"I was there, Shann. Well, not there. But afterward. I saw him. It was at Ann and Mike's twenty-fifth wedding anniversary party, wasn't it? It was Evan Radford."

Shann was pale and could only shake her head.

"Oh, Shann. I heard him. He was talking to that red-haired friend of his, Caleb Dean. They didn't know I was there, and Evan said he was going to show that bitch. He took something from Caleb, and Caleb said it was too risky. Then Evan said that no dyke was going to mess with his girlfriend."

"You heard them say that? Evan and Caleb?"

Angie nodded. "I couldn't leave it alone either. I stepped up to them and said I was amazed all women weren't lesbians if they were the only alternative. Then I stalked off. Oh Shann, tell me they didn't have anything to do with it."

Shann couldn't speak. Evan had drugged her? How could that be?

"Did Evan rape you, Shann?"

Shann shook her head. "No. He did get me a drink, but I didn't finish it. I only had a few mouthfuls. Then someone bumped me, and I spilled it all over my shirt. I was all wet and I was feeling sick so I headed for the bathroom. I left Evan and Caleb with Leigh, and I took a shortcut through the garden." Shann stopped and swallowed convulsively. "I've never told anyone," she said, fighting back tears.

"You don't have to tell me if you don't want to," Angie said gently, but Shann shook her head and clasped Angie's hand tightly.

"He caught me there in the garden and pulled me into the bushes. I thought he was helping me. He held my head while I threw up. Then he said it was time to learn a few of life's lessons. I couldn't quite take it in. I was so dizzy." Shann's tortured memories surged forward as she told Angie the story she hadn't told anyone else, not even Gina.

"I feel sick," she'd said tearfully over ten years ago.

165

"Don't worry. It'll pass. Take a deep breath." His hand stroked her hair, moved down her back. "You know you're too old to be fooling around, Shann."

"Fooling around?"

"All that kid's stuff with Leigh Callahan."

He knew about that. Who could have told him? Her father? Ruth? Shann looked up at him, and he smiled. The bright moonlight lit his face and something in that smile sent a shaft of fear through her.

"I think I'll go back now. Maybe I should just go home." She went to move around him, but he was too quick for her, cut off her exit with his body.

"Oh, no. Not yet. We have to have our little lesson."

"Lesson?"

He nodded, pleased with himself. "You know I'm a bit like Queen Victoria. I don't believe there are such things as lesbians. Lesbians don't exist."

Shann wanted to retaliate, tell him that Gina and Cassie and her friends would beg to differ, but she made herself remain silent.

"No. Lesbians just need straightening out. They need a lesson."

"Please. Let me go back to the party."

"In a while. Take off your shirt."

"No. I want to go back inside," Shann choked out, hearing the panic in her voice.

He grabbed her, and they struggled. She fought him, but he was stronger, and being sick and dizzy seemed to have made her sluggish. Then she was on the ground, the sharp edges of stones biting into her back. He roughly pushed her shirt and bra up, hurting her breasts. One of her arms was somehow caught beneath her and he was on top of her. She tried to scream but he'd pushed something into her mouth.

With her free hand she scratched at him, her nails raking, and he swore and pinned her hand above her head. With his other hand he clutched at her bare breast, his fingers painfully squeezing her nipple.

She managed to free her other arm and tore at his hair. He slapped her and captured both of her hands in his and pinned them both above her head. Then he reached down, pulled her skirt up over her thighs and ripped off her underpants.

Shann panicked, tried desperately to fight him off, but she couldn't seem to gather enough strength. Her body was uncoordinated, and she was no match for him.

"Stop fighting, Shann, or I'll really hurt you. Now I'm going to begin our lesson. I'm going to show you what you've been missing, and there won't be any going back. Just relax. You'll love it."

He forced her legs apart with his, fumbled with his zipper, and then he was thrusting himself into her. Shann thought she'd pass out with the pain.

But she didn't. It went on for a lifetime of agony and shame. Eventually he grunted and was still.

"Lesson number one," he said thickly. "Now you're playing in the big league, kid."

Shann moaned, her body screaming in pain.

He stood up, left her lying there while he zipped up his pants. Then he bent down and pulled the gag from her mouth. He picked something else up off the ground and shoved it into his pocket with the gag.

Shann tried to scream, but her throat was raw.

"Clean yourself up. You'll thank me for this, I promise you." He went to walk away. "Oh, and Shann. Keep this our little secret. It'll be your word against mine, and I've already implied that you've been giving me the come on." He turned and left her.

Shann lay on the stony ground, shocked, aching, and bewildered. Eventually she sat up and rearranged her clothing. She felt around for her underpants, but she couldn't find them. Why had she let Ruth talk her into wearing a skirt rather than her usual jeans? It had been no barrier.

She climbed shakily to her feet and wrapped her arms around herself as she shivered in shock. She'd have to tell her father what had happened. But would he believe her? He was so angry with her since Ann Callahan had caught her kissing Leigh. He hadn't spoken to her for a week. How would he react if she told him she'd been raped? They'd have to call the police. She'd have to tell strangers—

She recalled a friend of Gina's who'd been raped and who had tried to get the police to lay charges against the guy. The court case had turned into a fiasco, Gina said, where the woman had ended up on trial.

As he'd said, it was her word against his. Who would believe her, a frightened seventeen-year-old who had just been caught kissing another female? She'd have no credibility. And what if it was reported in the newspaper? She went totally cold at the thought. Everyone would find out. Leigh would know.

Dashing away her tears Shann knew she wouldn't put her family or herself through it. She'd have to keep this evening's horrifying incident a secret. No one must ever find out.

She made her way through the garden, to the toilet block, hanging back in the shadows until she was sure there was no one inside. She quickly washed her face and tidied her clothes as best she could. There was a reddening patch on the edge of her jaw where he'd hit her. She'd have to think of something to explain that.

She looked at her untidy hair, and it all came back. She was vomiting into the toilet when her stepmother found her.

"For heaven's sake, Shann. What's wrong with you?" She caught the odor of the drink Shann had spilled on her shirt and she gave an exclamation of disgust. "Haven't you upset your father enough already with your abhorrent behavior without getting blind drunk? Come on, I was about to go home, and you'd better come with me before you make an even bigger exhibition of yourself. We'll have to try to keep this from your father."

She took Shann's arm and led her toward the car park.

"Hello, Ruth. Shann. They're handing out the cake inside," Angelina said as she headed for the toilet.

"Shann isn't feeling very well so I've decided to take her home.

I wonder if you'd tell my husband that's where we've gone," Ruth said.

"What's the matter, Shann?" Angelina's green eyes filled with concern. "Shall I get Dr. Fleming? He's inside. I could go and find him."

"No. No. That won't be necessary," Ruth said quickly. "It's the time of the month, and she's having a few cramps." Ruth started Shann moving again. "Just tell my husband we've left."

"Angelina, you shouldn't be out here alone," Shann managed to get out, her tongue feeling thick and rubbery. "We'll wait for you."

"There's no need for that," Ruth said, taking her arm, drawing Shann along with her. And they'd gone home.

Now, ten years later Shann looked across at Angie, trying to gauge her reaction to what Shann had told her. The moonlight shining through the mango tree leaves danced patterns on her pale face.

"Oh, Shann. I'm so sorry." Angie put her arms around Shann, holding her close. Then she smoothed Shann's hair back with her hands and, holding her face, gently kissed her. "Shann, that night, just before I saw you with Ruth, I saw Evan out in the garden. Caleb was trying to get him to go back into the hall. I heard him say what a waste it was, that it hadn't worked. Then Leigh came outside, and she said he needed coffee. Caleb and Leigh took him into the hall. He could have been talking about your spiked drink, but he *was* out there that night."

"It wasn't Evan. He might have been responsible for the drink, but he didn't rape me." She ran a hand over her eyes. "It was Billy Cleary."

169

CHAPTER ELEVEN

"Your stepbrother?" Angie was obviously shocked. "Oh, Shann, I can't believe he'd do something so dreadful. I've never liked him but, rape? Shann, he should have been held accountable."

"I was too scared and too ashamed to tell anyone at the time." Shann told her. "For ages I honestly thought I didn't know who had done it. I must have completely blanked it out of my mind. Later, I even tried to tell myself it was Evan. Or one of his mates. They'd all been pretty dreadful after Ann caught Leigh and I together."

"But how did they find out about it?" Angie asked and Shann shrugged.

"I have no idea. I thought at first it had to be Leigh but then when I remembered it was Billy that night, I thought it might have been him. He wasn't there when it happened, but he came home a couple of times about then. Perhaps Ruth told him. He might have told Evan because Leigh was involved. Evan was certainly angry. He made that pretty clear from the start, he and his mates."

"What did they do?" Angie asked.

"Rang me when they knew I was at home alone and made obscene suggestions. Walked up behind me and whispered crude names. Touched me up at school in the hallways when no one else was nearby."

Angie shook her head.

"So it was easy to think it was one of them."

"What made you remember?" Angie asked, holding onto Shann's hand, gently rubbing her skin.

"Oh, good old Billy helped me out there," Shann said bitterly. "Most of the time I almost convinced myself it hadn't happened. I'd even pretend Corey's father was a really nice gay guy, that we got together to prove we were so-called normal. Then we'd decided we weren't heterosexual, so we went our separate ways. I wished it had been like that, if only for Corey's sake." Shann brushed away a tear, and Angie put her arms around her again, holding her comfortingly close.

"Billy should have gone to jail," Angie said as she rubbed Shann's back.

Shann sighed and lifted her head, keeping hold of Angie's hand.

"Didn't you say you'd scratched him? How did he explain that?" Angie asked.

"I didn't see him next day. I stayed in my room pretending I was asleep. He went back to join his Army mates. I think he was stationed in Darwin at the time. I remember Ruth saying Billy had been a little under the weather the night before and that he'd walked into a tree branch. She was clucking about the big patch on his forehead."

"It would have been evidence, Shann," Angie said softly.

"I know that now but at the time, I don't know, I was in total shock I think. By the time I was rational enough to think about it, it was too late. And I don't think Billy was that drunk, that was for sure."

"But it was acceptable to Ruth for Billy to be drunk," Angie remarked dryly. "Fine old double standards."

"Looking back, Ruth never took our side against Billy, no

matter how much evidence there was pointing to him. Billy was never responsible. Pat and I learned to keep out of his way as much as we could."

"How long was it before you saw Billy again? Was it before or after Corey was born?"

"After." Shann shrugged. "I didn't see him for over two years. He was passing through Sydney, and he called in. Aunt Millie gave him my address, I opened the door of my flat, and there he was." Shann unconsciously tightened her hold on Angie's hand. "I can't say I was thrilled to see him, but he was my stepbrother so I invited him in, reluctantly, and made him coffee. He told me his marriage was on the rocks, and I commiserated. He said it was Janice's fault, of course."

"Of course," Angie said. "I remember Ruth telling Ann something the same at the time."

"Then Corey woke up. I'd left him asleep on his blanket in the bedroom. I was getting his things ready for the evening because I was on late shift, and some friends babysat him for me. Well, Corey came toddling out carrying his favorite teddy bear, calling out for me. I picked him up, and he looked at Billy and buried his head in my shoulder."

"Sensible Corey," Angie remarked and Shann grimaced.

"Exactly. Billy was a little taken aback because apparently Ruth hadn't told him I was pregnant. He sort of smirked and asked me if Corey was mine. When I said he was he laughed. Then he said that his little lesson must have worked. When he said that, about the lesson, I knew. It all came flooding back to me. The whole thing flashed before me."

"The bastard. Did you confront him?"

"I couldn't—I was so shocked I couldn't speak. Then he took something out of his pocket and held it up." Shann swallowed. "It was my underpants. From that night. He'd taken them with him as a souvenir. Can you believe that? I was shattered. I accused him of raping me. And he just laughed."

Shann felt the moment closing in on her. "I got so angry I could have physically attacked him. I would have, but Corey started to cry. I probably squeezed him too tightly. By the time I'd settled him in his highchair with a drink, Billy had relaxed back in the lounge. I told him to leave, and he said he was at a loose end and planned on staying the night. I was terrified by this time so I told him my boyfriend was due home. He said he didn't believe me, that he'd stay so he could meet him, give him the once over."

"What did you do?"

"I opened the door and, luckily, Chris, the guy from the flat upstairs was walking up the stairs. He was a rugby player, six-foot-two, muscles on his muscles, and happily married. I threw myself on him, welcomed him home and called him darling. I tried to let him see my concerned expression, and it must have worked because he didn't resist when I dragged him into the flat.

"I told him Billy was my stepbrother and that he was just leaving. Chris summed up the situation and played the part for me. Billy decided discretion was the better part of valor and left. That's the last time I saw him."

"He was killed a few years ago, wasn't he?" Angie asked, and Shann nodded.

"In a truck accident. Apparently he swerved to miss a couple of pedestrians. Liz told me Ruth considers he's a hero."

"Some hero," Angie remarked and pulled Shann back into her arms. "I'm so sorry, Shann. I wish I'd told someone about what I'd heard the night of the party."

"I doubt it would have helped. I'm convinced no one would have believed me."

Angie kissed her gently and then ran her finger along the line of Shann's jaw. "You know I always wondered what you meant that night, about me not being out there in the garden alone. Now I know." She kissed Shann again and then sat back against the seat, her arm around Shann's shoulders. "Are you ever going to tell Corey?"

"I don't know. Not all of it, that's for sure. I've let him think his father was already married. That's not untrue. Billy and Janice had been married the year before it happened." She sighed unconsciously. "And I've told him his biological father is dead. Some day I'll tell him how he died. As to the rest of it, I don't know how, when or even if I'll tell him."

Angie nodded. "I've just realized Corey is Ruth's grandson."

"That's what bothers me the most. Have I got a right to keep that from her? When she returns from the UK I'll have to make a decision about that. It's all so complicated."

"Well, anyone would be pleased to claim Corey as a grandchild. Look how absolutely besotted your father is with him. He's such a great kid." Angie laughed. "I think I've said that before. He's smart. He's got a great sense of humor. Just like his mother."

Shann felt a surge of pleasure that Angie was so impressed by Corey. "You're starting to sound as biased as I am."

"I think I am, too. But it's not difficult." She tried to smother a yawn.

"We should go inside. You're tired and you have to work tomorrow. And we had a late night last night."

Angie gave a soft groan. "Would that I could be late like that every night. Tell me I didn't dream last night, Shann. It did happen, didn't it?"

"If it didn't then I seem to have had the same fantastic dream."

They merged together, and their kiss was long and deep.

"Will I—?" Shann paused. "Will I see you tomorrow?"

"I'll call over when I get home from work, but I have to go out to dinner tomorrow night."

Who was Angie going with? Shann wanted to ask but knew she didn't have the right. They hadn't spoken about—

"It's Mike's birthday in a week's time so we're going out to dinner with some friends of his. Leigh and Evan had hoped to be here, too, but Ann tells me Evan can't get out of his business meetings. I suggested we postpone the dinner until they got back, but this is the only weekend Mike's friends are free." Angie shrugged. "So it's still on. I wish you could come, too."

"As much as I want to spend time with you, I think I'll take it slowly with your aunt and uncle," Shann said ruefully.

"Pity. It will be a long night I suspect. And it will probably be too late for us to get together afterward. Then I have to speak at that conference, and I have some business appointments in Melbourne on Monday and Tuesday so I'm booked to fly out on Sunday evening." Angie pulled a face. "Absolutely worst timing, but maybe we could have lunch on Sunday, hmmm?"

"I'd like that."

"I'm going to miss you so much." Angie kissed her again and sighed, her forehead resting against Shann's. "I guess we should go to bed." She laughed lowly. "Now there's a thought."

"A thought that will be sure to keep me awake," Shann told her, and they both laughed. Shann stood up, pulled Angie up beside her and into her arms. "Maybe one quick hug first."

On Sunday Shann, Angie, and Corey went over to Southbank for lunch. They sat at a café overlooking the river and watched the City Cats on their journeys up and down the Brisbane River. Afterward they walked along the river eating ice cream before heading home and a few hours later, Shann drove Angie out to the airport to catch her flight to Melbourne.

"I wish I didn't have these appointments tomorrow." Angie put her hand on Shann's jean-clad thigh. "I won't be back in time to see you before you leave for the Muster on Tuesday."

"I'll be counting the hours till you get up to Gympie on Friday."

"Mmm. Me, too." Angie moved her hand on Shann's thigh and groaned. "I would have cancelled this trip, but it's been on the calendar for months, and I'm contracted to speak at the conference on Tuesday morning."

"Don't worry." Shann covered Angie's hand with her own. "Think of the anticipation of seeing each other again on Friday. Of course, on the down side by Friday my excitement level will be so high it will be unwise for me to operate heavy machinery and/or drive a motor vehicle."

Angie laughed and then sobered. "I'm really going to miss you."

"And I'll miss you." Shann pulled into the short-term car park and switched off the engine. "I could just drop you off but I need a hug here in relative seclusion."

She pulled Angie into her arms, nuzzled her earlobe, found her incredible lips. When they drew apart Shann rested her forehead against Angie's. "Much more of this and the windows will start to fog up."

"I think they already have." Angie held her wristwatch to the glow from a nearby overhead security light. "Damn! I should go."

Shann nodded, kissed Angie quickly. "Until Friday."

"Until Friday," Angie said huskily.

Shann left for the Muster after she'd dropped Corey off at school on Tuesday morning. She had packed the four-wheel drive with her clothes and Corey's, and sleeping bags for the three of them. Although it was hot during the day up in the National Park, the temperature plummeted at night. In a suit bag she had her stage outfits laid carefully on top of her guitar.

She headed up the Bruce Highway to the Sunshine Coast, and then she turned off toward the Amamoor State Forest. After the small quaint township of Amamoor the road went from bitumen to well-graded gravel.

At the main gate she registered and collected her meal vouchers and colored wristbands that were clipped on her arm. These stayed on for the duration of the Muster and were Shann's ticket to the various areas of the site, including the secure area especially for performers.

After getting directions she drove through the public camping area where tents, campers, trailers, and vans nestled in every nook and cranny of the forest. She knew people came to secure campsites weeks before the Muster and some had the same sites each year. There were people everywhere and at the weekend the population would more than double.

Shann passed through the next checkpoint and drove around behind the huge main stage that was still being erected. In front of the stage was the requisite mosh pit and then the sloping hillside rose in a natural amphitheater.

Parking the car beside a white camper with green and yellow stripes, Shann switched off the engine and whistled. It was far bigger than she expected. She unlocked the door and stepped inside. There was a spacious kitchenette at one end, a short hallway with bunks on one side and a separate shower and toilet at the other, and through a door at the other end was a bedroom with a large comfortable double bed.

Shann sat on the bed and bounced. Definitely comfortable. She glanced at the bedhead, the two pillows, and she saw Angie's wonderful naked body stretched out, her green eyes twinkling, her lips smiling invitingly, her firm full breasts, flat stomach, the gleam of her navel ring, the triangle of fair curls, and her long smooth legs. She groaned softly. It would be three days before Corey and Angie joined her.

With a sigh of regret Shann set to unloading her car and stowing her clothes in the closet space. Then she went out to explore the huge Muster site and catch up with the organizers of her shows and the band that would be backing her.

She walked over to the lower side of the site and checked out the CD store, which held a comprehensive range of merchandise. Then she wandered through the various stalls selling Western gear and souvenirs. She bought T-shirts for Corey, Angie, and herself depicting the most popular country music radio station in the southeast.

Her first and second appearances were at the Tavern which was on the far side of the site, so with a couple of hours to spare before she was expected on stage, she walked back past the main stage to the high side of the site. She watched technicians setting up the small stage set where they were going to film the television show *Muster Eye for the City Guy*. Apparently they'd chosen a woman and three guys from the city and for the duration of the Muster they were going to film them performing tasks such as stock whip cracking and tent site decorating, as well as the requisite singing of a country song.

There were more souvenir and hat, boot and clothing stalls, as well as food areas run by various charities. The Apex Club of Gympie was responsible for the Muster, but many other clubs were fund raising as well.

Next door to the Tavern was the huge marquee that was the Muster Club, the venue for Shann's third and main show late on Friday. Further down was the large Crowbar and up the hill past more souvenir and food stalls was the Blues Club.

There were many people wandering around exploring like Shann was, and considering that the Muster hadn't officially started, the lead-up shows were very well patronized.

Shann's first show went exceptionally well, as she told Corey when she rang him from a public phone down near the Tavern. Here in the forest her mobile phone had no reception so she told Corey to tell Liz not to try to call her, that Shann would phone them each evening. She also tried ringing Angie's mobile, but it went to message bank, and Shann could only tell her she was missing her.

That night Shann lay in the double bed snugly zipped in her sleeping bag. After temperatures in the nineties during the day, the mercury dropped to freezing during the night. As the music from the late shows at the Crowbar and the distant blues venue floated over the site and the mist insinuated itself among the trees and tents, Shann drifted off to sleep thinking of Angie.

Over the next two days Shann saw some great shows and performed again herself to a packed venue. The television company making *Muster Eye for the City Guy* sought her out for an interview. She performed the theme from *The Kelly Boys* for them and they told her the show was to air on the cable Country Music Channel.

And then it was Friday, and Shann sat on a fallen tree trunk watching passers-by and waiting for Angie and Corey. When she caught sight of them walking toward her, her heart swelled. Corey was pointing out the banners strung between the trees and Angie was caught up in his conversation. Then she looked up and saw Shann and smiled.

The smile lit Angie's face and hit Shann in the region of her heart. She drew in a steadying breath as she took in Angie's healthy good looks, the natural grace of her tall body, the wonder of that incredible smile. Shann stood up, hurrying toward them, breaking into a jog until she could wrap her arms around both of them.

"I missed you both so much," she said unevenly, a lump in her throat.

"We missed you, too, Mum," said Corey, squeezing her tightly.

Angie smiled and nodded. "It's been a very long week."

Shann showed them around some of the large site, pointing out the Muster Club where she would be performing later that night. Then they headed over to the trailer.

"Wow!" exclaimed Corey when they stepped inside. "This is as big as our flat in Sydney."

Shann laughed. "Just about."

"Is this my bunk?" Corey asked, dumping his backpack on the lower bed.

"Sure." Shann nodded and slid a quick look at Angie. She swallowed. "And that's the bedroom." She indicated the open door past Corey.

Angie walked down the hall and looked into the bedroom.

"I thought you might be more comfortable in the bed," Shann continued. "I'm not sure you could stretch your legs out in the bunks."

Angie raised one dark eyebrow, and a small smile played around her mouth.

Shann felt her cheeks warm.

"Which side of the bed do you want?" Angie asked with a grin, stepping inside the bedroom.

"Whichever." Shann stopped in the doorway.

179

Angie set her backpack beside the bed and turned to look at Shann. "It really has been a long week," she repeated softly.

"Angie, come and look," said Corey. "It's got a proper bathroom, too."

Angie laughed and walked back to the door, brushing past Shann as she went into the hallway.

Shann's stomach muscles clenched as her body reacted to Angie's touch, and she drew a steadying breath. She had to wipe the silly smile off her face before she turned back to Corey and Angie.

Shann's show that evening was wonderfully well received, and she was kept busy afterward signing T-shirts, caps, programs, and to Corey's amusement, the bulging biceps of a young man who was so obviously smitten. As the numbers of autograph hunters diminished Shann glanced up, looking for Angie, to see her talking to her friends, Alex and Jo.

Shann greeted them with pleasure and introduced them to Corey. Alex and Jo congratulated Shann on her performance and as they set off to have a cup of coffee, Alex told Shann she'd taken some photographs of her performing and would print them up for her. It was after midnight before Shann, Angie, and Corey returned to their trailer.

By then the temperature had dropped, and they stepped thankfully into the relative warmth of the trailer. Shann organized a sleepy Corey into the shower. She unfolded his sleeping bag, and she was suddenly warm at the thought of being with Angie again.

Corey came out of the bathroom and dived into his sleeping bag. Shann zipped him up and bent under the top bunk to kiss him goodnight.

"I've had the best time," he said sleepily. "You were the greatest, Mum."

"Thank you, kind sir. See you in the morning," Shann said.

Angie insisted Shann take first turn in the bathroom, and she gathered a warm tracksuit to put on after her shower. When she returned Angie had zipped their sleeping bags together.

"Hope you don't mind," she said a little uncertainly, and Shann laughed softly.

"Not at all. I was hoping—" Shann watched as Angie swallowed.

"Well, I'll have my shower."

"Hurry back," Shann said huskily. She snuggled into the sleeping bag, waiting in anticipation for Angie's return.

Soon Angie was back in the bedroom, quietly closing the door behind her. "You were right. Corey's fast asleep already." She crossed to the bed and slithered into the sleeping bag beside Shann. "Brrr. Pity it's so cold."

"Let me warm you up." Shann slid her arms around Angie, nestling her close.

"I've been thinking about this moment for a week." Angie laughed softly, her breath stirring Shann's hair. "I have to kiss you now or I'll go mad." She put her cool lips on Shann's.

Shann slid her hands under Angie's sweatshirt, murmuring appreciatively as her hands molded Angie's breasts, and Angie arched against her, sliding her leg between Shann's.

"I feel like I'm going to explode," Angie whispered and fumbled with Shann's top, her questing hands finding Shann's aroused nipples.

Their lips met again, their kiss deepening, tongues tasting.

"This is so deliciously restricting," Angie said with a low chuckle, and Shann gave a soft laugh. "Oh, Shann." Her fingers teased Shann's nipples. "I kept thinking about this every night and at some very inappropriate times during the day. And now I'm so . . ." She drew a steadying breath. "If I don't touch you soon I'll explode."

She moved Shann onto her back and helped her pull the waistband of her sweatpants down. Then she gave a throaty moan as she slowly slid her fingers into the wetness of Shann's center. Shann arched as Angie found her clitoris and when Angie's mouth moved over her breast to tease one rosy peak, Shann strained against Angie's hand. Her rhythm quickened, and Shann cascaded into her orgasm.

"Angie," she sighed brokenly, finding the softness of Angie's lips again. "That was indescribable."

181

"Indescribable is what I aim for," Angie said thickly, making Shann laugh softly.

"And I think I'll have to give you all night to stop doing that."

Shann moved slightly, her fingers brushing Angie's breasts, her mouth replacing her fingers as Angie's breath caught in her throat. Shann slipped her hands under the waistband of Angie's track pants, moving slowly downward until her palm cupped the soft curls. Angie moaned into Shann's mouth as Shann's fingers stroked, teased, circled. Then Angie's body tensed, and she fell into her release.

They kissed gently, reverently, and Angie sighed, moving her weight from Shann's body.

"You have incredibly magic fingers, did you know that?" she said huskily, and pulled Shann against her.

Shann felt the erotic nubs of Angie's breasts slide over her own bare breasts and her fingers traced the curve of Angie's firm buttocks. "I love the feel of your skin against mine. You feel divine." She murmured low in her throat, and Angie shivered slightly. "You're not cold, are you?"

"I'm too cozy to be cold." Angie laughed softly. "That shiver was a I'm-ready-to-have-you-ravish-me-again sort of quiver. In fact I'm more than warm enough to want to make love again."

"Quiver? Shiver? Ravish? You know you have the very best ideas," Shann said against her lips.

Eventually they fell asleep, and Shann woke with Angie still cuddled in the circle of her arms. She had her back to Shann, and Shann could feel the warmth of her smooth skin, the curve of her buttocks against her stomach. Their clothes were still in disarray and one of Shann's hands cupped one of Angie's full breasts, her other hand resting on Angie's stomach.

She drew in the clean fresh scent of Angie's hair, and desire clutched at her again. She moved her hand down to mold the triangle of soft curls, and Angie stirred.

"Mmmm. Is that a pipe in your pocket or are you just pleased to see me?" She asked with a credible Mae West accent as she turned into Shann's arms.

"Definitely not a pipe, but I do have an ache I know only you can take care of," Shann whispered.

The three of them spent the day enjoying the Muster and as Shann wasn't performing that night, they huddled together on the hill overlooking the Main Stage, watching the show featuring some of Australia's top country artists. As the temperature dropped Corey snuggled between them, and they wrapped themselves in a blanket until the end of the show. And later Shann and Angie slid into their sleeping bag and into each other's arms.

Reluctantly, Corey and Angie left late on Sunday afternoon so Corey could go to school next day and Angie to work. Shann stayed over till Monday morning as she had appointments with some of the artists interested in her songs as well as with a representative for a well-known record label. On Sunday night, wrapped in her sleeping bag, she missed Corey, and she missed the warmth, the nearness of Angie.

"Angie's home," said Corey as they walked passed the Callahans on Monday afternoon after Shann had collected him from school. Angie's green MG was parked in the Callahans' driveway behind Ann's small sedan.

"She must have left work early." Shann smiled as they turned into their driveway. With a welcoming woof Tiger bounded up along the side of the house to Corey, lurching to put his paws on Corey's shoulders, tongue licking his cheek.

"Down, Tiger. Down!" Corey pushed the dog off his shoulders. "What are you doing over here in our yard, boy?" Corey rubbed his ears and then his tummy. "Sit, Tiger. Sit."

The dog put his rump on the ground.

"Good dog." Corey took hold of the dog's collar. "We better put you back in your own yard."

As they started down the side of the house to the gate between the properties, Shann heard voices. She looked up toward the back deck, stopping in surprise when she saw Angie leaning on the railing, her face in profile. She didn't seem to be taking part in the conversations on the deck but rested back against the veranda post, her arms folded across her chest. Liz must have visitors.

"Angie." Shann called her, and the other woman turned and paused before lifting her hand in a half wave. Her smile was only fleeting as well and Shann's step faltered.

Corey caught sight of Angie then, and he waved eagerly. "Hi, Angie! Watch this!" He settled the dog and said, "Sit, Tiger. Sit."

The dog bounced around and then sat, looking up at Corey, tongue out, mouth open, as though he was grinning.

"Good dog," Corey wrapped his arms around the dog and hugged him. "Did you see that, Angie?"

Angie had turned to face them, her hands on the railing. "I saw it. It's totally amazing." She smiled at him.

Ann Callahan appeared beside Angie and leaned over to smile at them. "That's marvelous, Corey. You're very clever."

"He's really a smart dog, Mrs. Callahan," Corey told her and started forward, the dog following.

Shann also continued around the side of the house below where Angie and her aunt were standing. Perhaps Angie's reticence had something to do with her aunt. Had Angie talked to Ann? Surely not if Ann was so forthcoming.

They started up the back steps. Halfway up Shann realized Angie and Ann weren't alone on the back deck. Liz and their father were sitting at the table with a man, a woman, and two children.

Corey took hold of the dog's collar again as he reached the top of the stairs. Shann had stopped, too, several steps behind Corey, and across the deck her gaze met oh-so-familiar light blue eyes.

CHAPTER TWELVE

She had changed, had grown older. But then, Shann conceded, she had too, in the ten intervening years. Her fair hair with its darker streaks wasn't as long as she used to wear it, for it barely touched her shoulders, and it was fashionably mussed. A small smile lifted the corners of her mouth as she held Shann's gaze.

A rush of memories flashed before Shann. Walking with her, hand in hand, into class in grade one. Playing beam with a tennis ball on the bearers beneath the second-story classrooms. Skipping rope together. Playing softball. And then their first kiss. That wonderful, exhilarating kiss that had felt so unbelievably right.

Shann made herself continue up the stairs until she stood on the deck behind Corey. She rested her hands on his shoulders, needing the warmth, the reality of the present, needing to simply touch him.

Liz stood up, smiling with studied nonchalance. "Shann. Corey. We have visitors. Evan and Leigh arrived from Melbourne this afternoon and they've just come over to see Dad."

Ann Callahan walked back to the table. "It's Mike's birthday tomorrow, and Leigh thought it would be fun to surprise him and be here on his birthday. He's not expecting them until the end of the week so he'll be over the moon when he comes home tonight." She glanced at Shann. "But where's my manners? Shann, of course you know Evan and Leigh, but these are my grandchildren. Antony's a very grown-up seven and Michelle is almost six."

Leigh's children were both fair-haired and blue-eyed, and Shann could see their resemblance to their mother, especially the little girl, who was a carbon copy of Shann's memories of her mother.

"Leigh and Evan and the children live in Cairns so we don't see as much of them as we'd like," Ann continued.

And Shann felt sure Ann Callahan was just a little uncomfortable with the situation, but she was determined to get past it. Shann's gaze went from the children to Leigh's husband, Evan Radford.

He sat beside his wife, an arm draped casually around her shoulder. Gone was the long blond hair, the wispy goatee, the tattered clothes that had been Evan Radford ten years ago. His hair had thinned, and it was clipped into a crew cut. He was clean-shaven and wore steel-rimmed glasses and his T-shirt bore a designer label on the sleeve. Liz had told Shann that Evan had made a lot of money designing a part for a harvesting machine of some description. He looked successful.

"Leigh. Evan." Ann Callahan was saying. "This clever young man is Shann's son, Corey."

Corey walked across and held out his hand to Evan. "Nice to meet you."

Evan looked a little taken aback, but he shook hands with Shann's son.

Corey then shook hands with Leigh as she held out her hand to him.

Not to be outdone Tiger loped across and put his paws on Evan's knee, giving a happy, doggy woof.

"Sit, Tiger. Sit," commanded Corey, and the dog obeyed.

"Did you see that, Dad?" said Antony. He slid off his chair and came around to face Corey. "How did you teach him to do that?"

Corey shrugged. "I got this book from the library about training dogs."

"Isn't that marvelous, Evan?" asked Ann. "And it's only taken Corey a short time to teach the dog that."

"Maybe there's hope for the mutt after all," Evan remarked with little interest.

Shann shoved her hands in the back pockets of her jeans and out of the corner of her eye she saw Angie move slightly. She turned to look at her, but Angie was intent on inspecting a loose thread on the embroidered nametag on the pocket of her work shirt. Her face had a closed expression and although Shann willed her to look up, she didn't meet Shann's gaze.

"Liz was telling us you're a famous songwriter now," Leigh said, and Shann made herself look back at the other woman.

"Not exactly famous, but I've had some success recently," Shann told her disconcertedly, feeling the unsettling weight of the whole situation pressing heavily upon her.

Liz gave an exclamation of disbelief. "Honestly, Shann! Don't be so modest. She's doing exceptionally well. Some of Australia's top recording artists are performing Shann's songs on their albums."

"Mum *is* famous," Corey reiterated. He reeled off some of the artists who were singing his mother's songs.

Evan Radford looked bored. "I can't say I've heard of any of them."

"They're modern country music artists," Shann told him, and he shrugged.

"That accounts for it. I don't care for the country twang. I prefer blues or jazz myself."

"Shann performed at the Gympie Muster last week," Liz added and, as if on cue, Corey drew a dog-eared booklet from his pocket.

"I was showing this to my friends at school today." He walked around and held up the Muster program.

Evan barely glanced at it, but Leigh took it from Corey. He

187

looked over Leigh's shoulder as she spread it out on the tabletop. Corey pointed to the studio photo of Shann.

It was a full-length shot, and she was standing almost side on to the camera, looking back into the lens. Her guitar stood beside her, and she had both hands resting on the top of it. Her dark jeans accentuated the length of her long legs, and the red shirt she was wearing showed off more of Shann's cleavage than she was comfortable with. On her head was her trademark dark Akubra hat, set at a jaunty angle, and she was half smiling at the camera.

"See, I told you," said Corey, pointing to the photo. "Mum looks great, doesn't she?"

"It is a great shot," Leigh said, looking up at Shann with the smile Shann remembered so well.

Shann shifted from one foot to the other. "I think there was some airbrushing involved," she quipped.

"It says," read Corey, "well-known newcomer, performer and songwriter, Shann Delaney, will make her first appearance at the Muster with three shows. Shann is the writer of the popular theme from the television hit *The Kelly Boys* which has been nominated in three categories in the upcoming Golden Guitar Awards which will be held over the Australia Day week at Tamworth."

"Corey!" Shann admonished her son lightly. "No need to read the entire promo."

Liz laughed. "Didn't I tell you she was far too modest?"

Leigh smiled across at Shann. "You should just enjoy your success, Shann."

"From what I've seen in the music industry you might as well enjoy it while you have the chance," Evan put in disinterestedly. "Singers seem to fade away as quickly as they rise."

Shann stiffened, unconsciously drawing herself up to her full height. Evan was still sitting at the table and, standing, Shann was at an advantage. She gave him a level look. "My success didn't come overnight," she said evenly. "It's taken me ten years of hard work to build up my name in the industry."

Corey reached out and took his treasured program. He moved

around beside his mother. "And Mum's very talented," he said solemnly, giving Evan Radford a measured look, his young face set.

Angie walked over and squeezed Corey's shoulder. "Shann's shows at the Muster were packed and she was amazing. But then again, Corey, I can't say I'm surprised your mother's been so successful. I used to listen to her singing and playing her guitar all the time when we were younger, and I knew back then she was tops." She moved her hand from Corey's shoulder to Shann's and Shann could feel the warmth of her fingers. "I'd listen to her playing every afternoon, and I thought she was pretty fantastic."

"Right," said Corey. "She is fantastic."

Shann saw Leigh's gaze go from Angie's hand resting on Shann's shoulder to Angie's face then back to Shann, and one of her dark eyebrows rose slightly.

"So you all went to the Muster?" Leigh asked, and Corey nodded.

"I thought I would miss it because Mum had to go early and I had exams, but Angie took me up on Friday and we stayed all weekend. And"—he paused for effect—"we got to see Mum's show on Friday night. It was excellent."

"It sure was, kiddo," Angie agreed, and Corey grinned up at her.

"It was so cool that you could drive me up there, Angie. And I don't care what Mum says, I'm going to marry you."

Angie chuckled and kissed his forehead. "And I just might accept that proposal."

Everyone laughed, except Evan Radford. "I told you you should play hard to get, Angie," he said.

Angie raised her eyebrows at him, but she made no comment.

"Now, don't you two start bickering," Leigh said lightly enough. "I'm sorry we missed the Muster." She turned back to Shann. "Especially since Evan's company has accommodation there each year. If we'd known we could have gone, too."

Evan rolled his eyes. "Pity," he said, and his smile didn't reach his eyes.

Leigh slapped him playfully on the arm. "Stop teasing, darling. You know you would have enjoyed it if we'd gone." She leaned across to kiss him on the cheek, but he turned his head so her lips touched his mouth. When she drew back her eyes met Shann's, and Shann saw her flush just slightly.

"Well, we had fun," put in Corey. "The Muster Club where Mum was singing was huge, and they had this dance floor in front of the stage. Everyone was dancing, even Angie and me."

"Oh, so you have your own band and everything?" Ann remarked.

Shann nodded. "I did have a band backing me. A drummer, a bass guitarist, and two guys who can play just about everything. It wasn't my personal band unfortunately, but I have worked with most of the guys before so that was good."

"And are any of these young men special to you?"

Shann didn't understand what she was asking for a moment and she heard Angie bite off a soft laugh.

"I mean romantically," Ann explained. "These bands are usually made up of handsome young men from what I've seen."

"Handsome married men usually," Shann said dryly.

Corey looked at her and opened his mouth. "Mum's not into—"

Shann gave him a nudge. "What Corey's trying to say is that I make a point of not getting involved with band members. It makes things too complicated."

Corey grinned at her a little sheepishly and put his hand over his mouth.

"Very sensible of you, Shann," Ann was saying. "Doesn't do to mix business with pleasure." She stood up. "Well, I think I should be getting home. I need to put together some salads for the barbecue. Oh, Shann, you're all coming over tonight for a birthday barbecue for Mike. Now, Jim," she turned to Shann's father, "you're sure you'll be able to manage the steps?"

"I'll be fine, Ann." He got slowly to his feet. "But I think I'll have a short rest now so I'll be all right tonight. I'm looking forward to it."

Liz stood up, too, and passed her father his crutches, watching him as he maneuvered himself inside.

"We should get going as well," said Evan, keeping his arm around Leigh as they all started for the stairs. Antony grabbed hold of Tiger's collar, and the dog walked with him. Ann took Michelle's hand and looked back at Angie. "Are you coming, Angie?"

"Sure, Ann. I just want to have a quick chat to Shann and Liz. About some stuff they ordered from the shop."

Ann nodded, and then they'd all left.

Corey leaned over toward his mother. "Sorry about, um, you know," he whispered. "Nearly telling our secret."

"That's okay. No harm done." She ran a hand over his dark hair. "Now, if we're going out what say you go and have your shower."

"Okay." He bounded into the house.

"Your secret?" Liz raised her eyebrows, and Shann rolled her eyes.

"Before we came up here I asked him not to bandy the word lesbian around in conversations."

Liz chuckled. "Oh. I see. So that's what he didn't say. Mum's not into male guitarists."

Shann smiled. "Something like that."

"And talking about secrets, Angie. What exactly was that stuff I ordered?" Liz asked and laughed again when Angie flushed. "We'd better settle on stakes for my tomato bushes. Have to get our story straight."

"No pun intended," Shann remarked dryly, and even Angie smiled.

Liz stood up slowly. "Ann wants me to make my famous rice salad for tonight so I'd better go and get it started."

"I can make it, Liz." Shann said, and Liz waved her hand at her sister.

"Don't fuss, Shann. I'll be fine. If I need you I'll call you, I promise, Miss Worrywort." She disappeared inside.

"Liz is the most stubborn person I know," Shann said with a shake of her head.

Silence fell between them and Shann swallowed, her throat dry.

"This was quite a surprise," she managed at last.

"Yes." Angie moved slowly over to the other side of the deck, turning to rest back against the railing. "Ann phoned me at work, and I came home early."

Shann walked over to join her. She didn't know what to say, didn't know what she wanted to say. She'd just seen Leigh for the first time in ten years, and she felt numb, as though her emotions had shut down.

"I tried to ring you on your mobile," Angie was saying. "I thought you might appreciate some warning."

"I'm sorry! The battery needs charging. But thanks," Shann added, wondering if it would have made any difference if she'd known who was sitting here on the back deck.

Angie gave a crooked smile. "I was of two minds about trying to tell you as you and Corey walked down the side of the house, but my mind went blank. I couldn't seem to say a thing."

"That's okay. I was a little taken aback I guess," Shann admitted.

"I thought you might be," Angie said softly.

"Angie, it's all right. I'm all right. It had to happen some time. It didn't seem to faze Leigh so—" Shann shrugged.

"No. What about you though?"

"I don't know." Shann was honest. "It was all so long ago."

"I don't know that time makes much difference." Angie sighed. "I was concerned—" She shook her head slightly. "You don't have to come over to the barbecue if you don't want to."

"It might seem strange if I don't go."

"We could say we have a date," Angie said lightly, and Shann laughed.

"I'm not sure that would be such a wise revelation just at present. I think Ann has enough on her plate." She looked at Angie. "But I wish we did have a date," she said softly.

Angie gave a quick smile. "That gives me some measure of hope."

Shann bit her lip. "Angie, I just need some time. This has been a shock. I mean, I knew Leigh could turn up, but I wasn't expecting her so soon."

"Take all the time you need," Angie reached over and gave Shann's hand a squeeze. "But just don't shut me out. Okay?"

Shann nodded. "Angie, there's no need to worry. About Leigh, I mean." Shann looked away, not wanting Angie to see in her eyes the confusion she still felt about Leigh. "We both made our choices years ago."

"And later we may regret the choices that are sometimes forced on us when we're kids. And that's all you and Leigh were."

"Perhaps. But I was old enough to get pregnant, and Leigh was old enough to marry Evan. And that's the bottom line for me, Angie. Leigh's happily married."

Angie gazed at her, then her eyelids fell to disguise the expression in her eyes. She turned to look out over the back garden. "What if she was unhappily married?" she said softly.

Shann paused. "Are you asking me if I'd be interested if Leigh wasn't married? Angie, that's hypothetical. And it has been ten years. My relationship with Leigh wasn't really what I'd call a relationship anyway. Besides, she seemed happy enough," she added carefully. "And, if she is unhappy, only she can do something about it."

"I know." Angie hesitated. "Things didn't seem to go too well when she first got married, but I think it's been better these past few years. The first couple of years were rough for her, and then she was a bit overwhelmed when she fell pregnant with Michelle. She went into early labor, and they nearly lost the baby. It seemed to pull them both together." She turned back to Shann. "Did you think she'd changed?"

"Not all that much, but we are all ten years older." Shann grinned. "Now if you'd asked me if I thought you'd changed I'd have to say, most definitely."

Angie gave a quick smile. "For the better I hope."

Shann stepped forward and slid her hand over Angie's where it rested on the railing. "Absolutely," she said softly.

Angie looked at their joined hands and then at Shann. "Shann, what if I said—?"

193

"Angie?"

Shann and Angie drew apart with a start to see Leigh standing at the top of the steps.

Had she seen their hands entwined or their sudden guilty movement as they separated? Shann rather thought Leigh had.

"Oh, there you are, Angie." Leigh said lightly. "Mum wants you to make that carrot salad you made last time we had a barbecue."

Angie pushed herself off the railing. "Sure. I was just coming home anyway. I'll see you later, Shann."

"I'll be there soon," Leigh said brightly. "I just thought I'd take a few moments to catch up with Shann before I have to share her with everyone later."

Angie's step faltered and that same shuttered expression settled on her face. She gave a nod, and she was gone.

"I should go in and help Liz," Shann began walking across the deck, but Leigh stood her ground.

"Oh, come on, Shann. What's a few moments? We haven't seen each other for ten years. Can't we have a talk before everyone gets into the swing of the barbecue?"

Shann hesitated. "Where's your husband?"

"Gone to pick up some beer and spirits. He'll be back soon. Why don't we sit down out here in the open where everyone can see us?" she added dryly.

Shann reluctantly agreed. She waited for Leigh to sit down before she sat on the other side of the table. Leigh shook her head exasperatedly and moved around until she was beside Shann.

"You look fantastic," she said, her gaze holding Shann's.

"You do, too." Shann said sincerely.

"Thanks, but the mirror tells me otherwise."

Although Leigh was smiling Shann knew she believed it.

"You were pretty cute back ten years ago, and you've definitely got cuter."

"Leigh—"

"No. I mean it, Shann. But enough of that. I can see it makes you uncomfortable."

"Why wouldn't it?" Shann made a negating move with her hand. "I think it's best we keep the conversation—" She paused.

"Superficial?" Leigh suggested, and Shann nodded. "All right. We can try." Leigh gave a quick smile. "It was great to meet Corey. I couldn't believe he was so grown up." She sighed. "He's so much like you, Shann."

"So everyone tells me."

"And everyone says Michelle's like me. Antony's more like Evan. They're all great kids. We've been lucky, haven't we?"

"Yes, I'd say so." Shann relaxed a little.

"Who'd have thought we'd be sitting here ten years later, respectable matrons, raising three potential world leaders?" Leigh laughed, and Shann joined her.

"Enough of the matron bit. But we are fortunate."

"I know I sometimes look at my two, and I can't believe they're part of me, Leigh Radford, who hasn't had the most blameless life."

Shann thought she knew what Leigh meant. "Maybe our three are all that's good in us. That's how I feel when I look at Corey, that he's the best part of me."

"You never did tell me who his father was," Leigh said softly.

Shann looked back toward the house, could hear Liz pottering about in the kitchen. "I'd rather not discuss that here. It's too, well, public."

"Then let's walk down the back. Just for a few minutes." Leigh stood up. "I think we need to do this, Shann. Don't you think?"

Reluctantly Shann nodded and followed her down the steps, through the vegetable garden and down toward the mango tree, just as she'd followed Angie a week ago.

Leigh stopped by the bench and sat down. She patted the seat beside her but Shann remained standing. Hitching up the leg of her jeans she lifted one booted foot to rest it on an upturned plant pot.

"About Corey's father—you know I used to worry that what happened with us made you, you know—"

"Go out and try a guy?" Shann finished for her, and Leigh nodded. "Nothing could be further from the truth so you can clear your conscience there. I wasn't curious," she finished flatly.

"That's good." Leigh paused. "After you left I really missed you. I kept thinking you'd come home and, I don't know, that we could go on like before. I knew we couldn't, but I hoped. But you didn't come back and I married Evan." She looked up at Shann and away again. "Marriage wasn't exactly what I thought it would be." She grimaced. "I used to fantasize about you coming to take me away from my life." She gave a derisive laugh.

"Leigh, I don't think—"

"Shann, please. Can you just hear me out? I think . . . no, I know I loved you back then, and I wanted more than what we had, those kisses, those wonderful kisses."

"Oh, sure you did," Shann remarked derisively. "That's not how I remember it."

"I know. But I did want to make love with you."

"You were the one who set the limits, Leigh, if you also remember."

"I was scared about how I felt about you." Leigh sighed. "I was never as brave as you were. I couldn't cope with being different. When Mum found us together I couldn't face the truth, let alone own up to it. I told Mum it was you, that it was all your idea, that you'd kissed me. I guess it was easy to convince Mum because that's what she wanted to believe."

"It was all a long time ago. Does it matter now?"

"It does to me, Shann. I need to tell you, try to explain. I was a total coward. I was terrified our friends would find out, too, so I thought I'd get in first, before someone else did. So I told Evan you had tried to kiss me."

"I see." Deep down Shann knew she'd always suspected Leigh had told him.

"I just thought he'd laugh, that we'd joke about it. But he went crazy, totally berserk, and that really frightened me. I even thought he might—" She swallowed. "Did he say anything to you?"

196

"He didn't have to. He told his mates. They did his dirty work for him." Shann remembered the phone calls that came when she was home alone, the snide remarks whispered from behind her, the supposedly accidental jostling in the hallways and the rough hands on her body.

"Oh, Shann. I'm sorry. What did they say to you?"

"Just the usual. Nothing original, that's for sure. I've heard worse."

"I didn't know he'd do that. I feel so responsible, and I suppose I am. I just wish we could go back, replay it. I know I would have acted differently."

Shann wasn't so convinced about that. Without hindsight, she thought, everyone would react in exactly the same way.

"What happened to Corey's father? Do you still see him?" Leigh asked.

"He's never been in the picture, Leigh. It was never an option."

They were silent for long moments.

"You really were raped, weren't you?" Leigh asked quietly, and Shann nodded. Leigh bit her lip. "And I didn't—" She shook her head.

"You didn't believe me. I know."

"It was too horrible for me to even consider." She hesitated. "You also said you didn't know who was responsible for it. Did you really not know who did it?"

"I didn't know who had done it. Not then. I do now. Eventually, it came back to me." With a little help, Shann thought bitterly, but she wasn't going to tell Leigh that. She took a deep breath. "But the best thing to come of it was Corey. I wouldn't be without him."

"I can see that. And, as I said, he does remind me so much of you. It's a shame he can't know his father. Is there any chance—?"

"No. None. And apart from that, Leigh, I'm a lesbian. I always was, and I always will be."

Leigh looked away for a moment. "Is there anyone special?" she asked softly.

"I think so. Yes."

"I thought there might be. I recognize the, I don't know, aura you have. You used to look at me like that." She gave a faint smile. "Eons ago."

"It *was* a long time ago," Shann said flatly.

"I know." Leigh held Shann's gaze. "And you can't go back, no matter how much you might want to."

"Leigh, I—" Shann paused, trying to find the right way to tell Leigh she wanted to leave the past where it was.

"It's all right, Shann." Leigh stood up and put her hand on Shann's arm, her fingers warm and firm, and then she released her. "It's Angie, isn't it? The someone special? I see the way you look at her, the way you look at each other."

"I'm not comfortable talking to you about this," Shann began, and Leigh gave a soft laugh.

"Why not? I know Angie hasn't come out to Mum and Dad yet, but I've known about her for a while. I even met her last girlfriend."

Shann's eyes met Leigh's and the other woman looked a little disconcerted.

"I'm sorry. I didn't mean that the way it sounded. I meant . . . you know what I meant." She shrugged and glanced across at Shann. "Angie had a huge crush on you all those years ago. I suppose she told you that? I used to tease her about it, but it didn't seem to bother her. Although I remember one time she did get pretty angry with me. She said you'd come to your senses and realize I wasn't the one for you." Leigh laughed derisively. "Which you did."

"With a little help from you," Shann remarked dryly.

"Yes. I . . . I guess that reminds me that all this wasn't really what I wanted to say. There are so many things I want to tell you. I've missed having you to talk to. We used to talk all the time. In the good old days."

"I've missed that, too," Shann admitted.

"I'd just like us to be able to talk to each other, the way we used to. There's never been anyone I could talk to the way I could to you. Tell me about the ten years, Shann."

Shann raised her eyebrows. "Not much to tell really. I stayed with Aunt Millie until I had Corey then I found a job and a flat. I worked, wrote songs, performed when I could, and raised Corey. That's about it."

Leigh laughed. "Very concise."

"What about you?" Shann asked a little reluctantly.

"When I married Evan I think I had this, oh, crazy idea that the marriage certificate would make some miraculous change to my life."

"That everything would be all right on the night," Shann suggested lightly, and Leigh smiled a little sadly.

"That's not far from the truth. And, well, it wasn't. I hated it, and I wanted to leave Evan. I tried, but he was devastated and begged me to reconsider. Then I was pregnant with Antony. After he was born I was too busy to do anything except function. When I found out I was pregnant again I just fell into a complete heap."

"How far apart are they?" Shann asked.

"Fifteen months. Everyone said at least I'd get all the nappies and broken nights over together, but I was frantic. I didn't think I was coping with one baby, let alone that I'd have to cope with two. I got . . . I had a bit of a breakdown and Angie came up to look after me until I had Michelle."

Angie had mentioned that to Shann, and she hadn't been surprised. It was something Angie would do.

"Angie was wonderful," Leigh continued. "She saved my sanity. Evan's, too, I guess. She told him he was so busy living his own life he didn't even realize how badly I was feeling. And she made me see that deep down I was blaming Evan for everything when I should have been looking at myself."

Leigh turned and leant back against the trunk of the mango tree. "I thought I didn't want another baby until I nearly lost Michelle. I went into labor five weeks before I was supposed to. It was touch and go for a week. The longest week of my life. And Evan's. It made me realize I was only putting part of myself into our marriage, and I decided to change. That's when I stopped wishing Evan was you."

"Oh, Leigh, I don't—" Shann shook her head. "I don't know what to say."

"It wasn't your fault, Shann. It was all mine. I'd sent you away, and I'd chosen Evan, when I really wanted you. But I knew I had to put all that behind me. It was the only chance we had to make our marriage work. Evan loves me, Shann. And I've learned to love him, too. Our marriage isn't perfect, but it's all we've got. We love the kids, and we've got a good life."

Shann examined her feelings about Leigh's revelations. Before she came home she suspected her heart would have been bruised if Leigh had said that to her. Now she only felt a certain relief. For them both. "I'm glad you have, Leigh, that things are good for you," she said and knew she meant it. It was as though the final strand of the rope that tied them together, that small frayed end, had finally unraveled and allowed Shann to slip away.

Leigh sighed. "I think I heard Evan's car so I guess we should go back." She smiled at Shann. "I'm so glad we've made contact again."

"I am, too," Shann agreed.

They started walking slowly back up the garden.

"I wish we could have had a life together, Shann," Leigh said softly. "But I wasn't strong enough to live it, and I'm probably still not strong enough. Not like you." She leant over and kissed Shann on the cheek. "You and Angie deserve to be happy, and I wish you that." She smiled crookedly. "If I can't have you myself then I'm glad you'll be in the family."

And Leigh turned and walked away.

Shann stood at the bottom of the steps and the hard lump of tears stuck in her chest. She thought about what Leigh had said, and she knew Leigh was right. They'd both moved on, made separate lives, and seeing Leigh again meant Shann could put the past behind her and go on with her life. One tear overflowed and trickled down her cheek. She wiped it away and sighed, knowing in that small corner of her heart where she'd kept Leigh Callahan, she was saying a final good-bye to her.

Surprisingly the barbecue went reasonably well. Shann's initial meeting with Leigh's father was a little stilted, but Ann and Liz made light conversation and soon everything settled down.

Corey and Antony played with the dog until dinner and, after they'd eaten, the two families sat around laughing and joking the way they'd used to when Shann was a child. Shann could almost imagine they were back ten years, before life got so complicated.

Since her talk earlier with Leigh, Shann felt far more relaxed with her, although she noticed Evan stayed close to his wife, hovering when she got up to get meals for the children, sitting beside her, watching her. However, the tension Shann was feeling now had far more to do with Angie. Shann was sure the other woman was avoiding her, and her gaze rarely met Shann's.

Corey came over and leaned over Shann's chair from behind her, arms around her neck. She turned her head and kissed him on the cheek. "Mum, Antony says we can visit Tiger when we go up to Cairns. Can we go?"

"Cairns is a long way away," Shann began.

"You can come up any time you like, Shann," Leigh said lightly. "We have plenty of room, and we live right on the water. Corey would love it. Evan's usually working so the kids and I could show you around."

Shann murmured noncommittally, and she noticed Evan made no comment.

"We so enjoy our stays up there, don't we, Mike?" Ann turned to her husband.

"The fishing's superb. I've been meaning to show you some photos, Jim. I'll go and get them." Mike Callahan went into the house. When he returned he and Shann's father swapped fish tales while Ann and Leigh talked about the beauty of tropical north Queensland and the Great Barrier Reef.

By eight-thirty Corey's eyelids were beginning to droop so Shann excused herself to get him into bed. Her father decided to go home, too, and they made their good-byes with Ann urging Shann to return and have a cup of tea.

Shann saw her father and Corey into bed and wished she could simply go to bed herself. She was tired from her full-on week at the Muster, and she suspected she was somewhat emotionally drained from seeing Leigh again. But Liz would expect her back at the Callahans, and she knew she wanted to see Angie again. They needed to talk.

She walked down the back steps and headed for the side gate between the two properties. As she stepped into the Callahans' yard a dark figure detached itself from the shadows and took hold of her arm.

Shann's throat constricted on a scream, and she instinctively pulled back. As she did so she recognized Evan Radford and that fact did nothing to reassure her. She felt as though he had been glowering at her all evening.

"Sssh! Don't overreact," he said urgently.

"What do you want?" Shann got out, moving toward the back of the Callahans' house and the lighted deck.

"I just want to talk to you," he said flatly.

"I'm sorry, Evan, everyone's waiting for me." She stretched the truth.

"This won't take long. I want you to—" he looked away, and then his hand gripped her arm again "—come out the front."

Shann stiffened, suddenly alert, preparing to flee. But what could he do? Both families were nearby.

"Where's Leigh?" Shann asked him.

"She's putting the kids to bed. But I want to talk to you alone."

"I don't think we need to talk about anything, Evan, alone or otherwise."

"I think we do. Come on. It's Leigh I want to talk about."

Reluctantly Shann followed him, and they stood by the front veranda in the dull glow from the streetlight. Shann could hear the faint murmur of conversation from the back so she knew the others would hear her if she needed to call out.

"I don't want you to start anything with Leigh," he said through clenched teeth. "I want you to leave her alone."

Shann stared at him, totally nonplussed, but before she could reply there was a slight noise above them and they both looked up. Someone moved toward the front door, and Shann was sure she'd caught a glimpse of Angie's short fair hair as the figure entered the house.

CHAPTER THIRTEEN

"I said I want you to leave her alone," Evan repeated, and Shann drew her attention back to him.

"Look, Evan, it's not necessary for us to be having this conversation."

"And I know it is." He leaned toward her and lowered his voice. "If you think I'm going to stand by and let you try to—"

Shann held up her hand. "Back off, Evan. I'll only ask you once."

He hesitated and then moved back a step. "Are you still a dyke?"

"I don't see that that's any of your damn business."

"Well, where's your kid's father? I didn't think lesbians wanted kids."

Shann felt like slapping him. "Corey's father is also no business of yours. And being a lesbian has nothing to do with wanting or not wanting children," she added through her teeth. "Now, I'm not going to stand here and trade insults with you, Evan. We're not kids any longer so stop acting like one."

"I'm not—" And just as suddenly his bravado left him. His face was drawn and pale in the shadowy light. "Leave Leigh alone, Shann. If not for me then for our kids. You've got a son of your own. You'd know what it's like—" He drew a steadying breath. "I'm prepared to do anything. If you want money—"

"Evan, please." Shann held up her hand. "I have no idea what you think is—" She shook her head.

"And I'm prepared to apologize for what I did back then," he continued.

Shann stilled. "Apologize for what?"

"For stirring the guys up, telling them you were a dyke. And for the night of Leigh's parents' party."

"The party?" Shann swallowed.

"When Leigh told me about you coming on to her I was furious. You must understand that?" He appealed to her. "I'd had too much to drink at the party and calling you names and the rough stuff, it wasn't enough. I was . . . I couldn't bear the thought of losing Leigh. And losing her to you, well, that was worse."

He glanced at Shann and away again. "This guy Caleb knew gave him some stuff you put in drinks. It . . . we wouldn't have used it, but we were pretty drunk. I put some in your drink."

"You drugged me?"

"I was angry, mixed up, and I'd had too much to drink. I know that's no excuse but—I feel like shit about it, okay?" He ran his hand over his short hair. "When Leigh was trying to sober me up Angie came inside and said you were sick. I knew it was from the drink we gave you, and I'm sorry about that, too. I want you to know I wouldn't have done anything. Neither would Caleb or the Kingston twins."

Anger rose in Shann. "Can you say that for certain?" she asked him clippedly.

"Well, I all but passed out, but Caleb swore to me next day that they didn't." He hesitated. "Did they?" he asked uncertainly.

Shann ran a shaky hand over her tensed jaw.

"Fuck! Leigh told me no one knew who got you pregnant. Tell me it wasn't Caleb or the other guys after we put that stuff in your drink."

"It wasn't Caleb or the others," Shann said flatly.

"I never thought . . . I didn't even think . . . Look, Shann, I'm sorry. But I loved Leigh." He gave a negating exclamation. "I love Leigh. She's my life. And our kids. They're our life." He held Shann's gaze. "I couldn't go on if she . . . if Leigh left me. I know how she feels about you, and I'm asking you to leave her alone."

Shann sighed. "You have nothing to fear from me, Evan."

"But before, out the back, I saw her kiss you," he got out brokenly.

"On my cheek," Shann told him. "Like friends do. I'm not in love with Leigh in that way and she, well, she loves you, Evan. She told me that."

He barely moved, and Shann had a feeling he was close to tears. "She said that?" he got out thickly and Shann nodded.

"Yes, she did. Now, I do have to go, Evan. Liz will be wondering where I am." She stepped past him and strode back along the side of the house.

She desperately wanted to see Angie. If only she could hold her, tell her how much she loved her. But when she rejoined the others, Ann told her Angie was tired and had gone to bed. Leigh had finished putting her children to bed, too, and Shann could only accept the cup of tea Ann offered her. When Evan finally came back out onto the deck Shann decided she'd had enough. She found she couldn't meet his eyes, and she had no desire for further conversation with him. When she suggested to Liz they call it a night Liz agreed, and they said their good-byes and went home.

Yet sleep was a long time coming for Shann. She wanted to apologize to Angie, say all the things she'd held herself back from saying. She wanted to tell Angie she loved her so much, and that she wanted the two of them to spend the rest of their lives together. In the morning, she promised herself, she'd do just that.

But, of course, by the time Shann had dropped Corey at school and returned to settle her father and Liz it was midmorning. She felt totally on edge, wanting, and yet just a little apprehensive, about talking to Angie. What if Angie had overheard Evan and misconstrued what he had said? She paced up and down the deck trying to decide what to do, what to say to Angie. She'd have to go over to the store, talk to her.

"Shann, your tea's getting cold," Liz was saying as Leigh hailed them.

She walked up the steps to join them. "Am I in time for a cuppa?" she asked brightly, looking across at Shann.

"Shann's just made some," Liz told her and poured Leigh a cup.

Leigh sat down. "Great. Thanks, Liz. Dad and Mum are at work and Evan's taken the kids and the dog down to the park. Peace at last." She laughed.

"Come and sit down, Shann," Liz admonished. "You've been prowling like a caged lion."

Shann crossed the deck to sit at the table and took a sip of her cup of tea. "I guess Angie's at work?" she asked Leigh, and Leigh's eyebrows rose.

"Yes. She was off bright and early this morning," she replied dryly.

Shann flushed a little, knowing she was being hopelessly transparent, and when she slid a glance at Liz her sister gave her a piercing look.

"We had such a nice time last night, didn't we, Shann?" Liz said pointedly. "It was like old times."

"Apart from all the extra wrinkles." Leigh laughed. "Shann and I were discussing those yesterday, weren't we?"

"Yes." Shann stood up, suddenly coming to a decision. "Um, Leigh, I wonder if you'd mind staying with Liz for an hour or so. There's something I need to do."

"Shann, I don't need a babysitter," Liz protested. "I'm fine and Derek's in with Dad."

"Of course I can stay," Leigh agreed. "I haven't seen Liz in ages, and Evan won't be back any time soon. The kids will talk him into going for an ice cream from their favorite shop so take your time."

"Thanks, Leigh." Shann turned to her sister as she felt in the pocket of her jeans for her car keys. "I won't be long, Liz." She could see Liz wanted to ask where she was going, and Shann gave her sister a quick grin. "I'm going to check up on the tomato stakes you ordered from Angie," she said, and then she hurried out to her four-wheel drive, leaving Liz to make what she wanted of that.

Shann walked through the hardware store toward Angie's office. She tapped on the door and poked her head inside. A young woman was sitting at Angie's desk using the computer, earphones over her ears.

She looked up, lifted the earphones, and smiled across at Shann. "Can I help you with something?"

"I was looking for Angie."

"She's not here at the moment, but she'll be back this afternoon. Can I give her a message?"

"No, thanks. I'll call back later." Shann closed the door, and her heart sank. She walked back past the coffee shop, the delicious aroma of the coffee reminding her of Angie. How was she going to wait for hours?

"Hello, Shann. How are you?"

When she saw Joe Radford approaching Shann cringed. "I'm fine, Joe. I'm in a bit of a hurry."

"I guess you've caught up with Evan and Leigh," he said chattily.

"Yes. Last night. Well, I'll see you later."

"Don't forget to give Wade a call, will you?" he followed Shann as she tried to move off.

For a moment Shann wasn't sure what he was talking about and then she remembered his recently divorced older brother. She was trying to formulate a noncommittal reply when he continued.

"As I said to Angie when she was heading over to her unit, I think you and Wade would have so much in common."

Angie was at her unit? "How long ago did Angie leave?" she asked Joe as casually as she could.

He looked earnestly at his watch. "Oh, I'd say about forty minutes ago."

"Oh. I'll catch up with her later then. See you, Joe." Shann left him and hurried back out to her four-wheel drive.

It didn't take her long to get over to Angie's unit and park outside. She hurried into the foyer and before she could allow herself to think about it, she pushed the buzzer for the penthouse.

"Yes."

At the sound of Angie's voice Shann's legs went weak. She swallowed to clear her throat. "It's me. Shann. Can I come up?"

There was a moment of heavy silence.

CHAPTER FOURTEEN

"I'll come down," Angie said.

Eons later the elevator doors opened and Angie stepped into the foyer. She wore her work clothes, dark blue slacks and paler blue tailored shirt, and she was so beautiful she took Shann's breath away.

"Hi." Shann managed, feeling extremely gauche.

"There's nothing wrong, is there?" Angie asked, a frown of concern on her face.

"No, of course not. I just—" Shann swallowed again. "I wanted to talk to you." She made a movement of her hand to encompass the foyer. "Could we go upstairs? This is a bit public."

Angie hesitated, and then she gave a small nod. "Sure." She pushed the button for the lift and the doors slid open again. They stepped inside, and Angie used her key card to activate the elevator. "I've just had a curtain company measuring up. Now I have to choose the fabric."

As they moved upward a strained silence fell between them. The cubicle seemed to fill with a heavy tension as Shann's nerve endings clamored their unease. She tried to think of something to say, but her mind went completely blank.

The lift came to a halt and the doors opened. Shann followed Angie into the unit, and her gaze went straight to the couch in the middle of the room. It was still covered by the colorful blanket they'd left there. Shann's heartbeat accelerated as memories of their lovemaking catapulted into her mind. She saw their naked bodies, arms and legs entwined, and her skin grew hot. Was Angie thinking about that night? Shann slid a quick glance at her, but the other woman had moved over closer to the breakfast bar and her face was in profile. Shann wanted to go to her, kiss her, make love to her. Yet something made her hold back. Angie's face was pale, her expression closed.

"I went to see you at the store, and Joe Radford told me you were over here."

The corners of Angie's delightful mouth rose in a faint smile. "I don't think the old saying loose lips sink ships features anywhere in Joe's sphere of reference, do you?"

"No." Shann smiled, too. "And I believe he's still peddling his brother, Wade, as a possible suitor."

"Oh, yes." Angie grimaced. "Wade Radford is still up for grabs apparently."

Shann gave a chuckle, nerves still bombarding her composure. "I think I'm going to have to be pretty blunt there. I—" She took a steadying breath. "I told Liz I was going to your shop to check up on her order for tomato stakes," Shann got out, her voice thin in her ears.

Angie raised her eyebrow. "You did?"

"Yes. So by now I'd say she's formulating the direction of her next interrogation."

"Most probably," Angie said carefully.

"I left her drinking tea with Leigh."

"I see." Angie's gaze dropped. "Leigh said she'd had a talk with you yesterday. A long talk." She leaned back against the kitchen counter, her arms folded across her chest. "She said you talked about old times."

Shann nodded. "She called them the good old days." Shann pulled a face. "I suppose calling the past that depends on how you enjoyed it back then."

"Or which angle you were seeing the game from at the time." Angie had crossed one booted foot over the other now and was giving the toe of her shoe her attention. "From my position off in the left field, so to speak, it wasn't so great. I watched someone I cared for get desperately hurt by someone I also cared for, and I couldn't do a thing to stop it."

"The responsibility wasn't yours, Angie. You were little more than a kid."

"So were you and Leigh," Angie said dryly.

"I suppose we were. We certainly weren't old enough to handle the emotions of the situation. I know I wasn't," Shann added. "I'd say kissing Leigh was a fifty-fifty mix of pleasure and pain."

"You know, back then, I was burningly jealous of my cousin," Angie said flatly. She looked at Shann, her expression inscrutable, then she looked away again. "I wanted you to kiss me."

Shann swallowed. "I was far too immature to be kissing anyone."

"All very clear with hindsight, don't you think?"

Shann laughed humorlessly. "Most probably."

"I nearly told Ann about you and Leigh back then, but I couldn't bring myself to do it. When I saw how angry she was when she caught you I was glad I hadn't." Angie shook her head. "I did tell Ann that Leigh was lying about it all being your idea. That was something of a tactical error, too, because she realized I'd known about you and Leigh. She turned on me then for not telling her about what she referred to as your abhorrent behavior. On top of that I was in trouble because she decided I was telling lies about Leigh as well. Phew!" She moved her shoulders as though her muscles were tense. "As you said, the good old days that weren't so good."

"I'm sorry you got pulled into it all," Shann said. "I didn't know about that."

"For the record I thought Leigh behaved pretty badly blaming you."

"We talked about all that. Leigh explained why she'd done it and apologized. We made our peace."

Angie's gaze met and held Shann's. "Leigh also tried to tell me you weren't interested in her anymore." She looked down at the floor again. "I believed her because I so desperately wanted that to be true. But then I overheard you and Evan last night."

"I thought that was you on the veranda."

Angie looked up into Shann's eyes. "Why did he ask you not to start anything again with Leigh? Why did he feel he had to ask you that?"

"I was going to explain about that, but when I went upstairs you'd gone to bed."

"I'd had more than enough emotional beatings for one day," Angie said flatly. "I wasn't sure I could take much more."

Shann walked over to join Angie at the breakfast bar, standing close but not touching her. "Evan did ask me not to start anything with Leigh. He was upset because he'd seen Leigh kiss me before dinner. It was a kiss on the cheek, nothing more, nothing less. It was a good-bye, if you like. I told him he had nothing to fear from me and that Leigh loved him."

Angie turned to look at Shann. "Leigh told you that?"

Shann nodded. "Yes, she did. She said she'd made her life and that she was content with it." Shann's heartbeat raced as she saw the flutter of a pulse beat at the base of Angie's throat.

Angie swallowed. "And Evan knows this?"

"He does now. He admitted he'd spiked my drink, and he apologized for that, and for all the horrible stuff he and his friends did back then."

"I'm glad," Angie said thickly, and that same heavy silence fell between them. "And I'm glad you came here this morning, Shann," Angie said at last. "I wasn't sure if I was going to seek you out tonight." She swallowed again. "I wasn't sure you would want me to."

"If Joe hadn't told me you were here, I'd have still been cooling my heels in the coffee shop. All that caffeine would have had me awake for a week."

Angie gave a broken laugh. "I've been totally miserable since Leigh arrived home. I thought that perhaps seeing her again, you might have—" She shrugged. "I didn't want you to feel you had to choose between us."

Shann wanted to reach out to her, take her in her arms, but she also wanted to explain her feelings to Angie, get everything out in the open. "The way I felt about Leigh, well, I think I clung to that to help me get through those first years after I left home. I don't know, perhaps it got to be a habit, a nice memory I took out every so often, and then put away again.

"When Liz asked me to come home I know I hesitated because I knew there was every chance I'd have to see Leigh again, too. Deep down I think I knew that what I'd felt for her was a thing of the past, but a part of me didn't want to let it go. It was a comfortable skin I'd worn to protect myself from being hurt again.

"I tried a couple of times to start a relationship, but every time it died a swift death because I had no desire to shed my protective skin. I had a fair suspicion that seeing Leigh again would mean I'd have to face a few cold hard facts," Shann shrugged. "Reality, I guess. And that meant admitting that that old skin wouldn't be as effective as it had been. I was terrified I'd be left vulnerable. Then you walked back into my life and I realized just how vulnerable I could be."

Angie bit her lip, her expression concerned. "I never would have hurt you, Shann."

"I know that now but I was—" Shann shook her head. "Once I arrived home all the memories, good and bad, flooded back, and I was hesitant to take the chance." She gave a half smile. "I wasn't used to existing without my emotional protection. Because I knew that the way I felt about you, well, I could be very hurt."

Angie said nothing, but Shann saw her swallow convulsively. She moved away from Shann, putting space between them, stopping beside the couch. Turning, she sat on the armrest, facing Shann again.

Shann yearned to go to her and unshed tears constricted her throat.

"I suppose you knew that I had a huge crush on you ten years ago. Actually, I think it was more than an adolescent crush. I lived in hope that one day you'd notice me." A flush colored Angie's cheeks. "But I knew it was Leigh you were interested in back then. I spent what seemed like a lifetime worrying that you and Leigh would end up together. I was sure your parents' and Ann and Mike's disapproval would only cement your relationship, push you closer together. And then something worse happened. You went away."

"I had to get away, Angie. It was too complicated to stay."

Angie nodded. "I see that now, but I didn't know about your pregnancy then. I badgered everyone about where you'd gone. Eons later Liz finally took pity on me and said you'd gone down to Sydney. She also told me you had had Corey. I was devastated." She held up her hand when Shann went to say something. "Not because of Corey, Shann, but because I thought you'd started a relationship with a guy you'd met in Sydney. So I stopped asking Liz for news about you because it hurt too much. Things got easier and life went on. I threw myself into my work, building up my business.

"Then, not long ago, Liz said you were coming home. I thought I'd buried my feelings for you but those few words, *Shann's coming home next week*, brought them all back to the surface." Angie made a negating movement with her head. "I wasn't sure how I felt about you coming home. I told myself it would be great to see you again, that we'd all moved on, that what I'd felt for you was kid stuff, a schoolgirl crush. As far as I knew you could have been happily involved with Corey's father. Then I heard myself asking Liz if your husband was coming home with you."

Angie grimaced. "Liz told me you'd never married, that you and Corey lived alone. I can't begin to describe how wonderful that sounded. And how terrifying."

"Terrifying?"

Angie nodded. "I was terrified you'd decided, well, that you weren't a lesbian. I desperately tried to warn myself that you might have been simply experimenting with Leigh and that you'd decided you didn't prefer women. I told myself that we were all older, that we all change. But I was afraid I hadn't." She paused, bit her lip. "When I saw you I knew I hadn't.

"After that night, here in the unit," Angie swallowed, "I let myself hope that you could love me, too. But when Leigh came home I was so desperately afraid seeing her again would make you . . . I was sure you still had feelings for her. When you walked up the steps and saw her you went pale. You couldn't take your eyes off her and I . . . well, part of me just withered and died." Angie straightened, moved away from the couch, stood with arms folded facing Shann. "I didn't know what to do. Me, cool, together, always in command of the situation, Angie Callahan. I wavered between gracefully stepping aside if Leigh was what you wanted, and making a fight for you. And I've been like that ever since. Standing ineffectually on the side, watching you."

"Never ineffectually." Shann laughed softly. "But you did hide your feelings so well I was worried you'd changed your mind about me."

"Changed my mind?" Angie rolled her eyes. "I've loved you for so long, Shann." She gave a hiccuping laugh. "I was so afraid you and Leigh, well, I couldn't bear the thought of you getting hurt again." She stopped and ran a shaky hand through her hair. "I love you so much, Shann."

"And I love you, Angie Callahan." Shann walked across to her, gently pulled her into her arms, held her close, breathed in the familiar delicious scent of her. And then she lifted her head, looked into Angie's shimmering green eyes. "Right now I want to kiss you within an inch of your life, make love to you so you'll never want to leave this unit," she said huskily. She leaned forward and kissed

216

her, gently at first, and then they strained together, desire rising in them both, until they drew breathlessly apart.

"I think I need to sit down," Angie said brokenly, and they moved back over to the couch, sinking down onto it, arms entwined, and they kissed again.

"I think I'll have to keep this old couch," Angie said some time later when they sat back in each other's arms. "It's become something of a family artifact."

"Definitely an heirloom. Shall we get a plaque?" Shann giggled. "Although I'm not sure what we could write on it that would be suitable for general exhibition."

"Censored due to possibility of arrest?"

They laughed and then sobered, and their lips met again.

"I can't believe you're here in my arms," Angie said. "This morning I was so sure I'd lost you."

"You never did lose me," Shann told her. "I was just slower at working things out than you were. But I'm here, and I'm staying right here if you'll have me."

Tears glistened in Angie's green eyes and she dashed them away. "I've been so—" She sighed. "I just wish I could have read our last page first," she said. "It would have saved me loads of heartache."

"I'm sorry, Angie." Shann gave a crooked smile. "Maybe there's some way I can make it up to you."

Angie gave a soft laugh. "Without getting us arrested, do you mean?"

"I'm sure Liz would bail us out," Shann murmured lowly, and slowly pulled Angie's shirt from her waistband, sliding her hand upward over Angie's midriff to cup a full, lace-covered breast. Angie moaned and arched against her.

"Tell me there are no more curtain measurers due to arrive and interrupt us."

Angie shook her head. "We're all done with measuring. Unless you'd like to help me choose fabrics. I have a pile of swatches—" Her fingers began to unbutton Shann's shirt.

"I'm afraid I can't say much for my ability to make color coordinated choices just at the moment." Shann watched as Angie reached the top button, pushed the shirt open, let her fingers tease Shann's nipples as they thrust against her bra. She drew a steadying breath. "And please tell me you don't have to get back to work any time soon," she continued thickly.

Angie undid the press-stud at the waist of Shann's jeans, pulled down the zipper. "I think I'll risk the boss firing me. What do you think?"

"You have the cutest boss, did you know that? I could really make a play for her. She's absolutely gorgeous. Her kisses are exquisite." Shann drew in the scent of Angie's skin. "She smells divine. And I think she rather likes me."

"Oh, I'd say she more than likes you." Angie kissed her eyebrow.

"You know, I think you should consider giving Joe Radford a raise. Otherwise I wouldn't have known you were here."

Angie gave a soft laugh and drew back to look at Shann. "Only on the condition you tell him in no uncertain terms that you're not interested in his obnoxious brother Wade." She held Shann's gaze. "Or anyone else well-meaning family and friends try to match you up with. Especially handsome members of any and all bands."

"I'll put the word around that there's only you."

Angie held her gaze. "There is?"

"Absolutely. I love you, Angie Callahan."

"And I love you. Always . . . and forever."